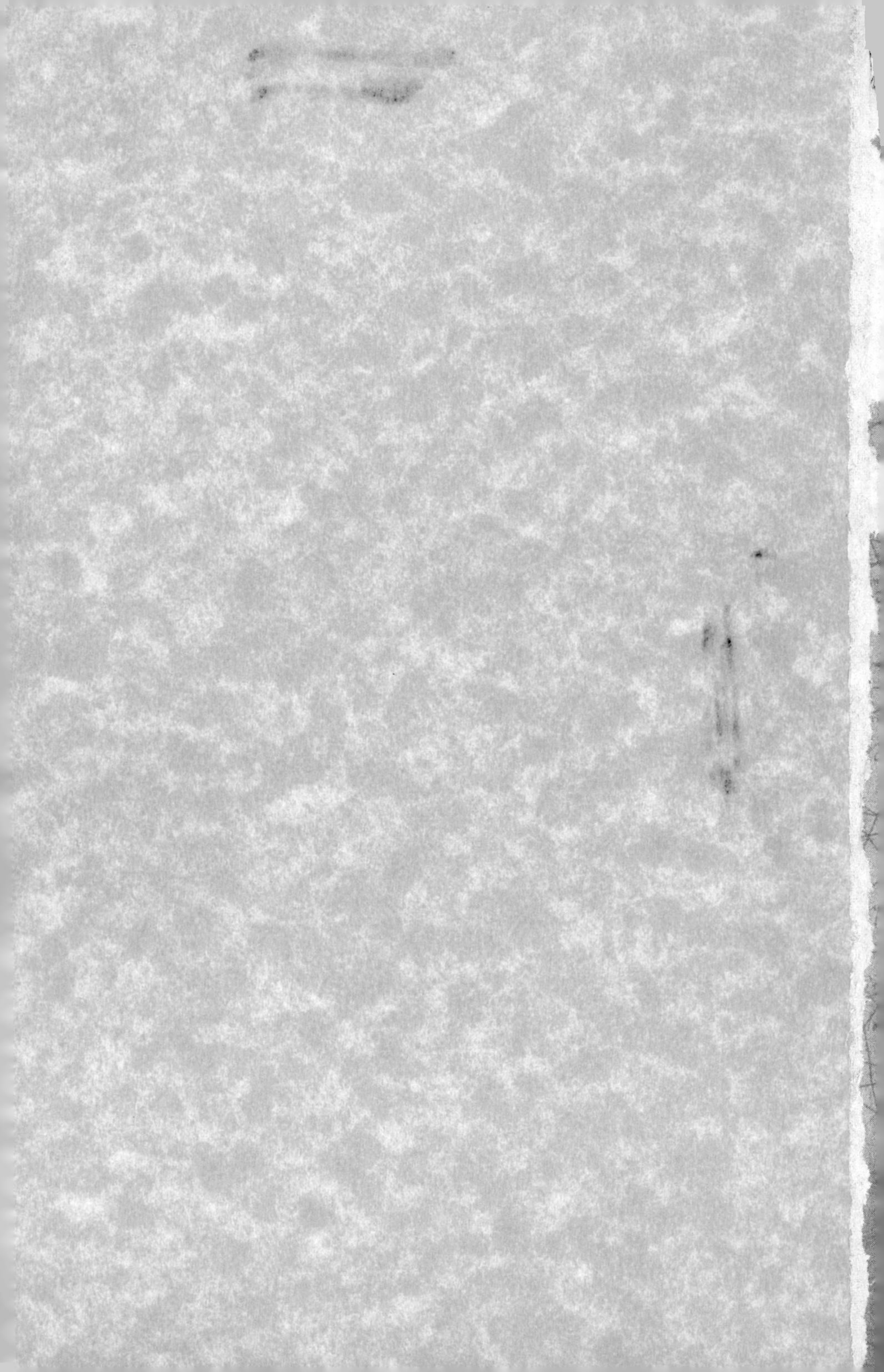

RAIDERS' Ransom

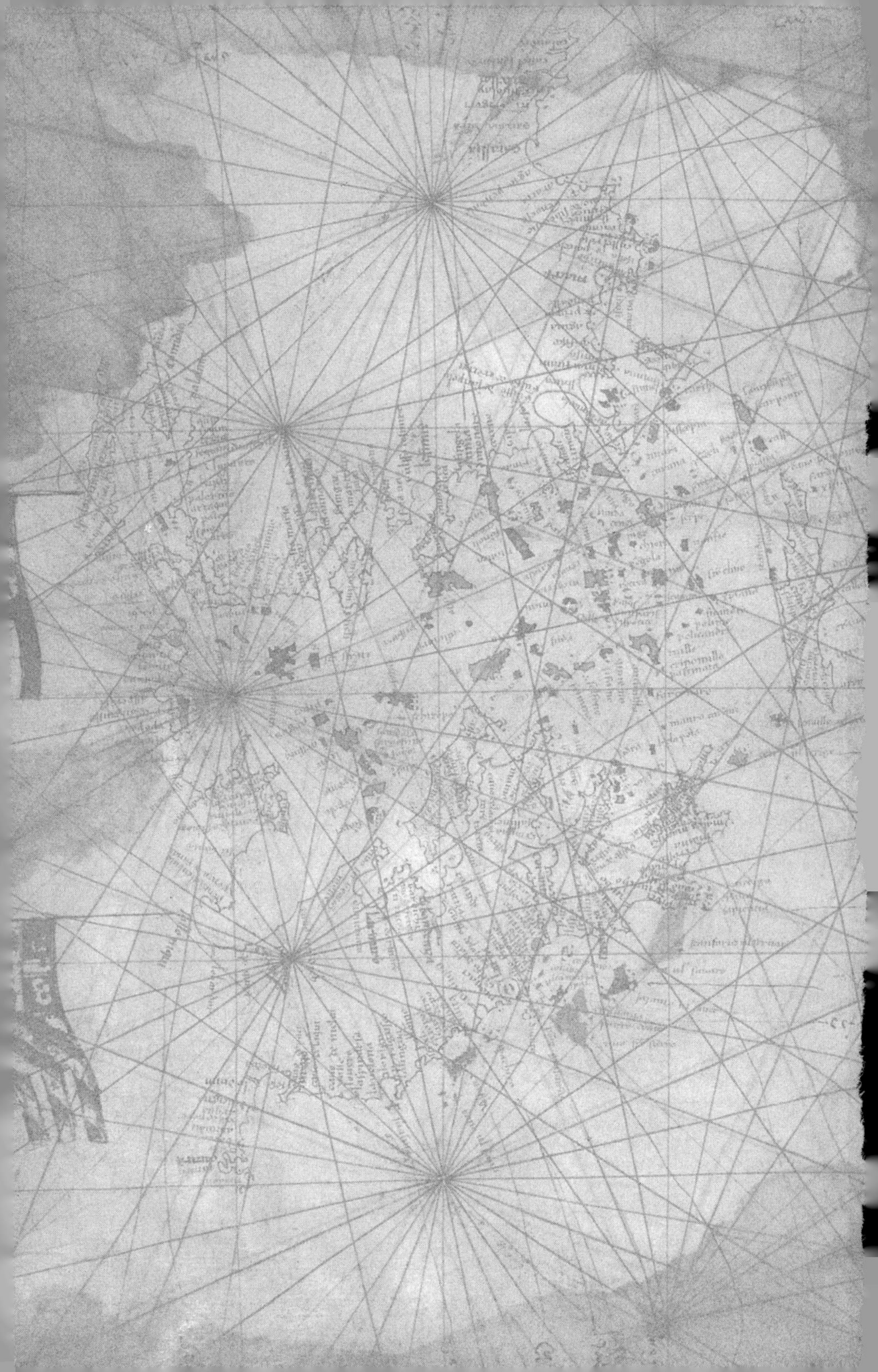

RAIDERS' Ransom

EMILY DIAMAND

Chicken House
SCHOLASTIC INC · NEW YORK

www.scholastic.com

First published in the United Kingdom by Chicken House,
2 Palmer Street, Frome, Somerset BA11 1DS.

www.doublecluck.com

Library of Congress Cataloging-in-Publication Data
Diamand, Emily.
Raiders' ransom / Emily Diamand. — 1st American ed.
p. cm.

Summary: In 23rd-century Great Britain, where climate change has caused vast flooding, the piratical raiders kidnap the Prime Minister's daughter, and thirteen-year-old Lilly Melkun, an English fishergirl, takes her seacat on a daring rescue attempt, with a mysterious talking jewel from a past computer age tucked in her belt as ransom.

ISBN-13: 978-0-545-14297-7 · ISBN-10: 0-545-14297-0

[1. Adventure and adventurers — Fiction. 2. Kidnapping — Fiction. 3. Pirates — Fiction. 4. Cats — Fiction. 5. Computers — Fiction. 6. Environmental degradation — Fiction. 7. Great Britain — Fiction. 8. Science fiction.] I. Title.

PZ7.D5415312Red 2009
[Fic]—dc22

2008043692

10 9 8 7 6 5 4 3 2 1 09 10 11 12 13

Printed in the U.S.A. 23
First American edition, December 2009

The text type was set in Cochin.
Book design by Chris Stengel

For Mum and Dad

N
W
E
S
Edinburgh
Map of my travels out of the Last Ten Counties. I put on London, even tho it's mostly drowned, and the raider marshes, even tho you'd be mad to go there.
Lilly Melkun,
April 2216
GREATER SCOTLAND
York
RAIDER LANDS
Islands and tidal marshes
Norwich
Birmingham
Cambridge
London
Black Waters
Angel Isling
Cardiff
SWINDON
LAST TEN COUNTIES OF ENGLAND
Chichester
MY VILLAGE

CONTENTS

·1· THE RAID

Cat puts up his nose to sniff the breath of wind barely filling the sail, and opens his small pink mouth to speak.

"Yow yow," he says, and I know what he's thinking: We're nearly there.

He's in a funny old mood: twitchy and nervous, like when a bad wind's coming. Maybe it's just us being out a whole day with nothing caught, which ain't like us. I'll get some stick for it from the captains when I get back: "What have you done to that cat, then, stuffed his nose with sand?" Another excuse to keep me off the big boats and stuck in this dinghy with hardly room for nets and baskets and us, as well.

We're running along past the coastline, as fast as this little wind will push us. Round here it's all hills, cliffs, and thin pebbly beaches. None of the wide brown marshes or fallen-in towns you get farther east. Not long we'll be at the headland,

and as soon as we peek round it, we'll see the little rocky harbor. And our village climbing up the hillside away from it.

Maybe Cat can smell fish? Fish guts curling off the harborside into the water; fish scales decorating the stones like pearls. Scrape, slice, pack: the daily chore of fisherfolk. And Cat's a favorite, with his pretty gray markings and his seaweed eyes. Any one of 'em, man or woman, would give him a tidbit, hoping to steal him away. He makes the most of it, gets a bellyful whenever he can, but it doesn't matter what they do, how much fish they give him; he'll thank 'em, eat it neatly, then come straight back to me.

I swing the sail out a bit more, trying to catch the sharp, salty wind. But we're only jogging through the water, jouncing over tiny waves, sparkle-bright in the sun.

Cat meows again.

"What's wrong?" I ask him, but he won't tell me. Just puts his front paws on the bow and stands there, flicking his tail, like he can't get home soon enough.

Back home, Granny'll be waiting. She doesn't make it to the harbor these days, what with her rheumatics, but she'll see us from the window.

"I'm just watching the sails," she always says. Watching the boats go out and counting them back in again. Every day, she always counts them back. "Cos you can never trust the sea." And I reckon she should know, what with Grampy going down the way he did.

Granny was a fisher herself when she was younger — worked with Captain Grayhand on the *Annie May.* But she doesn't want me to do it.

"Wears you down and wears you out," she says. "Look at me — fifty-four and crippled with rheumatics. Is that really what you want, girl? A hard, windy life and not much more than rusty joints at the end of it?"

But what else is there? Life in a cobbledy old village, gutting and scraping and earning tuppence a week? Or having to marry a farmer and go and plow fields? Well, no thank you! Not for me. Anyway, Cat picked me, didn't he? That's got to say something.

The little wind pushes us past Station Point, a dank green lump of land with the sea eating at its roots. In olden times, before the Collapse, there was a great building there with huge towers and steam coming out all day long. Used to make lights and heat for all the houses in all the land. But maybe that's just one of Granny's stories, cos the old power station's nothing but moldy old concrete now, and every winter a bit more falls into the sea.

Cat turns his head and looks back at me.

"Yow yow, prup yow," he says. But I still don't know what he's trying to tell me. He drops down from his perch and leaps daintily over.

"Mee yow!" he says, looking right in my face. And then he reaches up and sinks his teeth right into my hand on the tiller.

"Ow!" I cry. "What was that for?" But all I can work out is he's upset about something. Could be anything: a storm; whales; me missing a good shoal of fish; him thinking I'm not going fast enough.

"Tell me what the matter is!" I say. But he's too worked up, just paces in circles, growling.

I should be able to work out what Cat's saying by now. That's the whole point, cos a seacat's meant to help with sailing and fishing, to tell what's rumbling in the sea and sniff out good catches under the waves. But I still haven't got it. Lun Hindle says that's all the more reason why I shouldn't be allowed to keep him. Went round pretty much everyone in the village, telling how Cat should be taken off me. But luckily Granny stood up for us, and there's none of them captains who'd cross her.

"He chose Lilly hisself. And you know it can't be undone if the cat chooses." That's what she said; hobbled her way down to the Old Moon where everyone was drinking and smoking and discussing it. I wasn't allowed in, of course, what with "being only a girl," but I peeked through the window and saw all the captains nodding in agreement, like the Wise Men at Christmas. Lun kept on grumbling and whining, though. He even went to ask the vicar about it — probably hoping I'd get cast out as a witch or something. Andy was clipping the grass edges in the churchyard, and he told me about it.

Lun comes running up: "Vicar Reynolds! Lilly Melkun's gone and swiped herself a seacat — lured it from the litter with fish!" As if I did any such thing! "And I've been waiting for two years now, had my name down and everything!"

And ever wonder why you've been waiting so long, Lun? Probably no cat would have you, that's why.

Anyway, Andy told me the vicar just said it was God's will if it was anything, and then went off in a huff. I don't know what else Lun was expecting; I should think the vicar would denounce seacats as the Devil's helpers if he had a church inland. But he can't hardly do it in a fishing village, can he? Not when everyone depends on them to keep safe.

It's when we're level with the tip of the headland I see it. An angel's head, bobbing by on the water. It's carved out of wood, not very well, and its hair is painted a strange reddish color, like you've never seen on a real person. I only know it's an angel head cos it's usually stuck on the front of Andy's dinghy, which he named *Angel*. But Andy'd never take it off his boat! He carved that head himself, sitting out on his doorstep, whittling away. Even when the old boys who sit down by the harbor laughed and said it looked more like a pig than an angel, he still kept on at it.

By now Cat's growling and yowling and leaping about like a crazy thing. It's all I can do to keep him from climbing up on top of my head. And while I'm fighting him off and staring open-gobbed at the head, which is floating south, headed for Espana, I hear a noise like *whump*. Up on the headland. And the old station's on fire.

Of course, the station ain't actually burning. It's the beacon. A great pile of wood and kindling kept dry and stacked up on a raised platform. Cos a fire at Station Point can be seen at Wytham, and then they'll light their beacon. And then the fires'll be lit all along the coast until they reach the garrison at Chichester.

But there's only one reason to light the beacon, and that's raiders.

Now I know why Cat's been in such a frenzy, and my hands go sweaty cold. And when we turn the point of the headland, I can see the broken boats in the harbor and the smoke rising from the village. Too much smoke, smoke like houses on fire.

I look from the smoke to the wreckage of the village boats floating in the water to the beacon blazing on the headland, and I can't hardly believe it. I only went away for a day! How could this have happened in just a day?

More scrips and scraps of wood come floating by, then a fishbasket, then a slick hummock of something floating in the water. My breath stops in my mouth, till the waves move again and show it's just clothing, not a body. But it could have been. And there's probably bodies in the village right now if the raiders came down with no warning. Oh don't let it be Granny, or Andy, or Hetty, or . . .

Don't let it be anyone, not even Lun.

I turn the tiller and head fast as I can, fast as this stupid little wind will take me, for home.

* * *

To get into harbor, I have to push my boat through a tide of broken wood. On the quayside there's a great gang of fishers — just standing, not sorting fish or mending nets. They're dressed in the browny woollens and raggedy trousers that every fisher wears under their oilskins. Like they jumped straight up from their beds and ran down to the quay. And they're all staring out over the water, like they ain't ever seen it before. I'm staring, too, cos there ain't one boat left whole. The whole fleet is sitting half out of the water, or leaning with their masts broken. It looks like a giant reached down to the village and crushed all the boats for matchsticks.

"Lilly! Lilly!"

There's Andy, waving and shouting my name, his curly black hair sticking up like a mushroom over the other heads. First off, I'm so happy to see him alive and well, but then my stomach knots up. Cos why is he waving and shouting at me?

As we get in near the harbor wall, the only sound's the crunching and creaking of the wood-filled waves. I can't get close, what with all the wood, so I stand up and throw out a coil of rope. And I'm pulled in by half a dozen fishers, even Captain Ainsty, who ain't done any work himself for twenty years. I step out of the boat and climb up the stone steps to the quay, Cat trotting behind me. Everyone just looks at me with thin, pinched faces. A few shake their heads.

"Raiders?" I ask. And I get some nods.

"A terrible, terrible day," says Captain Ainsty, and for once he doesn't sound full of his own importance.

"They just came in this morning, no warning, out of the early mist," says John Greenstick. Everyone nods and moans.

Captain Ainsty claps his hand on my shoulder.

"Lilly, this has been a terrible day. You must be brave."

Brave?

I look around panicky at the sea-roughened faces, but their eyes flick away from me. Only Andy holds my gaze, and I know he'll tell me.

"What is it?" I whisper, and the tears start dropping from his charcoal eyes.

"Oh Lilly," he says. "It's your granny."

And he doesn't have to say any more, cos now I'm pushing and struggling my way out of the crowd.

"Let me through!" I'm shrieking, and then I'm running, feet pounding over the smooth gray cobbles, racing two at a time up the little steps. Past the black and charred front of the carpenter's workshop, around broken furniture, over a torn mattress, fluffy stuffing spilling out onto the flagstones. Behind me, Andy's calling my name, but I ain't slowing for anything.

Then I'm home. Chest burning, lungs panting. And the front door's standing open, an axe-sized hole in its middle. And when I run inside, there's Granny lying out on the table: arms crossed, eyes shut, lips blue. Hetty's sat next to her on a chair, her face bloated from crying. She jumps up as I crash in, and for a moment she doesn't say anything, her mouth hanging open. Then she wails.

"Oh Lilly! They'd heard about Cat! Half a dozen of them broke off from the rest and came straight up here! You should have seen Granny — like a fiery fury she was! But there was one of them, young and nasty. He wouldn't believe Cat was out at sea. Kept going on and on, said she was lying and hit her with his sword . . . And she fell down, and she never got up again . . . Oh Lilly, I tried to save her, I did, but the blood just kept on coming . . ."

And she's crying, and I'm crying, and Andy comes in and he's crying. And Cat skitters in, and he's mewing and mewing.

And I put my arms around Granny's poor cold body, hold on to her like I've done so many times before. But she doesn't hug me, or stroke my hair, or tell me everything is all right. And still I hold on to her, hold her tight in that dark little room, cos how can I ever let her go?

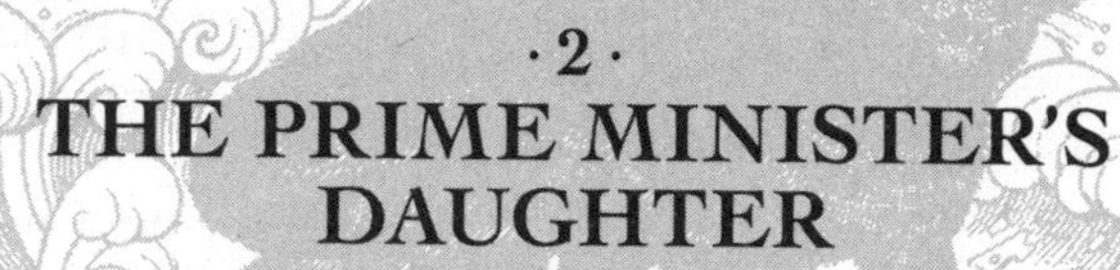

·2· THE PRIME MINISTER'S DAUGHTER

The next few hours is just crying and misery. I don't want to say any more about it. But eventually I have to pick myself up, cos Hetty says, "We've got to get her laid out proper." And she's right; people are poking their heads in, wanting to pay respects.

The vicar arrives when it's getting near to dark.

"Your grandmother was a good woman," he says. "She was honest, hardworking, and never let herself be lured into the bad old ways. She'll be getting her reward for her good life." And that's something I hold on to, hoping he's right.

Andy says, his voice wobbling and strange, "Vicar, do you want help with the grave?" and Vicar Reynolds nods, all solemn. Then he takes Andy away to help with the digging in the churchyard. Just one hole. Just for Granny.

"It really is something of a miracle no one else was killed," says the vicar before he leaves, "but it seems the raiders had other things on their minds. Even the two soldiers at Mrs. Denton's will recover from their wounds."

And I hate him then, for saying Granny's death is a miracle. So I don't ask him what he means.

The late afternoon draws into evening, and people come in ones and twos to sit with us and say their good-byes to Granny. Then comes night, passing in an age and a flash, both at the same time. And when the first light creeps in rosy through the parlor window, the fog in my head starts to lift, leaving an empty, horrible hole.

We dress Granny in her best clothes and wrap her in a winding sheet. The church bells start to toll, and Andy comes back, with James the carpenter in tow. They set Granny on a wide plank and carry her out of our house for the last time, with me and Hetty following behind. As we walk to church, first one person, then another, then another comes out of their smashed-up houses and walks quietly after. I look over my shoulder and see fisherfolk and captains, all marching solemnly behind us. Fishing caps off their heads, eyes down, wearing their best clothes. Even shoes, if they have them.

When we reach the church, the vicar leads the service. I sit through it in a front pew, everyone's eyes on the back of my head.

"The raiders fester in their marshes," he roars, "fleeing from decency and righteousness, just as their ancestors fled from London. Their forebears were the scum of that terrible city, and the raiders have descended even further into depravity!" I keep hoping he'll say something nice about Granny, but he just keeps on about the raiders leading wicked lives, and everyone in Greater Scotland being not much better, cos they won't renounce technology, and how us being poor and hungry is good for our souls.

"Only in the Last Ten Counties has any virtue survived the floods, storms, and destruction that have rained down over these lands!"

When he does finally give a word to Granny, he just says what he did before. How she was kindhearted and honest. Like he can't think of anything else to say about her, even though she's been going to this church since before he was born.

When he's finished, we go outside and lay Granny in a deep, dirty hole. Next to the little stone for my ma and pa, lost at sea. It's over so quick, and I'm left looking at a mound of silent earth. It's while I'm stood there, wondering if I'll ever be able to move again, I overhear the captains talking behind me.

"I reckon they must have known she was visiting the village, tho who knows how."

"Worth a pretty penny, I suppose."

"But snatching the Prime Minister's daughter? Them raiders're getting crazier every year. They'll more likely get a war party than a ransom. Randall won't take it lying down, that's for sure. There'll be a fine old ruckus once word gets to Swindon, you wait."

"Strange how they knew where the girl was. Even the pillaging wasn't much – they just rushed in and straight out again."

"I think I'd prefer pillaging to smashing all the boats in."

"Maybe they was worried we'd chase after their hostage?"

"Not I!"

"Not for Randall! He ain't a patch on his father – now *he* were a good Prime Minister."

"And his granddad before him."

"But this one, he's just in it for hisself!"

"Hush up. Ears might hear and tell on us for saying such things. We don't need any more trouble."

"I reckon we'll be getting it, tho."

"'Tis a terrible shame about Melkun's old missus."

"She were a fine woman, and a good fisher in her day."

"How did they know there was a seacat in the house?"

"Same as how they knowed little Alexandra Randall was here, I suppose."

"It just goes to show, there's no good comes from a young girl having such a beast. If he'd gone to a captain with a proper-sized boat, he wouldn't have needed a home on land, and the raiders wouldn't have thought they'd a chance of getting theirselves a seacat."

"The cat *was* out at sea."

"But that ain't the point, is it? Hers is the only seacat lives ashore. And the raiders heard about it and thought they had a chance."

"That'd be sense — they knows the value of 'em, just like we do."

"Aye, seacats is rare. Should be on a decent-sized boat with a proper cat's mate. Not some flimsy thing run by a little girl."

"I allas did think maybe Lun was right about the cat. Should've been given to someone suited to it. Melkun's missus would be alive today if it had."

Their voices roll out over the crowd. By the time the captains have finished, every other conversation has kind of fizzled out, and everyone's just staring at them, and at me.

"Cat chose me!" is all I can think to say, the words popping out of my mouth into the silence. People near me cough and look embarrassed, but Captain Ainsty's wife pulls herself up like a ship in full sail and glares at her husband. Who suddenly looks right cowed and scuttles into the cover of the other captains.

"Now is not the time for this discussion," she says, in her ordering-everyone-about voice. "Mrs. Melkun was a fine woman who deserves our respect. And the taking of the Prime Minister's only daughter by raiders — and a little child of seven at that — is a dreadful disaster. I think you'll all agree gossiping does nothing to help things along."

The captains bow their heads meekly and walk off in single file. But they're heading straight for the Old Moon, and I know they'll be going over this every which way for a month.

* * *

After the captains leave, everyone else trickles off, too, shaking my hand and saying how sorry they are. In the end, I'm on my own, stood by Granny's grave. I look around, and the only people left are Andy and his ma and pa, stood a bit away. Andy comes over to where I am.

"Don't listen to them, Lilly," he says, his dark eyes narrow. "Them captains are old fools; they never think any further than boats and fish."

I shake my head.

"It was me went to sea, leaving Granny all alone."

"You had to go fishing, just like everyone does in this miserable village!" And I know Andy's right, 'cept . . . seacats *are* meant to be on the boats all their lives. That way they get to know every lump and hush of the ocean. That way they can tell when something's up and warn the captain or the cat's mate. But I couldn't hardly leave Cat down at the harbor in my little open boat, and, anyway, he followed me home right from the first. Ten years old I was — all puffed up to be chosen by a seacat — thought I must be something really special.

Well, that was three years ago, and now how special am I? Special to lose Granny to the raiders? Special to be left an orphan?

Andy clears his throat, then says, "Do you want to stay with me and Ma and Pa for a bit? You know, so you won't be alone?"

I smile a bit of a smile, and he takes hold of my hand. Our fingers link together, making a pattern of browns. Darker and lighter, like the strong joints on a wooden chest.

In the evening, Andy's ma makes us beachy stew. She must have walked the whole afternoon to find all them mussels, cockles, winkles, and whelks. Andy's face lights up to see such good food. And then she plumps on the table a steaming bowl of potatoes.

"Here, Lilly," says Andy's pa, "have some of these. I got 'em special from Will, works at Burnt Tree Farm."

Beachy stew and potatoes! We don't get that hardly once a month; most days it's oat porridge and dried fish. And even though we laid Granny into the ground this morning, my stomach still growls for such a feast, and I put the food into my mouth. While I'm eating, Andy keeps on trying to cheer me.

"You'll see, things are going to get better, I promise. I'll make sure of it."

And it does give me a tiny bit of cheer to think of me and Andy, saving up to get our own rig.

"We'll be the best fishing boat in the village," I whisper, cos that's what I always say. 'Cept the words seem hollow and dry now, without Granny. Cos she was the one going to be proud when me and Andy started bringing in big catches. She was the one going to be proved right for standing up for me and Cat.

At least I still got Andy. Maybe not everything's ruined, cos me and Andy's still got all our plans to get on with.

But a couple of days later, when I can finally bring myself to go back home, I feel worse all over again. I push at the still-open door of our house and go inside. The fire's out, which makes the whole house feel wrong, cos Granny always kept it chattering. And there are muddy footprints on the floor, which Granny would never have stood for.

Near the wall by the fireplace, there's a large stain, crusty and red on the gray flagstones. I remember what Hetty said, and I get a feeling inside, like I've been tossed about in a stormy sea. I run from that dark room into the street and stare out at the distant wave tops, sparkling with sunlight and tears. I can't believe Granny's not here. I keep thinking I'll hear her come out and start washing the step, like she does every morning. But she doesn't, and the step's all dirty.

I'm still stood staring when Mrs. Ainsty comes marching up, all rustle and bustle.

"Lilly Melkun! The very person I was searching for."

And before I have a chance to run, she's got hold of my hand, with a grip like a crab, and she's got her doing-good look on her face.

"Now dear," she says. "I've something very important to say to you. I've been talking with some of the other wives about what to do with you."

Do with me?

"I can look after myself," I say. I try and shake her off, but her grip's like iron.

"Oh my dear," says Mrs. Ainsty. "You don't think we'd let the granddaughter of Captain Melkun run around like a wild thing?"

"I got my boat. And Cat."

Mrs. Ainsty tuts.

"You don't seriously think you can carry on fishing, do you? This ain't your grandmother's day. If you spend your life wearing fisher's overalls and hanging around with fishermen, well, you won't have a reputation worth a penny."

"I don't need a reputation."

"And that just goes to show how much you need a guiding hand. Someone to look after you and set you on the right way. I know your grandmother indulged your whims — letting you go out fishing and all, but you're hardly a child anymore. Why, I've already been to see Susan Wheeler."

"You never!" I cry.

Mrs. Ainsty looks at me all kindness and raised eyebrows.

"You don't have to thank me, dear. Of course I've been to see the matchmaker for you. And very helpful she was, too. You must be . . . twelve?"

"Thirteen."

"So! Quite old enough to be married! I'm sure between Susan Wheeler, myself, and the other ladies, we can get you wed in no time at all. And after all, you have your seacat. He's a valuable dowry. I don't think we'll have any trouble getting the Hindles to accept you for their son."

"Lun Hindle! But he's spent the last two years trying to get Cat taken from me!"

"Which just shows he'll accept the animal as a dowry."

"But he's lazy. And stupid! And he's only got a boat cos his pa sorted him one."

"That's enough!" snaps Mrs. Ainsty, looking cross. "Do you think you've got the pick of every man in the village? You'd do better than many if you marry into such a good family as the Hindles. So you'd better change your mind about Lun, as there'll be no one who'll want to listen to such vile comments when you're his wife!"

"I won't change my mind, cos it ain't never happening!" I cry, and I finally wrench my hand from hers. Then I'm running again. But this time it's away. Away from our house without Granny in it. Away from Mrs. Ainsty wanting to marry me off. Heading for the harbor, where my boat's waiting.

And that's how come I'm down there just when there's a great clattering of hooves and a soldier comes riding in.

Of course, I ain't the only one to see it. There's a great gang of folk already down at the harbor: fishers hard at work, trying to rescue what they can of sails and nets, hauling boat remains from the water. And the captains, in the ale-stained innards of the Old Moon, taking a bit of drink before they come out and start ordering folk around. Soon as the soldier gallops in, there's a bearded face peering out of one of the pub's windows, mouth round at the sight of the blue uniform, jingling with silver and braid, and the gleaming chestnut horse. Then the face disappears, and next second all the captains come out of the pub, puffing out their chests and muttering importantly. The fisherfolk stop their work, and there's just the sound of the sea and the gulls flying overhead.

"Who's in charge here?" shouts the soldier.

There's a bit of shuffling from the flock of captains, then Captain Ainsty puffs himself forward.

"You can talk to me," he says.

"I'm here on the orders of the commander of the Chichester garrison," says the soldier, "to determine why your beacon was lit for no reason. As it caused no little panic down the coast!"

Everyone looks at everyone else in surprise. Captain Ainsty pulls his chest right up and flings his arm out to the smashed-up remains of our fishing fleet.

"No reason!" he cries, all outrage. "You call the destruction of our fishing fleet no reason?"

The soldier looks around, like he's noticed all the wreckage for the first time. He smiles, and it ain't a nice one.

"You're claiming the raiders came and destroyed your *boats*? And left all the other villages on the coast untouched? I find that rather odd."

"The raiders came down upon us three days ago. Of course they wrought this terrible damage. Who else could it be?"

Everyone nods and mutters, but the soldier just smiles his nasty smile.

"I'd say I was looking right at the most likely perpetrators. After all, the raiders don't attack single villages and then flee. They'd have ravaged the coast and slaughtered the lot of you. Yet you claim your village alone was attacked, and you were all left alive."

Something just boils up inside me at that. "My granny! They killed my granny!" I'm shouting. The soldier looks around at me, but his smile doesn't break, even for a moment.

"You expect me to believe the word of some urchin? I wouldn't be surprised if you did this all yourselves in the hope of compensation."

"No! No! Never!" come the shouts.

"I'll make a report," says the soldier coldly, "then we'll see what happens."

John Greenstick steps forward from the fisherfolk and takes his cap from his head.

"Excusing your pardon, Your Honor," he says. "But you've got to believe us. We're honest folk here, and loyal to the Prime Minister. And we need help. We'll starve if we can't get our boats sorted."

"Aye, what's the Prime Minister going to do to help us?" shouts someone in the crowd.

The soldier's smile turns to a sneer.

"Isn't that just like you peasants? Sly and greedy, every one. All you want is your handouts, but you'll get nothing if it turns out you scuppered your own boats."

And then everyone's in an uproar.

"It was raiders done the damage to our fleet!"

"We ain't scroungers!"

"What'll my children eat if we don't get nothing from His Majesty?"

"Shame on you! Shame on your hard heart."

The soldier's horse starts to skitter about at all the shouting, and the soldier roars out, "Enough! Haven't you read His Majesty's new declaration on attacks? Haven't you understood it? Go and read the notice up at your church if you want to know what's coming to you."

But no one needs to go up to the church, we've all got that notice by heart, all read it dozens of times since it got pinned up last month.

In view of recent increased attacks by picaroons out of Eastern Anglia *– named by commoners as raiders –* His Glorious Majesty *the* Prime Minister *of the* Last Ten Counties *of* England *has concluded that compensation payments have been acting as an incitement to collaboration and fraud.* His Majesty *therefore commands that punishment, not compensation, shall be the reward for such attacks in the future, unless certain proof of commoner resistance is provided.*

By his might and right, His Glorious Majesty *makes this judgment for the benefit of all.*

And at the bottom there's a big squiggly signature.

The soldier glares about at the crowd. Everyone's still mumbling and fizzling with anger, but the shouting quiets down; no one wants the Prime Minister to punish us, not on top of being raided.

"Well now," says the soldier, "since that's cleared up, I will get on with my main business here." He looks around. "Which way is it to the house of Mrs. Clare Denton?" A hush falls over us, like we all stop breathing at once. "Come on! I haven't got all day. I'm charged to lead Miss Alexandra Randall's escort back from her aunt's house to the Prime Minister's palace in Swindon. And we need to leave in good time."

No one says anything. Captain Ainsty and John Greenstick sneak back into the gaggle. The soldier looks around at everyone, and you can see a dawning of something on his face.

"Is there some problem?" he barks.

Eventually Captain Ainsty pipes up.

"You can't see Mrs. Denton," he says nervously, "because I hear the poor woman is laid up in bed with the hysterics . . . And you can't take little Alexandra Randall back to her father, because the raiders have her."

·3· ANGEL ISLING

My father! He's back!

Everything's in ruck and noise, servants and slaves running all over. In the kitchens they're breaking their backs to get the cooking done.

Coz Father's home, so we'll be having a feast!

The great doors of the main hall — facing east, facing the sea — is pushed open. I run outside; I want to see Father sailing in. But it seems like everyone who's been left behind — wives and concubines, old men and too young — is already out there on the main deckway. Five, six, seven deep against the railing. I try pushing, try jumping up. But the only person who even gives me a look is Ananda, skank wife of Enrique.

She just scowls out, "Stop pushing, Zeph, have some respect!"

"Respect you, pig features?" I say, then leg it before she can hit me.

She would never have spoke to me like that if Mother was still alive.

I go here and there behind the crowd, but no one's letting me through. And I need to see Father!

A thought comes in my head. It's bad, but it gets right in, not letting go.

"So what if it's forbidden?" it says. "Ain't you the son of the greatest Boss in all the Families?"

I make sure no one's checkin' me, then I pull open the north gate of the wind gallery. Just a crack. Just enough to squeeze through.

I shut it behind me, and I'm into the dim half-dark of the wind gallery. The spirits will punish me for sure — bad dreams, bad luck, bad skin. And I'll get a nice beating if Ims catches me. But who cares?

All four windgates are shut, the red spirit-flags hanging limp, but the willow lattice walls let in light through cracks in the weave. North, all I can see is the crowd on the deckway. South is the marshes, curving away into green. West is the carved wooden walls and high thatched roof of Father's hall, but east, toward the sea, is all specks of blue — dark sea below, light sky above. And there's a bit of red.

Red sails. Father's dragonboat!

I get quick to the northeast corner, press my eyes to the gaps. And now, through the blurry pattern of woven willow stems, I can see Father coming home.

It's quiet in the wind gallery, even with the whole Family right near me on the deckway. Only the *splash, splash* of water beneath the hall, lapping at the stilt-legs, and the wind spirits brushing and breathing against the wind-gallery walls. But I'm all right, they can't get inside unless the gates is opened.

This is a good spot. Through these little holes I can see everything: the seven islands that sit between the hall and the open sea; the sea channels — wide and sky-gleaming now the tide's full in; the reeds flicking waves of green across the marshes.

Most important, though, I can see Father's dragonboat. Red sail billowing, red flags fluttering, shields stacked at her prow. The foredeck's like a forest of swords; even from in here I can hear the cheers of the warriors.

Which means success!

Everyone on the deckway is cheering as well now. But I have to keep my mouth shut — I don't want Ims finding me. Or worse, the Windspeaker. He'd spike me for sure!

Father's ship cuts easy through the water, the dragonhead carved in her prow snarling and showing its teeth.

"Medwin! Medwin! Medwin!" shouts the crowd on the deckway.

"Angel Isling! Angel Isling!" shout the warriors on Father's warship.

Boss and Family.

Which is everything that matters.

The dragonboat's red sail is being furled, but she's still sliding through the water. Thirty long oars lift and pull with a creaking, splashing sound — like insect legs, powering her along. The holes in the lattice wall ain't showing blue or green now, just the brown and red of Father's boat. And the shining steel of the warriors' swords, and the red of their leathers, and the dull gleam of the helmets and armor. There's shouts and calls as the oars are raised, and the warriors on deck put their swords down and get ready to moor Father's dragonboat. One of them throws a rope to the deckway. It's red-haired Eadan, leaning right out from the prow. He looks well proud.

Straightaway, his mother's going on, "Oh my son! My wonderful son!"

Eadan's four years older than me, and this was his first journey as a warrior.

I wish it had been mine.

More lines are thrown from the boat and get caught by slaves, standing ready. But Eadan's mother grabs a rope and starts hauling it, which gets a laughing cheer from the warriors on ship. And soon everyone's pulling in my father's warship, not stopping until she's moored tight to the deckway.

Then it's like the crowd falls into waiting. Everyone's silent. The warriors on board move aside, making way.

Making way for Father.

And he's smiling, calling out as people press forward, trying to touch him. Steps off the dragonboat, onto the deckway. But he don't go into the hall, and now he stops smiling, looking around. He crosses his arms: frowning; searching. He sees I ain't there. He's wondering where I am!

"Where is Aileen?" he shouts.

Not me! Why not me? All he cares about is his skanky concubine, and the stupid mare's not even here. Like always.

There's the sound of footsteps out from the hall, and when I put my eyes to a different hole, I can see Aileen, walking out to him.

She's got a smile on her nasty face, probably coz everyone's looking at her. It ain't right: She's only his doxy! A slave, sold down by some Scottish smuggler. But she's got her claws in, for sure. If my mother was still here, she'd slap her into place in a second. But she ain't here. Nor Saera, neither. My mother and my little sister, both floated out into the marshes three years back. Sometimes I wonder if Father even remembers them.

"Here I am, my lord," says Aileen, in her stupid Scottish accent.

And my father opens his arms and takes hold of her. Squeezing her.

"You're a sight to make a man happy. And I've got a sight as fine to show you, too. You'll never guess what luck we had."

The smile on Aileen's stinking face gets bigger.

"Did you get it?" she asks.

"What a sweet time we had!" cries Father. "Those villages is like oysters ripe for cracking. And what a pearl we found inside!"

"So did you get it? Can I see it?" pants Aileen.

"This is the start!" shouts Father. "Everything starts from now!"

The warriors on the ship start laughing and shouting. I put my eye to a different hole, and I can see them pull something across the boat toward the deckway. It struggles. It wails. It's a well miserable, thin-faced little girl, with bare blue legs poking out from a white nightdress, ropes binding her arms to her sides. She's about the same age Saera was when she got sick. And she looks half sick herself.

Aileen pushes out of Father's arms.

"What is that?" she snaps. "Where's the jewel?"

"Forget the jewel!" says Father. "This little girl is far more valuable."

"I want to go home. Please!" wails the little girl.

Aileen's fists are clenched. "Why didn't you do what you were meant to?"

My father laughs at her.

"Don't worry, my love. You can have all the jewels you want, but later. First let me introduce you to Miss Alexandra Randall, daughter of His *Glorious* Majesty Archibald Randall — Prime Minister of England, defender of their useless Last Ten Counties!"

Aileen's mouth drops open.

"What have you done?" she whispers.

"I've got one over that fool! Now let's see if the whining English puppy dares to leave his palace and test himself against real warriors!"

"But you were only supposed to get the jewel!" cries Aileen. "This will bring a war party down on us!"

"I pigging hope so!" shouts Father. "And then we'll give the English such a pounding! Those backstabbers have been wanting a war for years, so I say let them have one!"

A war with the English! My father is the greatest Boss in all the Families!

The crowd on the deckway starts cheering, and the warriors on the boat are cheering, and even I start cheering, here in my hiding place.

The only people who ain't happy is Aileen, who looks well sour and frowning, and the little English girl, who starts to cry.

·4· LISTENING IN

Finding out about Alexandra Randall being kidnapped sends that soldier off in a hurry. He doesn't even stop to ask more questions — just turns his horse and gallops away. He races back to the coast road, whipping his beautiful horse like it's a wooden top.

And I suddenly realize what everyone else has been thinking on these last two days. The raiders came and kidnapped the Prime Minister's daughter! Which means it won't just be the captains at the Old Moon talking about the attack. Once that soldier gets word to Swindon, the Prime Minister and parliament and generals and who knows what other important people from all over the Last Ten Counties, they'll all be talking about our village.

Everyone's even more twitchy and jumpy now.

"No good's going to come to us from all this," says Andy's pa, as we're sat round that evening, watching the fire fade to embers in the hearth.

"It'll be all right, you'll see," says Andy's ma, knitting away. "The Prime Minister knows we're good folk. He'll look after us." She looks my way, like the Prime Minister's going to take special care of me.

"His father might have, but I ain't so sure about this 'un," says Andy's pa. "And that soldier was right, there's something odd in all this. It ain't like the raiders to only attack one village." He shakes his head. "I don't reckon the Prime Minister and his kind'll go looking far and wide for folk to blame. Not when they've got us right here."

"Hush about it, then," says Andy's ma, giving him a stern look. "Haven't these children seen enough bad things already?"

There's a knock at the door, and we all jump at the sound. But it's only Hetty's boy, Charlie. He's grinning his little head off.

"Guess what?" he says. Andy's pa smiles back.

"I can't guess. You tell me."

"I got a penny," says Charlie.

"That's very nice," says Andy's ma. "Maybe you should go and give it to your ma."

"I can't, not yet," says Charlie, "cos I got to tell Lilly."

"Tell her what?" says Andy.

"About Mrs. Denton. Martha gave me the penny. She told me to tell you to come and see Mrs. Denton. Tomorrow." He beams proudly. "I done it now." Then he shuts the door with a *bang,* and he's gone.

"Mrs. Denton?" I say, wondering what's going on. "Why'd she want to see me?"

"She's a good kind woman," says Andy's ma. "She must wants to help you somehow. So you go along and be respectful."

And I suppose she's right. Seems all the fine ladies of the village want to help me now I'm an orphan.

Next morning, Andy and his pa go down to the harbor to carry on patching their boats. Me and Cat ought to be helping, but instead I'm off to see Mrs. Denton.

I knock on the back door, like Andy's ma told me to, and it's opened by Martha, Mrs. Denton's housekeeper.

"Oh, it's you," she says, not looking very happy about it. "I suppose you'd better come in."

The door's newly mended, with planks nailed over the middle. The raiders must have smashed it in, cos around the mending there's still chinks and chunks of axe marks. Just like our door at home. It makes me shiver, and I don't want to go through. But I have to, and as I do, I get a sudden memory from years back.

There was a night when beacons got lit down the coast, and Granny woke me from sleep.

"The beacons is lit, we have to be going."

Maybe it was waking into darkness, or Granny's face lit by a candle, or all the tales I'd heard of raider savageness, but straightaway I was screaming and crying, "Don't let them kill us! Don't let them kill us!" I can remember how scared I was, like a cold sword against my back.

But Granny just hugged me and said, "Don't you worry, Lilly-girl. We'll be gone before they gets here. Anyway, raiders ain't interested in little children, they want gold and boat cargoes and anything they can steal. Why, they'd see a little mite like you and pass right on by."

And I always took that as a comfort.

But what about Alexandra Randall? She must have been woken out of sleep, and not for comforting words and a safe escape, but to the sound of the door being broken in, heavy boots tramping, and raiders shouting inside her own house.

I saw her once in the village with her ma: an overfrilled little girl being paraded about by a fancy lady in silks and ribbons. I reckoned then how she must be the luckiest girl I'd ever seen, to be so rich. Even when Granny told me a year back how her mother had been taken ill and died, I hardly felt sorry for her. But now I wonder if she hid under her bed when the raiders got in the house? I wonder if she screamed for help that never came? I wonder if they let her put warm clothes on, or just bundled her up in her nightgown, her bare feet kicking in the cold morning air?

* * *

Martha takes me into a big, flagstone kitchen, with a great oak table, heavy cookware, and a range glowing with fire. Then she turns to look at me, and scowls.

"First off, we'll get things straight. Mrs. Denton asked for you to come and visit, but that doesn't make you more than a fishgirl, nor her any less of a fine lady. So you'd better keep to your place, cos one wrong step and you're out on your ear."

I nod meekly, cos Martha ain't one to cross. When we was little, scamping through the village, me and Andy knew just who'd smile at our chubby little faces and who'd give us a smack for sassing back. And Martha was always the smacking kind.

"And another thing," says Martha, scowling down at Cat. "That animal of yours better not drop any fur on the furniture."

Then she pushes me through a door into a wide, dark hallway. At one end is the brown wood of the front door, and at the other a set of wide, dark stairs. Facing us are some tall double doors. Martha knocks quietly twice on one of them doors, then turns to me. She pinches my arm and whispers harshly.

"Mrs. Denton's in her sitting room, so in you go. But mind you're quiet and meek as a mouse. She wants to see you cos of your granny, but that only shows how good she is, thinking of others' troubles when she's suffering herself."

Then Martha opens one of the doors, and Cat trots in like he lives here.

Mrs. Denton's parlor is the loveliest room I've ever seen. It's so big, with pale yellow walls and a picture over the fireplace of a young man and woman holding hands. And there's sofas and soft chairs to sit on, and a carpet over the floor. But the curtains are closed, and the room is all shadows and no air. It smells a bit like lavender, a bit like sour breath.

Mrs. Denton's sat on one of the sofas, her head leaning to one side. There's a handkerchief over her face, and she's snoring quietly. At the sound of me and Martha walking in, she startles and squawks.

"Who's that? What are you doing? Help! Help!"

"Hush, madam," says Martha. "It's only me. And I've got that Lilly Melkun, like you wanted."

"Oh yes! Lilly Melkun!" Mrs. Denton smiles. "How silly of me! It was just a fright to wake and have someone in the room, it made me think of . . ." She shakes her head and pushes herself up from the sofa.

"And you brought your cat. How lovely of you to think of cheering me. Here, pusskin!" Martha rolls her eyes and stomps out. Cat carries on sniffing about and doesn't even look at Mrs. Denton. I keep an eye on him, thinking of his claws in all them carpets and cushions.

"Go and see the lady," I say. But Cat hardly ever listens to me, and now he just sits down on her carpet and starts washing his butt.

Mrs. Denton coughs, looks away quickly, and says, "Be a dear and let some light in."

I go over to the window and pull back a curtain. The morning light breaks into the room, picking out the dark circles under Mrs. Denton's eyes, the deep lines running across her forehead, and her hair all ragged and mussed.

She puts out a hand.

"Come and sit by me, Lilly." There's tears in her eyes. "We two have gained something in common this last week."

She takes my hand in hers and pulls me down onto the sofa right next to her. Her head comes forward, like a heron sighting for fish.

"You know, I think you're the only person in the village I can bear to see right now . . . The only one who could understand what's happened to me."

And she's proper crying now, wiping at her face with her handkerchief. This ain't what I want! I've had enough crying of my own these last days.

Maybe I could say Cat was sick and we have to leave? But he looks pretty healthy, licking away at himself, one leg in the air.

"Oh Lilly," sobs Mrs. Denton, "I can't sleep for worrying over Alexandra and what she must be suffering. And when I do sleep, I am tormented by nightmares. I keep thinking what they may be doing to her."

And then I don't know who's worse off, me or Mrs. Denton. I'll never see Granny again, but at least I know she ain't suffering. Cos everyone knows raiders chop up their captives a bit at a time and boil them for stew, or hang them in cages and use them for shooting practice.

"I'm sorry about Alexandra," I say, and Mrs. Denton gives me a watery smile.

"You're a good girl, Lilly." She sighs, and wipes at her eyes again. "I wanted you to come here so I could see if there was anything I could do to help you in your time of need." And I get a little bit of hope. But then Mrs. Denton says, "Except, you have to understand, I'm not a rich woman." Which doesn't sound so hopeful after all. "I married for love, not wealth, and against the wishes of my brother. Dear Eustace, my husband, was wonderful with everything except money, and he left me with almost nothing. It is only by an allowance from my brother that I can even live here. So I hope you understand that I can give you very little . . ." She puts her hands over mine, and stares at me. "But if there is any other way I can help you, just ask."

I'm trying to think of anything she can do if she can't give me money, but I can't. So I'm sat there, my mouth open like a fish's, when there's a great thumping on the front door knocker. *Clank clank clank!*

Mrs. Denton is up and fluttering in an instant.

"Oh! It's them! They're back!"

She almost makes me panic, too, but then my sense comes back.

"It can't be raiders. They don't use door knockers, they use axes."

Mrs. Denton sits down at that, flapping her hanky over her face.

"Of course, dear, how practical you are."

I can hear Martha's feet clumping as she heads to the front door, and then, as soon as it's opened, a loud voice says, "Let me in! I'm here to see my sister!"

Mrs. Denton's brother? The Prime Minister!

"Oh dear!" says Mrs. Denton, turning pale. "It's Archie!" She turns to me. "What will I do? What can I say to him?" And now she's flapping and flustering even worse than before. "He always had such a temper, even when we were children!" She starts pulling at me. "Quick! You can hide! Go in there and he won't see you!"

And before I can say anything, she picks up Cat, making him squawk as she pushes him into my arms. Then she shoves us through a door, not the one back to the hallway, but another one, and slams it behind us.

So now we're stuck in another room. A completely different kind of room. No sofas and pretty chairs here, just a big old desk by the window. And there ain't any pictures or mirrors on the walls, either. Instead it's books — shelves full of them, covering a whole wall. Them books make me think of what Granny said about Mrs. Denton's dead husband.

"Married some scholar, didn't she. Caused a great big scandal at the time, cos she ought to have been marrying some prince or such like. And him having such an interest in the olden times as well. That's how she ended up living in such a poor little place as this village, cos none of them lords and ministers and such would have anything to do with her after. And then Mr. Denton went and headed off on a tour of all the drowned places looking for his relics, and came back dying of the wasting plague. *I* could have told him no good would come of fishing about in them dead towns." I get a shiver.

In Mrs. Denton's sitting room I can hear her sobbing and crying. "Oh Archie, I'm sorry! So, so sorry!" And I know straight off I don't want to hear her. Cos she makes me think of Hetty, sat crying next to Granny's body. So I head off across the room and set about putting my mind to anything else.

Against the far wall are two tall cabinets with little labels pasted onto the front of all the drawers, as well as a glass-fronted cupboard, crammed inside with all sorts of jars and pots and stuffed creatures and a whole lot of other things that I don't know what they are.

Cat's struggling in my arms and saying, "Mwaaarow!" which means *let me down,* and he wriggles out of my grasp onto the floor. Straightaway he's sniffing around the cabinets. And since there ain't anything else to do while we wait, I end up doing the same.

It takes me a while to pick through the words on the labels. On the first cabinet, they all say stuff like MILITARY CENTERS

Drowned by Rising Sea Levels and Ruins of the Dust Plains. I know what some of that means, cos the vicar's always sermoning about how the sea rose up and swallowed whole towns, and the sun got hotter and frazzled the land, and all the crops died and turned to dust, and that's why we're hungry. He says it's punishment for the greed of the olden times, and that's why we've got to be humble. He says the olden-time people were wicked, and their machines were wickeder.

I wonder if Mr. Denton ever listened to the vicar's sermons?

Developments in Com Puting says the label on one drawer. I take hold of the handle and ease it open, but it's all just paper and close-set writing, so I push it shut again. Granny used to tell tales about puters, how the olden-time people used them to do their thinking for them. She said they probably was wicked to do that, but I shouldn't worry too much what the vicar says cos he's always in a fret about something.

"Think about it," she'd say. "Them Scots use all sorts of teknology, and they got their solar power and whatnot. Have they been cursed or struck by plague? Why, we have it far worse than them." And then she'd whisper, so there was no chance of anyone hearing, "Chances are, we'd be a lot better off if we lived in Greater Scotland." But we both knew there wasn't much chance of that, cos there's plenty of soldiers at the border to stop anyone who wants to try leaving.

Instead, I turn to the glass-fronted cupboard. Mr. Denton's strange collectings are staring out at me. There's little flat boxes in different colors, with two wires coming off, and buttons attached to the end of the wires. And there's a stack of thin silver discs with holes in the middle. There's curvy little boxes with knobs and buttons on 'em, just the right size for holding in your hands.

Some of the things are really strange. Like the statues of tiny women, with blond hair and long thin arms, staring out with big dead eyes. And there's another statue, of a fat old man with a white beard and dressed in red. He looks like a raider, cos only raiders dress in a single color, but on his stand the label says SINGING SANTA. Maybe he was a really nasty raider boss, who sang while he chopped up people?

But mostly it's just dusty old stuff. There's a whole half of the cupboard just filled with boxes: On the shelves near the floor, they're big and gray; on the middle shelves they're smaller and mostly black; on the topmost shelf, the boxes are no bigger than your hand, flat and sparkling, in different colors of pink and red and green. A bit like seashells. Next to them is a paper label, but when I manage to pick out the words, it says LATE TWENTY-FIRST CENTURY COM PUTERS. It's all a bit creepy, and I get another shiver. Can you catch the wasting plague from old-time things?

I'm still looking at them shell puters when I hear the Prime Minister shouting, "Don't be an idiot, Clare! I can't just pay a ransom!"

After that their conversation's so loud I can hear every word. At least, I can if I creep over and put my ear to the door.

"Why not? Don't you want your daughter back?"

"Of course!"

"Well it hardly seems like it! Just like you've hardly seemed interested in the poor little mite up until now."

"Don't be ridiculous. I have as much interest in her as a father should in a daughter. Why, only last week I met with Lord Brown to discuss options for her betrothal. And now I've dropped everything — matters of state you couldn't hope to understand — in order to rush to this wretched village and find out what's happened to her."

"Is that all she is to you? Marriage fodder? Another tool in your plottings?"

"Spare me your sentimental nonsense. Since she couldn't be a boy, getting married to my advantage is the most useful and important thing that child will ever do. Or would be, if you hadn't let her be taken by raiders."

Mrs. Denton lets out a sob.

"I never meant . . ." She takes a big sighing breath. "Archie, please, you have money. The raiders must have taken her for the ransom. Why not pay it, and then she can come back home."

"Don't be ridiculous! What message would that send?"

"It would get her back!"

"Which just shows how little you know of the real world. How could I, of all people, possibly make a deal with those outlaws who trade in terror? I assume this is another example of your willful naïveté. Like your wretched marriage."

"Please! If you won't pay a ransom for Alexandra, what's going to happen to her?"

"Maybe you should have asked *yourself* that before you pleaded with me to let her stay here with you. I don't know why I gave in, she would have been far better off at court."

"Don't you think I wish I hadn't asked? I've regretted it every second since she was taken. And the moment she was taken plays in my mind, over and over. But I just wanted her to be with family. She's become so quiet since Anne Marie died. I never imagined this would happen! Anyway, if you were so concerned, why did you only send two soldiers to guard her?"

"Because I foolishly assumed that Englishmen would fight to defend a member of the Prime Ministerial family. Instead these wretches just ran away!"

"No one in this village could be any match for the raiders."

"Because they're whining commoner scum!"

"For goodness' sake, Archie, they're just fishermen; they can't fight raiders. They need garrisons and protection, not punishment and persecution."

"That's enough! What on earth makes you think you're in any position to judge on this matter? When were *you* last in charge of defending the Last Ten Counties?"

"I just think —"

"No! I don't want to hear it! You had your way, and my daughter was taken by the raiders. Now I shall do things properly, and get my daughter back with force of arms, not force of money."

"But Alexandra —"

"Is daughter to a Prime Minister! She will be resolute and determined. She will learn fortitude."

"She's seven!"

"You were seven when Father took us with him on his marshes campaign."

"I don't remember it teaching me fortitude. I did learn what a soldier looks like when the top of his head has been sliced off and his brains are oozing out into the mud. Is that what you want your daughter to find out?"

"Don't be so pathetic! I'm recruiting the militia from whichever of these sniveling fishermen is worth pressing, and then I'm going on campaign, just like Father did, so there's an end to it as far as you're concerned. Now, order me something to drink from that servant of yours. The archbishop told me I have to forgive you for losing Alexandra. So I'm just going to have to sit here until I can bring myself to do it. And I should think it'll take at least a couple of bottles of wine."

·5· THE MAN IN BLACK

Through the door, I hear a heavy *thump,* which I reckon is the Prime Minister sitting down. Then a bell tinkling, more footsteps, and Mrs. Denton ordering red wine for him. Then nothing. Even when I put my ear right to the keyhole.

So I put my eye to it instead, and I can just make out the two of them, Mrs. Denton and the Prime Minister. They're sat, glaring at each other.

So much for Mrs. Denton's short visit. I could be here all day waiting, the Prime Minister ain't known for being much on forgiveness. Well, there's another door out of this room. All I have to do is sneak out through it, run down the hall to the front door, and then I'll be off. Cos I've got to warn Andy. The Prime Minister said he was going to press the villagers into the militia and send them to fight the raiders.

What if he gets Andy? The raiders will kill him, just like they always kill militiamen.

"Cat," I call. But he's nowhere. Not on the table, nor under it. Not climbing over the bookshelves, nor snoozing on top of the cabinets. And the window ain't open, so he can't have got out that way.

"Where are you?" I say crossly, and then I hear a muffled mewling. It's coming from behind the glass-fronted cupboard. I walk over and look inside, but he's not sat next to any of them boxes.

"Cat?" I call again, and get another mew. Sounding quite sorry for himself.

At one end of the cupboard there's a little gap between it and the wall of bookshelves. Just big enough so a person could squeeze in if they was trying to reach a book right at the end of the shelf. Easily big enough for Cat.

I step into the dark little space, which smells of wood and old paper, and straightaway I know where Cat is. Cos the cupboard ain't completely flush against the wall. There's a narrowing gap, no wider than my hand, and somehow Cat's got himself stuck in it. I can see his tail and his furry back legs. He's wriggling and trying to twist himself out, but he's just getting himself stuck tighter.

I crouch down, as best I can in the tiny space, and reach my arm behind the cabinet. But the tips of my fingers only brush his tail. I try pushing on the cupboard to see if I can move it a bit. But it's so heavy, it might as well be made of stone.

I'm crouched into this corner, practically behind the cupboard, and wondering what to do, when the door opens. Not the door to the sitting room, the door from the hallway.

"If you wouldn't mind waiting in here, sir," says Martha. "Mrs. Denton did say they wasn't to be disturbed . . ."

"No, no. It's really quite all right. I have no objection to waiting for a few moments." It's a man's voice, but no one I recognize.

"Well I'll tell Mrs. Denton and His Majesty directly they come out."

Then Martha shuts the door, leaving the man in here with me.

I can't exactly say why I don't tell him straight off I'm in the room. Maybe cos it looks like I'm hiding. Or maybe cos I don't want to admit how my seacat, who's meant to be so clever and special, has got himself stuck behind a cupboard. Anyway, whatever the reason, I just keep still and quiet, crouched between the cupboard and the bookshelf.

The man walks over to the door leading into the sitting room, and I get a look at him. First thing I notice is his hair — how short it is. Most men in our village have scraggly hair to at least below their ears. But his is so short he looks like he's been shaving his head as well as his chin. Next thing is his clothes. Cos they're nothing like I've seen here, either poor folk or rich. Fishers and farmers wear rough, practical stuff. Smocks and trousers, patched and darned on every corner. And the rich have their bright-colored dresses and jackets, with frills and flounces all over. But this man's clothes are made of something smooth, clean, and pretty much all black, apart from small strips of color running along the seams. It's like he's got the money to have really good stuff, but just ain't bothered about showing off. And when I peer at his face, it ain't young and it ain't old, and his eyes look like he's got something on his mind.

At first, he doesn't act that strangely. Does just what anyone would, putting his ear to the door into the sitting room, poking around in the cabinets and pulling open drawers. Like he's looking for something. If he is, he doesn't find it, and I have to crouch even farther into the corner so he doesn't see me.

Then he does something that makes me poke my head up to try and see better. He reaches into the blackness of his strange dark clothes and pulls out what looks like a little flat box. When he opens it, one half of its inside looks like it's made of dark silver, and the other has little buttons in a square pattern. He lays the opened box on the table by the window, in a patch of sunlight, and it makes a little chiming noise, like it's happy to get in the sunshine. He looks around at that, like he's checking no one's heard, but luckily doesn't see me hid in the corner. The little box chimes three more times, and the man taps on the buttons. Then he holds it up to his head. Next thing, he's talking. To himself!

"Hello, are you alone?"

Then he pauses.

"No, but you can't be too careful."

Pause.

"I know! Why on earth did that fool Medwin take the girl . . . No, hold on a minute. I'm not criticizing you. I'm sure you're doing what you can, but this is rapidly turning into a disaster."

Pause.

"I had no idea Randall's daughter was going to be here! He hardly sees her, hardly even mentions her, so how could I have known she'd been sent away?"

Pause.

"Well, this is hardly going to plan."

Pause.

"Don't panic yet. I'm in Eustace Denton's house, let's see where that gets us. I've already had a chance to take a quick look for it."

Pause.

"Of course I won't! But maybe it isn't even in the house. Perhaps he hid it somewhere else in the village. If only he hadn't gone and died before he could get it to us."

Pause.

"I'm afraid Medwin is *your* problem. See what you can do to bring him round."

Long pause.

"I know you want to get out, but remember how important this is. We need to find it. Denton said he was sure it was military; that was why we offered him asylum, why we're going to such lengths. Think what might happen if it falls into the wrong hands. Just a little bit longer, that's all we ask."

I'm wondering if the man is crazed, or drunk, when Cat gives himself a shake and shudder and with a great howling crash shoots backward out of the gap behind the cabinet, knocking me over and sending us both sprawling out from the hidey-hole, onto the floor.

The man spins round, puts his little box away so quick you'd think it had never been, and says, "Well now. What have we here?"

"I was just trying to get my cat. I mean, he got stuck behind the cupboard, and I couldn't get him out."

'Cept now Cat's washing his belly like nothing ever happened. The man frowns, and takes a step toward me.

"Were you spying on me?"

"No! I was just trying to get my cat. I didn't hear anything. I mean . . ."

The man smiles.

"I should think a little lassie like you would know when she needs to be sensible. When she needs to forget things? Let's see, how can I help you forget?"

I don't feel at all happy about that smile.

The man walks toward me, and there's nowhere for me to go but behind that cupboard. 'Cept it was hardly wide enough for Cat, let alone for me, to squeeze behind. I'm just about to open my mouth and start screaming when the door into

Mrs. Denton's sitting room springs open and there she is, with her brother looking red-faced and angry.

"What's happened? I heard a crash!" says Mrs. Denton, then stops, looking surprised to see the strange man in her study.

"Ambassador. What are you doing here?" says the Prime Minister.

The man in black turns and bows.

"Prime Minister. I was just waiting to speak with you. Mrs. Denton's woman showed me in here to wait, where I uncovered this little minx. A thief of some kind, I shouldn't wonder."

"Don't be ridiculous!" says Mrs. Denton. "This is Lilly Melkun, a tragic orphan girl. I asked her to wait in here for me."

I manage to stand up, holding Cat. I know there's all dust and fluff in my hair.

"Cat got stuck behind the cupboard," I say.

"How typical of you, Clare!" snaps the Prime Minister. "Spending your care on some urchin while you let your own niece fall into God knows what danger."

"That's not fair —" starts Mrs. Denton, but her brother just snaps his fingers at her.

"Jasper, I am glad you're here. I thought Greater Scotland's representative would be bound to have an opinion on how to deal with this traitor's nest of a village. I imagine the soldiers will have rounded them up by now. I was planning to go and see how many of them to hang!"

"Archie, no!" cries Mrs. Denton, but she may as well not be here for all the notice he takes. And I don't want to be here, either! I have to find Andy, find his pa. I have to warn them!

· 6 ·
FEASTING AND FIGHTING

My father puts down his cup, wine sloshing in the bottom. He looks angry.

"I gotta think on it, Zeph."

My mouth goes dry. Everyone stops talking; all I can hear is the reed torches hissing, lighting the feast hall with their flickers and smoke. Father's been well pleased since he got back from the raid, and he's ordered feast after feast. I thought this'd be a good time to ask, but he ain't saying anything, just checkin' me. And so is everyone else at the high table.

Faz — father's Windspeaker — he's frowning, like he always does. Next to him, Ims has got worry on his crisscrossed scar face. He wants Father to say yes, I know it! Ever since I can remember, he's always been on my side.

Across from Ims is Roba, my brother. My half brother. My stinking, lowborn, older-by-seven-years brother. He don't look too happy – but then, he never does if I'm anywhere near Father. And then there's Aileen, staring at me from her witch-green eyes. I don't know what she's thinking, but I bet it's nothing good for me.

I hold my breath, waiting for Father's answer. Then he grins.

"I thought on it, and you can come along! You're not far off being a warrior. You should start making your journeys."

Lunden! I'm going to Lunden! I'm so chuffed, there's a big grin all over my face. Faz nearly smiles. Ims says, "Nice one!"

Then Aileen butts in.

"Do you really think he should go?" she says. "After all, he's only a boy. And Lunden's a dangerous place."

My gut turns over. Ever since Father bought her, she's done nothing but try and turn him against me.

"I ain't a boy! I'm thirteen!" I say.

"Oh, so you're practically a man," she says.

Roba can't stop himself smiling at that, and I get ready for a smack from Father. Then, everything shifts. Father don't hit me. He don't even take Aileen's side. He just shakes his head. At her!

"Zeph's right," he says. "He ain't a child no longer. You must be thinking of your soft Scottish boys – Zeph's well old enough to go to Lunden."

I can't believe it! By her face, Aileen can't believe it, either, and Roba looks well put out. Father punches my arm, but like a joke.

"Family boys is out fighting when Scottish lads are still weakening their brains in school." He calls out to the whole hall, "Ain't that right? We make men of our boys, while the Scots make women out of theirs!"

And everyone's cheering and laughing. Maybe Father is finally getting his brains back from that Scottish wench? Aileen don't say nothing, but her eyes show what she really thinks — how she's so much better than us for being Scottish. Well all that tech stuff and learning didn't stop her ending up a slave, did it?

But who cares about her? Today it feels like things are changing for me: Father's back; we're going to war with the English; I'm sitting here at the feast; I'll be going to Lunden; Aileen has been put in her place.

"That's sorted, then," says Father, and he turns to the Windspeaker. "Hey, Faz, how about you bring our little guest of honor to see us?"

Faz smiles at that, showing teeth the same color as his bleached hair, then he pushes himself from the table and disappears. Off to the slave hall.

After a bit, Faz is back, towing the little English girl. She's still in her nightdress, but now the ropes is off her, and Faz is pulling her by one of her skinny arms. At the sight of the English girl, the warriors at the tables start shouting, laughing, banging their plates and knives together — *clang clang clang!* Her eyes get wide and frightened.

Saera had eyes like that. Toward the end, when she was so weak from the shivers she could hardly speak. "Don't let me die," she whispered in a little croaking voice.

And I said, "You ain't gonna, I'll make sure of it." But I couldn't keep my promise.

Faz stops in front of our table, and Father shouts out, "Let's hear it for Alexandra Randall! As fine a little doxy as ever came out of England, and all ready to start a war with!"

A great roar goes up, and a great battering of plates. The little English girl looks even more frightened, and she starts crying again. The cheering goes on and on, so it's hard to hear anything else. But I can see Aileen nagging at my father, and when the noise starts to die, he says, "All right, lady! Anything to shut you up!"

He waves at Faz. "Bring the little thing over here."

Faz pulls the English girl round the table to Father. She's crying so hard she ain't even looking at anything, and her bare feet stumble and slip. Father grabs hold of her and lifts her onto his lap. Then she stops crying! She goes rigid, her pale eyes wide.

"Now then, little madam," says Father, "my good lady here thinks you need a bit of kindness, coz you're a child. But I know how you fought and kicked when we grabbed you, so I think we should keep you locked up safe like an animal. What do you think?"

The girl turns her little face to check my father, and stares like she's waiting for him to slit her throat.

"Please don't toy with her, Medwin," says Aileen. "Can't you see she's frightened out of her wits?"

"And what do you want me to do? Wrap her in lambs' wool and sing her lullabies? I might have done that with my own daughter, but I ain't about to start with Randall's."

"She's only a little lass! Isn't it enough that you've gone against all the plans? Are you also going to take your hatred for Randall out on a speck of a girl?"

Father hisses and glares at Aileen.

"Don't speak to me that way, woman! I do what I want, when I want."

Ims steps in, checkin' Father with his dark eyes. It's all he ever needs to do.

"Maybe Aileen ain't so far out of line? After all, that Scottish agent wanted us to raid Denton's house for some jewel they're after, not the Prime Minister's daughter."

"Are you going soft on me, Ims?"

"Never!" says Ims with a laugh. "I like the idea of an English war as much as every man here. I just wonder how we're gonna sort the deal when we next meet up with the Scots."

"Let me worry about them and their schemes. When the Denton biddy started shrieking about the girl"— he chuckles —"how we wasn't to touch her coz she was Randall's kid . . . Do you think I was gonna miss a chance like that just for having shook the hand of some Scottish spy? I said it to Aileen, and I'll say it to them: I do what I want, when I want. Anything else is just slavery."

"What do they need some jewel for, anyway?" asks Roba. "They must have plenty of loot with all their tech and democracy and the other things they're always boasting on about."

Ims acts like he ain't even heard Roba.

"The Scots offered a crazy price for us to raid that village. You was right to break Family ways to make a deal with those northerners, coz the weapons smugglers is only interested in Scottish cash. But if we break that deal, they might tell the Family council . . ."

Father smiles one of his hard smiles. "Ims, you don't need to worry about the Chief and his Norwich cronies. I can work my way round that old fool any day. And he'd never believe the Scots, anyway; he hates them more than the English!"

"Why don't we just buy some cheap jewels in Lunden, and give them to the Scots?" says Roba. "Who'll know the difference?"

Now Ims notices him.

"Can we buy a seacat while we're at it?" he says.

"It weren't my fault the stupid thing weren't there!" says Roba, turning well red and angry. "That Lunden merchant swore there was a seacat living off the boats in that village."

"And you believed the tavern gossip," says Ims. "But at least you had your bit of fun, didn't you?"

"It were just some old lady. I didn't know she'd die so easy."

Ims shakes his head at Roba, like he don't matter, anyway, then turns back to Father.

"The seacat ain't nothing. Even without one, we're the best sailors in the channel. But I got a bad feeling about the rest of it."

My father's smile changes as he checks Ims.

"Ims, you gotta be the best Second any Boss ever had. But sometimes I think your sense of honor will be our undoing." He slaps Ims on the shoulder. "If this was a deal with another Family, it'd be different. But we're talking about the Scots! Where were they when Lunden fell? Did they help the first Families escape when everyone in Lunden was killing each other to get out? No! We got away from old Isling by ourselves, just like the Brixt and the Kensings got themselves out of their parts of Lunden. And when the first Families ended up in the eastern marshes, did the Scots help them find food or places to live? Did they care how many Family kids died before we got it sorted? No! They was too busy grabbing every bit of land from Carlisle to Birmingham, turning old England into Greater Scotland. They only left the Last Ten Counties coz they're full of stinking English peasants and leeches like Randall. Us Families are the only free ones left, so anything that helps keep us free, like getting better weapons, that's gotta be good, ain't it?"

Ims opens his mouth, then shuts it and shrugs his shoulders.

"As you say, Medwin. You're Boss, not me."

Father looks pleased at that. He turns to Aileen and pinches her cheek. Which she don't look pleased with.

"Lady, Ims thinks you spoke a bit of sense! For that, I may listen to your thoughts on our little worm here."

He gives the English girl on his knee a squeeze. Her face changes from red to white.

"Perhaps I should make the hook she's dangling on a bit less pointed! And maybe I will, if she works for it."

He lifts the little girl up onto the table, pushing her so her feet knock into the dishes. She ends standing in the middle, like a roast waiting to be carved.

"Not much meat on that bait," says Roba.

Father laughs. "It ain't the size of the worm, but how you dangle it! Come on, little maggot, I've been feeding you these last few days, now it's time for you to earn your keep. How about a song for your Uncle Medwin?"

The girl stares bug-eyed at Father. She makes me think of Saera again. Not how she was at the end, but how she looked when Roba was playing one of his games with us. Games that always ended with a beating — out of sight, where no one could see. The little English girl gulps, and then she starts to sing, in a reedy little voice, so quiet it's practically a whisper.

"Lavender's blue, dilly dilly, lavender's green, when you are king, dilly dilly, I shall be queen."

Roba bursts into laughter.

"Here's hoping, your ladyship. Who knows what marriage your father was planning for you? But don't count on it now!"

The English girl looks like she don't know what's going on, and tears start coming. I reach forward and grab hold of one of her legs. She squeaks, and spins round to face me.

"Come down," I say. "You can sit by me." The English girl don't say nothing, but she looks grateful in her eyes. Father ain't pleased, though; looks like he's thinking about slapping me. Aileen puts her hand on his arm.

"Let her down. She's frightened. And Zeph's a good boy, he can look after her."

Now I wish I hadn't done it, coz I don't want Aileen's praise, that's for sure.

"Getting yourself a little doxy?" says Roba.

"Shut up, slave son," I say, but quiet enough so Father don't hear.

The English girl climbs down from the tabletop and sits next to me on the bench. I can feel her shaking.

"Boss, what are you planning for the Prime Minister's daughter?" asks Faz.

She goes completely still next to me.

"Keep her here. Maybe I'll even demand a ransom," says Father, smiling.

"You'd let her go for money?" says Aileen.

Father's smile twists up a bit.

"If Randall gave me enough, I might think about it. Say, ten million Scottish pounds."

Aileen gasps; Ims chuckles.

"But the English wouldn't ever be able to raise that kind of money," says Aileen.

Ims and Faz is grinning now.

"I don't understand," says Roba. "Why'd you set a ransom the Prime Minister can't never pay?"

"Because he isn't going to let me go," says a little voice next to me.

"Exactly!" shouts my father. "Now you're showing your worth, little maggot! Why would I ever let you go, when by having you here I can guarantee your father will come sailing in for a fight?"

"But the English navy —" says Aileen.

"Is made up of a dozen ancient ships held together with paper, and manned by press-ganged peasants who wet themselves at the first sight of a real warrior!" says Father.

"So you don't want the money?" says Roba.

"Course I don't, lad. I want a fight!" Father grins. "I still can't believe what luck we've had."

"The Bosses of the other Families won't be pleased when they hear what you've done," says Ims.

"But they'll come round, even old Biter of the Dogs Family. They'll see the benefits of battering the English."

I feel something tugging at my arm. I look down, and the little English girl's staring up at me.

"Are you going to kill me?" she says.

"We ain't going to kill you," I say, hoping it ain't a lie. But Roba leers at her, rolling his eyes back in his head, twisting his neck and sticking out his tongue, like he's hanging on a gibbet.

The English girl starts shaking even more.

"Come on. I'll take you back," I say quickly, looking at my father. He frowns, then nods.

The girl looks up at me, still frightened, but maybe thinking I'm the best thing she's got going here, coz she puts her small cold hand in mine. We walk between the tables of noisy, laughing shield men, dodge the slaves and servants carrying platters of food and jugs of wine, and head out the cramped northern door of the hall into the starlit night. Outside, the marshes is talking their nighttime whispers, and the other huts and halls are just shapes poking out from the reeds. I lead the little girl down one of the narrow wooden walkways that's the only way of getting around without swimming, and the big lump of the slave house looms ahead in the darkness.

The girl walks slow and careful, holding tight to my hand; I guess she ain't used to this. Then we're out of the rustling, watery night and into the smoky, stinky murk of the slave house. I push through the sacking door and step inside, and the whole slave house falls silent. Not that there's many slaves in here tonight, coz most are working the feast. But them that are turn and stare at me. Then they look down quick, like they ought to.

A raggedy old slave woman comes quickstepping over to us.

"Oh lord, thank you, thank you. You shouldn't have troubled to bring the prisoner back yourself. One of us could have attended to it, lord."

"Well I did," I say.

"Then let me take her now," says the old slave. "I've got to put on her chain." She leads the little girl over to a dark corner where there's a big stone with a metal ring sunk in it. There's chains hanging off the hook, and each chain's got a shackle on the end. The woman takes one, and puts the heavy metal cuff round the girl's ankle.

"She don't need chaining, she's only a little kid!" I say, and the slave gives me a funny look.

"But it's the Boss's orders."

Then the old woman starts pushing and piling together a mess of straw. When she's finished, the girl sits down in it and the slave gives her a mangy blanket. The girl huddles down — knees pulled up, arms round her legs, shoulders hunched.

I know I shouldn't, but I feel sorry for her.

"You ain't gonna die, I'll make sure of it," I say quietly, after the old slave is gone. And I get a cold feeling, hearing those words coming out of my mouth again.

"But that man Medwin doesn't want to give me back," says the little girl, hunching up her shoulders. "So what else will he do but kill me?"

"He might keep you as a slave, or sell you on," I say, trying to cheer her up. But she don't look very happy at that, neither.

"My name's Zephaniah," I say, trying something different. "But everyone calls me Zeph. Medwin's my father. He's the greatest Boss in all the Families."

She blinks. Then she says, "My name's Lady Alexandra Persephone Olivia Randall. But my mummy always called me Lexy."

Then she pulls the blanket over herself, and lies down on the straw in a curled-up ball. She looks at me out of pale blue eyes.

"My daddy only ever talks about war and fighting. It used to frighten me, but Mummy said it's just the way he is, that a lot of scary things he says are just to make people respect him. Is that what your daddy's like?"

I don't answer, coz my father ain't nothing like that scumbag Randall.

So instead I say, "Don't worry. It'll be all right."

But when Lexy checks me with her eyes like Saera's, I know she don't believe me.

"I'm scared being on my own here," she says quietly. "Will you stay with me until I go to sleep?"

·7·
RETRIBUTION

Andy. I've got to warn Andy. It's all I can think as I run down the lane, Cat helter-skeltering after me. *Slap slap* over the cobbles, my feet take me fast as they can for the harbor; scrambling over walls, jumping through the Hendrys' backyard. Cos I've got to get there first. Got to get there before Randall. Got to let everyone know! The Prime Minister's here! In our village! And he's out to get folk. Out to hang them, or press them. And either way, they'll die.

I hop over a fence and skid round the corner of Fishnet Street, into the harbor. And straightaway I know I'm too late, cos the first thing I see is a line of men in blue uniforms, dead ahead. They've got their backs to me and their rifles raised and ready.

Soldiers. A whole company of them.

And the next thing I see is the ship. So big, my gob opens by itself. Three great masts, high as forest trees. Miles of rigging, sailors crawling all over. Her hull's a patchy gray, like she's made of stone, and she's anchored just outside the harbor, blocking any way out by sea. Her cannon ports are open, facing the village.

There's no point going any farther. Cat bounds up behind me, his tail arched in a question, and I scoop him up before he can run out among those soldiers. Who knows what they'd do to him?

All the men of the village have been rounded up by the Old Moon. They're surrounded by a ring of soldiers, like sheep caught in a pen. I can see Andy's head poking up from the middle, and his pa next to him. They look scared and angry at the same time. Then comes a clattering of boots on Broad Lane. Everyone turns to see the Prime Minister swaggering down to the harbor with a dozen more soldiers, and that strange, dark-suited Scottish Ambassador.

The Prime Minister's great fat belly is wrapped in a yellow silk waistcoat, with a bright blue jacket around, and his fat legs are stuffed into white stockings and pale jodhpurs. He's red and sweating, wiping his potato face with a handkerchief. He stops in front of the herded-up fisherfolk.

"So! Here are the brave villagers who stood by and did nothing while my daughter was being taken by raiders."

A few people look startled, and lots of people look down.

Captain Ainsty steps forward, cap in hand, and says, "Begging Your Majesty's pardon, we never wanted any harm to come to Lady Alexandra. We're loyal to the bone. But we had raiders rampaging through the village."

A couple of people shout, "Aye, that's right."

"Your kind of loyalty isn't worth a green penny!" roars the Prime Minister. "What use were you to my child when you let her be carried off?"

"We tried! But they was raiders, with swords and all!"

"They were smashing our boats up. What could we do?"

"You could have laid down your lives to protect the honor of your country!" shouts Randall. He stops, wiping his face. "I hear not one of you was even hurt. Which makes me wonder, are you cowards or traitors? Well let me tell you, if you've leagued up with those raiders, I won't stop until every one of you is dangling from a noose!"

Of course, that gets everyone really frightened, all shouting at once: "No! No! We'd never work with the raiders! We're loyal to Your Majesty!"

Which doesn't impress him much.

"Then you'll get your chance to prove it, with a spell in the militia fighting the raiders."

And everyone stops talking then, and looks frightened. Cos a choice between the noose and the militia is pretty much a choice of dying quick or dying slow.

But Captain Whitedove waggles his hairy head and dares to speak.

"Please, Majesty, we can't be joining no militia, not when the raiders has been through! Half our fleet's been sunk or smashed. We need every man to help with repairs. If we go on militia, how will we do that? Who'll feed our families?"

Prime Minister Randall turns beet red. "You should have thought of how you'd manage before you let the raiders take my daughter!"

Standing next to the soldiers is an officer with gold bits all over his uniform. He says, "Majesty, you needn't concern yourself about this rabble. I'll make it my task to establish guilt in the matter of the raider attack. If any of them had anything to do with your daughter's disappearance, we'll have the gallows raised and a row of hangings before nightfall."

Randall looks pleased at that.

"Good plan, Colonel. And if any of them are traitors," he sneers, "I shall relish every second of their dance from the gallows!" The Colonel bows to the Prime Minister, then sweeps a long glance over the crowd. He turns to another soldier. "I want a statement from every man here about what happened when the raiders came. Any who are shifty or clearly lying, pull them over for further questioning. Any that are honest and fit can put their marks on a militia contract."

Then the Scottish Ambassador speaks up.

"Prime Minister, may I suggest searching the village for signs of treachery? Such as, say, unusual wealth or booty? An investigation would be prudent before taking any of these men for the militia. The last thing you want is to conscript traitors."

"A sensible move, Jasper," says Randall, nodding. "See to it, will you, Colonel?"

Soon as the Scottish Ambassador's gone off looking for proof we're in league with the raiders, the Colonel disappears inside the Old Moon, and the interviews end up being done by three bored soldiers, who line up the fishermen in rows, taking turns to bawl questions at them.

I spend the day hanging around by the harbor, watching and listening, stomach tied in knots. And I ain't the only one. Cos pretty soon I'm joined by women come down from their houses, frightened about soldiers tearing apart their homes, or searching for husbands, fathers, and brothers who've not come back for their dinner. Not long there's more than thirty women stood around, wringing their hands and clutching at fears as the men are interviewed. And I'm the same, cos when the soldiers get to Andy, I'm praying on him to lie and say he's not fit to fight.

But he doesn't lie, only says, "When the raiders came I was up on Top Lane, and I tried to stop them harming Granny Melkun, but two of them held me fast and laughed while she died." And he shows them the bracelets of bruises all round his arms, given to him by the raiders. Then he says, "I'll be sixteen next May, I've not been sick since I was a boy, and though I've never held a rifle, I can throw stones better'n anyone in the village."

And the soldier chuckles and writes something in his ledger.

After most of the day's gone on sorting through the men of our village, and them soldiers have mumbled and scratched over their notes, the Colonel marches stiffly off into the village. Everyone waits, getting more and more nervous, then there's another tramping of boots down to the harbor, and the Prime Minister's back.

He swaggers down in front of the crowd, puffs out his chest, and bellows, "This village is now going to learn about generosity. My generosity. Which will see to it that none of you hang today." I hear someone start crying, must be with relief, and there's smiles and grins spreading across the faces of the men. "But don't think that means there won't be any payment for your disgusting, cowardly behavior!" The smiles get wiped off their faces. "For a start, all those who are able have been conscripted into the militia. So you'd better say your good-byes, lads, because you'll only see your families again if you fight the raiders like you should have done before."

The Prime Minister nods at the Colonel, who starts calling out names — twenty-seven in all. All around me is gasping and weeping as all the young men of the village get pressed to fight the raiders. And I'm crying with everyone else, cos the fourteenth name on the list is Andy's. Who takes it calmly, only telling his pa not to worry.

And the one I wouldn't mind if his name got called, Lun Hindle, well he ain't going anywhere. Turns out he's too lazy and stupid even for the militia. Even after he shouts, "My dad'll make you!" at the soldiers, they still don't want him.

When the twenty-seven men and boys have been huddled into a separate group, with rifles trained on them, the Prime Minister starts strutting about again.

"Do you think that's all you have to pay? Well it isn't, not by a long shot!" Everyone shuts their mouths, waiting for the next blow. "I said I was being generous, not a fool! There'll be no hangings today, but that doesn't mean there'll be none at all. Every man in authority, who might have been colluding with the raiders, shall be taken into custody. If we find my daughter, bring her back safely, and she testifies to their innocence, then they shall go free. But if she is not safely returned, or I find any evidence of treachery, then my justice shall be swift and terrible."

At that, the Colonel shouts, "Seize them!" and the soldiers wade into the crowd, pulling out Captain Ainsty, Captain Whitedove, Captain Beaufort, and all the other men who run the boats. Including Andy's pa.

There's screams and shouts from the crowd, and the women try to break through the line of soldiers. But there's nothing anyone can do against rifle butts and sword swipes. Andy and the other lads are marched down the harbor steps to waiting rowboats, then taken off to the ship. And the captains are pushed and battered toward one of the solid stone warehouses that line the harbor.

The soldiers lock them inside and post an armed guard at the heavy wooden door.

* * *

Randall's ship sails the next morning, taking Andy and the others away. Seems like everyone who's left of the village is down at the harbor, and most of us have spent the night there. Staring out at the ship, hoping every time a figure moves on deck that it's one of the lads, let up to wave good-bye.

The sky's fading from black to blue in the east, and the first red light of dawn is creeping in when there's a sound I've got to hating, the clattering of boots down Broad Lane. Everyone watches silently as the Prime Minister and the Scottish Ambassador come walking down to the harbor with their escort of soldiers. We watch as a boat's rowed out from Randall's ship. We watch as Randall and the Scot stroll down the harbor steps and settle themselves into it like they're off for a Sunday jaunt. We watch them get rowed away without even giving us a backward glance.

And once they're on board the ship, there's a load of shouting and bustle, and a great clattering as the anchor's raised. Then the mainsails are unfurled, snapping and flapping into place, billowing with the wind. The ship groans, the sea rushes under her bows, and she heads away from our harbor.

"What shall we do now?" I ask Andy's ma.

"Go back to ours, Lilly, get some rest."

But when I get there, it feels empty and strange. Cos Andy's not out in the yard, chopping wood, and his pa ain't sitting at the table, talking about fishing, and his ma ain't bustling about the stove. It's the same kind of emptiness as back at my house, without Granny. The kind of emptiness in the whole village, with so many people missing.

Nothing gets better in the next days. It's just frightened waiting, and taking food down to the warehouse, and trying to get Andy's ma to eat a little, sleep a little. But mostly she doesn't do either, spending all her time at the harbor, where the captains are being made to build a jail for themselves. And that's why I'm on my own at the house when there's a knocking at the door. Before I can even open it, Mrs. Denton's head is poking in. If such a thing had happened before, Andy's ma would've been beside herself if the house wasn't sparkling-shiny in every corner. But Andy's ma doesn't care a thing about cleaning now, and Mrs. Denton doesn't even notice the mess. She holds up a basket with a cloth over it.

"I've brought some food for you," she says, sounding like she ain't sure she'll be welcome. "I've emptied my cellar, and I'm taking all I can to feed the children of the village."

She looks at me.

"That's very kind," I say, even though I ain't hardly a child, am I?

"It's the least I can do, after all . . ." She heaves a great sigh and plonks herself down in the chair Andy's pa always sits in. Sat in.

"This is all so terrible," she says, her voice all wobbly. "Martha claims the men will be set to building the gallows tomorrow." Which puts an aching tightness inside me.

Mrs. Denton carries on, "Oh Lilly, I do feel I can talk to you. That you understand . . . You know, when Archie and I were children everything seemed so straightforward. Our tutor taught us that the raiders were evil, the Scots cursed for not throwing away their machines. And we believed it all." She smiles softly. "It was Eustace who taught me differently. Showed me things aren't always the way we think they are." Her face hardens again. "But my brother is just as pigheaded and arrogant as he was then. And that makes me afraid for Alexandra. It makes me afraid for all of us." She laughs, but it sounds sad, not funny. "You know, after she was taken, I came up with an idea of how to get my niece back. I hoped I could stop my brother taking us to war. It's all useless now, but I was going to provide Alexandra's ransom myself."

She stops again, and I ain't sure I'm even meant to answer. But I do. I say, "How were you going to do that?"

"I have something. An artifact. Eustace gave it to me on my birthday, the year before he died. I don't even know what it is; all I know is he found it on one of his expeditions, and it must be worth a lot, because he had a special box made for it, with a golden clasp. He told me it was the most important thing he'd ever found, that it would change our lives." She pauses. "So I thought perhaps the raiders would accept it as ransom. I was planning to ask some brave captain from the village to take it to London and contact the raiders there. Eustace had dealings with other antiquarians in London, and he told me of one who regularly bought antiques from the raiders. I hoped this man could help find the gang that took Alexandra. I even wrote out a letter requesting his help." She laughs her sad laugh again. "Of course, it doesn't matter now. My brother has taken away all the able men of this village and there's no one left to ask."

She shakes her head, like she's clearing cobwebs out of it. "Enough of this. I didn't come here to burden you with cares you can't mend. I have some much better news!"

She takes my hand. "Mrs. Ainsty called on me yesterday. Such a thoughtful woman, to think of others, even at this time. She has suggested, and I have agreed, that I stand in place of your grandmother for you."

She looks at me expectantly, like I should be jumping up and down or something.

"In place for what?"

"Why, your marriage negotiations. I'm so happy to be able to do something for you, and to bring some cheer in these dark days. I see no reason why it shouldn't go very smoothly, even now. You have the seacat for a dowry, and myself as a sponsor." She gives me a big smile, like she's wanting one back from me. "Mrs. Ainsty and I both agree it should be a fairly simple matter to persuade the Hindles to accept you as a wife for their son. And since he is one of the few men spared, you could be his wife in just a few weeks."

"A few weeks!"

"I know, isn't it wonderful?"

* * *

After Mrs. Denton leaves, I feel like I'll explode if I don't tell someone what her and Mrs. Ainsty's got planned. I end up at the harbor, cos that's where everyone is. And I practically run down Andy's ma, I'm that keen to find her.

"Mrs. Denton wants me to marry Lun Hindle!" I cry, soon as I clap eyes on her.

I think she'll laugh, but first she doesn't even seem like she's heard, then she looks at me out of tired eyes and says, "Well, maybe that ain't such a bad idea."

The other women in the crowd nod and agree.

"Lucky lass!" says one.

"And her an orphan, too," says another.

"But I ain't marrying Lun! I'm going to get a boat with Andy. We're going to be captains together."

Mrs. Whitedove tuts and purses her lips together.

"Lilly Melkun, terrible things have happened these last few days, so it's time you stop living in your dreamland!" she snaps.

"Lilly, how do you think we're even going to feed ourselves, let alone buy a boat?" says Andy's ma quietly. "Everything's wrecked, Pa's in jail, and Andy . . ." Her voice cracks. "He might not even be coming back."

Mrs. Greenstick butts in. "So if Mrs. Denton wants to help you, then you should count your blessings!"

All the women are tutting and huffing at me now.

"Ungrateful little thing."

"The girl's gone wild, I tell you."

"Out on her own in that boat, it goes to show . . ."

But I ain't standing around to listen. I've got to find someone who understands me. Who cares. And I know where he'll be. It's where I want to go, anyway. Back home.

When I get there, Cat's sat on the windowsill, tail neatly round his feet.

"Meow," he says when he sees me. Which means: Open up, I can't get in by myself. I open the front door, and Cat leaps down and trots inside. He walks over to the fireplace and looks at it, like he's expecting it to be hot.

"Granny ain't here," I say to him, and sit down at our table, feeling a chill from the cold, empty hearth.

"Everyone wants me to get married," I say to Cat, who looks at me, his ears flicked back. "They reckon you'll make a good dowry, and Lun Hindle'll get you for his seacat." His ears pull back a bit farther. "Lun probably won't even let me sail. And he smells. And what about Andy? What'll he say when he gets back?" A cold stone settles in my belly. "If he gets back."

"Mreow," says Cat, and starts licking one of his feet. Something about the sound of his raspy tongue makes me remember him sat on Mrs. Denton's fancy carpet, and the idea just pops into my head! I get so excited, I can hardly breathe, cos it all makes sense.

"So what if all the able men are gone from the village?" I shout. "I can sail as good as any of them, and I've got you.

We can take the ransom to the raiders!" Cat licks his other foot. "And if I saved Alexandra, the Prime Minister'd be sure to reward me, wouldn't he? Then I'd have enough money to buy a boat for me and Andy, and I wouldn't have to marry Lun! And Andy wouldn't have to fight, he could just come home with all the others. And Alexandra could tell how we aren't traitors and the captains would be set free and everything would be fine again!"

Cat turns around and starts licking his back.

"With you I could get to London easily."

Lick, lick, lick, is Cat's reply.

"All I'd need is Mrs. Denton's treasure and the letter. I'm going to tell Mrs. Denton right now." But that's when I get a sinking feeling inside. Cos I know there's no way she'll give me the ransom. Most folk in the village don't think I should even be sailing; all they think I'm good for is getting married to Lun Hindle.

Cat makes a funny little coughing noise, and spits out a bit of fur.

"'Cept . . . I could *take* the jewel and the letter. And it wouldn't be stealing, would it?" I ask him. "Not if I'm going to give it to the raiders and save everyone. It can't be stealing then?"

Cat doesn't answer, just lifts up a leg and starts cleaning his belly.

·8· LEAVING

Toward dark, I go back to Mrs. Denton's, Cat following behind. This time, when Martha opens the door, she doesn't even pretend not to be cross.

"Mrs. Denton ain't in. Leastways, she's resting in her room, and I ain't disturbing her for the likes of you."

"I . . . um . . . I left something when I was here before. Left it in Mrs. Denton's drawing room. I just wanted to fetch it."

Martha's eyebrows go up into arches. "I cleaned that room top to toe since you was here, and there weren't nothing ragged or dirty in it. So whatever you lost, you didn't lose it here." She starts to shut the door in my face.

"No. It was a locket. My granny gave it to me. I think the chain snapped and it fell on the floor. Please, it's only small, maybe you missed it? I've looked everywhere else."

I can feel a blush coming on, cos the locket's right here, hidden under my shirt. And the blush gets redder when I think what Granny would say if she caught me lying like this.

I'm waiting for Martha to catch me out, but she just goes frowny. Then she says, "All right, I'll take you in there, and you can look for your locket. But I'll be keeping both eyes on you, so keep your dirty fingermarks off anything that ain't yours."

"Thank you," I say, but inside I'm cursing cos my plan's going wrong already! Of course Martha ain't going to let me in by myself, and how can I get the jewel without her seeing? But then Cat solves the problem by trying to get into the kitchen.

"Hey! Get that scrawny beggar out!" Martha uses her foot to poke at Cat and flaps her arms about.

"I can't leave him outside!" I say, glad he never worries about invitations. "He's a seacat." Martha looks at me, then down at Cat. Her face goes a little bit more sour.

"All right," she says. "For your granny's sake, he can come in. But he ain't dropping his fleas on the carpet! I'll keep watch on him here in the kitchen. You go straight in the sitting room, find your locket, and come straight out again. And if you're any more than two minutes, I'll be in there finding out why."

I push open the door of Mrs. Denton's sitting room, my hand shaking ever so slightly. The only light in the room comes flickering from the fire, and it's nearly out. What if Mrs. Denton's locked her treasure away? I can't hardly ask Martha to get it for me. But I'm lucky, cos right on the mantelpiece is a dark wooden box with a golden clasp, and next to it a letter. I just have to step across and take them.

"It's not stealing," I whisper. "I'm just doing Mrs. Denton's mission for her."

I pick up the box and undo the clasp. When I lift the lid, I can't help but gasp. Cos inside, resting on a bed of white silk, is what looks like a huge jewel! It's a bit larger than an egg, and it's cut with lots of tiny edges that sparkle softly in the red glow from the fireplace. My hands are shaking even more as I take the jewel from its resting place, and when I pick it up, I gasp again. Cos I'm sure I can feel a little tingle as it sets in my palm, and there's a flash of light across the room, like lightning far away. Then it's gone, and the jewel lies still.

I look round, cos I can't believe Martha ain't seen, but there's no sound from away in the kitchen. My heart's beating so hard I can feel the blood pounding in my head, but I ain't got time to worry, so I just tuck the jewel into my shirt pocket and pull my coat round to cover the lump. Then I close the box, set it back on the mantel, and take the letter, stuffing it in with the jewel. Then I pull Granny's locket over my head and hold it out in my hand.

"Here it is!" I say when I'm back in the kitchen, holding up the locket for Martha to see. And I pop out her door like an eel out from under a rock, Cat scampering after, before she can ask me any questions.

Soon as I'm outside, I want to start running. But I make myself walk, cos I don't want to look guilty. Like a thief would.

"We did it!" I whisper to Cat.

"Prup," he says. And that's when I get a cold jolt inside me. What an idiot I am! First thing tomorrow, Mrs. Denton's bound to notice the envelope's missing from her mantelpiece. And when she does, she'll check her box. And when she's done that, it won't take Martha a minute to put the blame on me. So I've got to go now, tonight, or I won't be going anywhere 'cept the new jail!

And now I start running.

When I get home, I hurtle about getting clothes, oilskins, a knife, extra rope, my rope-splicing kit, and what food I can find. Which turns out to be a bag of oats and some hard sea biscuits. Well, I'll just have to catch the rest.

"I'm going on Mrs. Denton's mission," I say to the empty dark house. Hoping Granny's there somehow, hoping she can hear me. "So I'll have to take the money from the jar."

I put my hand under Granny's bed and pull out a small jangling jar. Granny's savings jar, where she'd hoard every extra penny for the winter storms, when it's too rough to go fishing. The coins rattle out of the jar, and I put them into Granny's purse, which hangs from a loop of leather. It goes round my neck, next to Granny's locket, and it ain't heavy, cos there ain't many coins in it. But it should last me. After all, things can't cost much in London, can they?

I pat my shirt where the bulge of the purse shows through. I reckon it should be safe from muggers, cos all that shows of it is a bit of leather at my neck. But what about the jewel? All it'd take is one peek and any thief would be on me. After a bit of thinking, I take out my fishing belt. It's got plenty of pockets for stashing spare line and hooks and all the other stuff you don't want to go searching for when you're out. I wrap the jewel in a dirty cloth, then I squeeze it into the largest pocket of my belt, where it just about fits. It looks bumpy, but I reckon it'll be safe. After all, who'd ever think there's a big jewel inside a fisherbelt?

I've got my bag on my back, and I'm heading for the door, when I catch a glimpse of my reflection in the dark window: round brown face, dark brown eyes, bundled up in stained oilskins, long hair tied back in a ponytail. Girl's hair. But Mrs. Denton said she was looking for a captain or a young lad to do her mission. I take the letter out of my bag and carefully pry it open, trying not to tear the envelope too badly. I read down through her scrabbly writing and all her fancy phrases. It takes me quite a while, but halfway down are the words that matter:

I commend this man to you.
Please give him any aid you can.

This man! I ain't a man! How will I explain *that* to Mrs. Denton's London trader? What if he guesses I took the letter and the jewel? He'd never help me then.

And that's why I take out Granny's kitchen scissors, use the window as a mirror, and start to cut my hair. When I've finished, I look into the window, and there's a boy looking back at me. I lift my hand to my short hair, and he does the same. I open my mouth at what I done, and he opens his right back. I'm a boy now. A boy who Mrs. Denton could have asked to go on a mission. A boy she might have given the letter and jewel to. The boy in the window grins at me, and he doesn't look like the marrying type.

Cat ain't very keen to go out sailing before it's even light. And he ain't going to be very keen on his disguise, neither, which is why I'm leaving it till he's trapped in the boat and can't get away. Thing is, he's gray, cos he's a seacat. The color is how they get spotted out of a litter of kittens. But if raiders came all this way to get a seacat, what might happen if I try and walk a gray cat through London? I can't risk him like that. So the last thing I packed was a jar of Granny's polish, which she made out of tallow and ashes and herbs and who knows what else. That polish stains something terrible; even with all Cat's washing, it should take him a week to get it off.

By the time I've raised the mainsail and set the lines, the eastern sky is fading from deep black to dark blue, and the first stars are winking out. Cat and me slip out of the harbor and along the coast eastward, with a sharp, helpful wind behind us. And by the time the sun's up, the hills give way to fly-whining marshes. A flat patchwork of greens and browns with birds flying up in spiraling flocks.

By late morning the blue sky's been eaten up by high gray clouds, and the breeze carries a twang of rain. But the clouds stay high and light, whipping over the sky, just damping us now and then with a bit of drizzle. The wind stays steady from the west, and we make good speed, slicing neatly through the dark reflecting waves.

Cat gets a bit snappy, cos he doesn't like the rain and the cold breeze over much. But he doesn't howl or meow, so there can't be any really bad weather or dangerous seas to worry about. Around midmorning, Cat meows out at the flock of birds bobbing and diving on the water. I slow us down and set out the fishing lines. Then I sail through where the birds are, and the shoal of fish they're sat on. The lines pull and sing, and in a few minutes I've caught half a dozen nice mackerel. Cat gets the first one, and starts purring loud like a drum. He doesn't mind the bits of rain so much after that.

By dusk on the first day, we're between the green hills of Wight Isle, out at sea, and South Ampton water, stretching away inland to where all the ruins are. This is the farthest east I've ever been, and it makes me jumpy to sail into waters I don't know my way round. But I know all the pilot songs, right the way to Clakton; Granny made me learn them all when I started fishing with Cat.

"What do I need them for? I ain't going that far," is what I said to her.

"A storm might take you anywhere, so you need to know how to ride it, and where you can find safe anchor. Do you want to end up like your grampy and your parents?"

"No, Granny."

"Then sing me all the wrecking stones between Bognor and Beachy's Head."

And now I'm glad she was so strict.

By the time we get to a safe-looking anchor, night's drawing in. On shore, there's some house shapes around the low headland. But even when it gets to candle-lighting time, none of them are lit up. Must be ruins; there's always plenty of them about.

After I've set us safe, and Cat's curled up happy, I don't feel much like sleeping. My head keeps going round what I got to do. I think about reading the letter again, but I can't now it's dark. Instead I get the jewel out, unwrap it from the dirty cloth, and hold it in my hand. It ain't sparkling like it was in Mrs. Denton's parlor, and it feels cold and smooth, with no tingle like before. I turn it about, and there's something perfect to how it feels in my hands. Like it wants to be held. And as I hold it, it starts to warm up, but not like it's taking the heat from my hands, more like it's getting hot from inside. Which doesn't make me feel happy at all, cos the vicar's always going on about how it was the olden-time people brought all the trouble to the world, and who knows why this thing is flickering and flashing. I reckon the best thing is to wrap it back in the cloth and leave well alone.

And I'm going to do that, really I am, but the jewel starts glowing. Not all over, but in ten little spots, just perfectly placed for putting your fingers on if you wanted to hold it. Before my head can think what I'm doing, my fingers have put themselves in the little glowing circles. There's a bright flash, a little clicking sound, and the jewel suddenly sprouts a head! It's level with my own, hanging in the dark air and glowing like a ghost. It's got a face that could be a man, could be a woman. It opens its mouth and says:

"DNA recorded and recognized. Interface locked to primary user."

· 9 ·
PSAI

You ain't never heard anyone scream the way I give it out! I drop the jewel like it's a hot ember, and all the clatter and screaming wakes Cat, who jumps up from his sleep and starts hissing and spitting. The head stays where it is, hanging in the air, watching me, Cat, and the jewel rolling in the bottom of the boat. After a minute, my screams stop and Cat calms down.

We both stare terrified at the floating head, which raises one eyebrow and says, "Sunoon Technologies guarantees this unit only if it is operated according to the manufacturer's instructions — see section 3.2.4 of the user manual. Use contrary to those instructions may lead to the artificial intelligence becoming unstable." It spins in the air like it's hanging on a gibbet and says, "And may I add that operation in a *boat*, out at *sea*, is almost certainly *not* covered by the guarantee."

"What are you?" I squeak. "Are you a demon?"

The head looks irked. "The Demon is a very basic unit, with extremely limited gaming facilities. I am the Play System A I unit 2457." It pauses. "I'm sometimes referred to as PSAI. With state-of-the-art artificial intelligence." It looks at me like I should be impressed.

"What are you talking about?" I say.

"For goodness' sake! Have you been living under a rock? We PSAI units have been very well advertised; in the factory they were saying there's an eight-month waiting list for us." It sighs. "Oh well, I suppose I could skip the rest of the legal stuff."

It shuffles about on its neck, like it's clearing water out of its ears, then says, "Please identify primary user."

I look at it blankly.

"What's your name?" it says, very slow and loud.

"Lilly Melkun," I squeak.

"*Thank you*. Now that we've cleared that up, I am your new system. What would you like to play?"

I can't help it, but a little groan comes out of my mouth. "I should have known better than to take some olden-time thing. The sea'll probably rise up and swallow us all just for you being here."

"I am unable to understand these instructions," says the head irritably. "Please provide more information."

"You're just supposed to be a jewel!" I cry. "You're just supposed to pay off the raiders so they'll give back Alexandra!

You ain't supposed to be some scary head! They'll think you're one of their spirits and kill us all!"

Now the head looks quite peeved. "Really, can you please be a bit clearer? Are you talking about a fantasy game? Because my strategy capabilities are well beyond that, you know. I can handle entire wars in real time."

"You're a puter, ain't you?" I say, suddenly twigging. After all, Mr. Denton had loads of them in his study. "But I thought you all got broke in the Collapse? How come you're still working?"

"What do you mean? What Collapse? Has there been a power failure at the factory? Is that why I've been offline for so long?" The head stops talking, and it gets a strange look on its face, like it's scared or something.

"There appears to be something wrong with my internal clock. It's saying I've been powered down for one hundred forty-seven years. But that can't be. Why would anyone leave me unplayed for so long?"

"You're lucky you're here at all," I say. "Granny said that after the Collapse, people got really angry about puters and all that stuff, and there was gangs of people going around smashing them. There ain't any left working anywhere, that's what the vicar says. He says they don't even have puters in Greater Scotland, and they've got solar-powered sunships."

"People smashing computers." The head looks sick. "But what about my friends, what about units 2435 and 1897?"

The head starts looking around, like it's trying to see every way at once. "Am I safe? Is someone going to smash me?"

"Well I ain't," I say, "though I don't know what the vicar will say if he ever finds out. You're my ransom for Alexandra, so I've got to keep you. But you can't go popping out like that. Most people would have thrown you in the sea by now."

"Well it's not my fault. You activated me."

"I did not. I just picked you up."

"I am designed to respond only to the DNA of my designated user when held. And if what you say is true, then it's rather curious that I was activated at all . . . Pick up my drive unit," it says. I stare at it, and it nods down at the jewel. "Go on, down there." I put my hand out, but then pull it back. "Just pick it up!" snaps the head. "It won't hurt you. Unfortunately."

I pick up the jewel, but with just my thumb and finger this time.

"Good," says the head. Then it stares off into the distance. A ghostly pencil appears in the air, floats into the head's mouth, and it starts chewing.

"Well, your DNA is certainly a match for the user I was due to be sent out to," it mutters. "Although there are some discrepancies . . ." It chews on the ghostly pencil a bit more.

"Aha!" it cries. "A descendant! Enough of a DNA match to allow activation!" It looks pretty pleased with itself and says, "Great-great-great-great-granddaughter by my calculation."

"I don't have a clue what you're talking about," I say. "You got to get back inside."

"Well, I'm not sure I wasn't better off, anyway." It looks a little bit sad. "You won't just leave me off, though, will you? I might as well have been killed like my friends if that's what you do."

Well, anything to get rid of it.

"Of course I won't," I say. "If it's safe, you can come out. Now, how do I get you back in?" I start pressing all the little glowing spots, trying to undo whatever I did in the first place.

"No!" cries the head, looking horrified. "Not like that!" It starts swirling and twisting in the air, fading and shrinking as it goes.

"I am being improperly shut down!" it wails, and it disappears into nothing.

After the head is gone, I wrap the jewel back in its cloth with shaking hands. I stare at it for ages, wondering what to do. I want to chuck the stupid thing in the sea, but I know I can't, cos then I'd have nothing to trade for Alexandra. In the end I decide I'll keep it safely hidden in my belt and not touch it again till I hand it over to the raiders. And I'll just have to hope the head doesn't come popping out again, cos I haven't the foggiest what I'll do if it does. I put the jewel away, then lie down and try to get some sleep. But my brain's even more full of whirling thoughts now, and I spend a long time staring up at the stars.

* * *

The next day, my head's claggy from not having much sleep, but there ain't any other sign of the strange glowing head. I feel a whole lot better now it's daytime, and last night starts to feel like a dream.

Even with the good wind, it'll take us four or five days to reach the mouth of the River Thames. We pass some more marshes, and little islands poking into the sea. And ruins. There's no houses round here, no smoke rising from chimneys or people moving about. Everywhere's empty, but then, who'd want to live with all the ghosts?

I ain't the only one sailing, cos we pass plenty of fishing boats, nets trailing. There's good catches round the flooded places, if you're careful not to get snagged on a drowned building. They all hail us, and I hail 'em back. But I ain't stopping, ain't telling 'em where we're off to.

That night we moor up in a sheltered inlet, far enough away from the shores that the ghosts can't get to us. I'm so tired, I just wrap myself up and lie down next to Cat. My eyes close, and I'm drifting into sleep when I feel a tingling at my waist, and a tiny high voice says, "System ready, system ready" over and over. In a moment I'm wide awake and I've got a cold feeling inside. Cos there's only one thing that'd be tingling and squeaking like that. I carefully pull the jewel out from my belt and unwrap it. The little spots are glowing on it, and I touch one gently. Straightaway the head pops out in front of me.

"Primary user identified. Welcome, Lilly Melkun."

"What are you doing?" I say. "Why are you out again?"

It looks hurt.

"That's not a very nice greeting. Especially as you're the one who put me on standby for twenty-three hours. If you had waited for me to provide instructions, I could have told you how to do things properly. Would you like me to engage the help interface this time?"

I nod, cos I don't even know what it's talking about. The head changes suddenly. Now it doesn't look like a human anymore; it looks like an animal. A puppy maybe, but with too big eyes and a large, grinning mouth.

"Arf, arf!" it says. "Let me help you to get the best from your new Play System with full artificial intelligence. You don't need to read the manual when I'm here. Arf! Arf!"

I practically jump out of the boat, I'm that startled.

"Ugh! Go away! Where's the head? Get it back!" Instantly the creepy puppy turns back into the head.

"Well, at least you've got *some* sense," it says. "I must say I always find the help feature totally demeaning."

"What's artificial intelligence?" I ask.

"It's being cleverer than the child who's somehow become my primary user, that's what it is. And I have to say I'm not entirely convinced by your story. You say that everything I know has been lost, but you give me no way of checking. For all I know, you could be hacking me at this very moment, with all this as an elaborate distraction."

"I ain't hacking you, whatever that is. I'm taking you to the raiders as ransom for Alexandra Randall so she can tell how our village ain't cowards and stop the war."

The head looks worried.

"Oh dear," it says. "I do hope this is a virtual simulation designed to test my flexibility." It pauses and looks at the dark waters lapping softly against the boat, and the lumps of land on either side of us, and the stars winking between the nighttime clouds. "Could I be losing rational integrity? Surely one hundred forty-seven years can't really have passed since I was last on?" It gives a little shiver, then looks straight at me and says, "Please, take me to the nearest Sunoon Technologies outlet. I am possibly malfunctioning, being hacked, or losing rational integrity. I require technical support with the utmost urgency."

"I ain't never heard of them sun and moon people," I say. "And anyway, I can't take you anywhere, cos you're my only way of getting Alexandra back."

The head purses its lips.

"All right, tell me about that, then."

I don't quite know why, but for some reason I tell that head all sorts of things. It keeps on asking questions, and before I know it, I've told it all about Granny, and the raider attack on the village, and Mrs. Denton's plan. It nods and looks interested, but it keeps on asking about the sun and moon thing. And every time I say I ain't never heard anything about such a place, it looks a bit scared.

"How can they all be gone?" it says. "Who will provide me with technical support now?"

And sometimes it says, "Would you like to play?" which is pretty strange, I reckon. So I tell it a boat's no place for mucking about.

Every day of sailing takes us nearer to London. And every night the head comes out for a chat. I keep telling myself I won't let it out, but every night I do, anyway. Cos it seems so sad, how it's lost everything it knew. By the third night it's almost like normal, having the head floating in the darkness in front of me. It wants to know about everything. What I'm doing, my plan, what the world's like. But I ain't sure it believes anything I say.

When I tell it about the drowning of London, it says, "But there were sea defenses. What happened to those?"

And I shrug, cos I don't know. "Maybe they weren't good enough?" I say, "My granny said in the olden times they never had storms like we get now. She said the bad storms coming and the sea rising up was all part of the Collapse."

And when we run out of talk, the head goes back in its jewel, and I lay my head down to sleep. But it feels like I'm leaving a dream, instead of going into one.

· 10 ·
A WRONGING AND AN EQUALING

Lunden! It stinks, like old cabbage and pig droppings. Every street that ain't underwater is covered in the thick oozing mud dumped by the Temz. It slimes around everywhere. In and out of the old buildings. Stone and brick buildings, and high as the sky! But they ain't so much now, and every one of them's broken: windows smashed; holes in walls; roofs fallen in.

"Watch where you're going, Zeph! You'll end up in the slop!" Ims laughs and nods at the mud underneath the wooden walkway.

Lunden is buzzing! The great wide River Temz is full of sails: red, blue, green, purple of the Families; gleaming silver of the Scottish sunships; even the odd white sail, though any English would be mad to show their faces now. And the banks are lined with piers poking into the water, everyone loading and unloading something different: fish, wool, hay, sides of mutton, wood, people, pigs, bales of cloth, barrels of beer, rounds of cheese — anything you can think of, seems like. And where there ain't traders, there's warriors. From every Family, in every color leathers you can think of. And all of them looking fierce as you like, ready to draw weapons, bristling to start a fight.

Even after four days here, I ain't used to all these people! They're everywhere — pushing along the walkways, wading through the mud with parcels and pots and bales and every kind of thing on their heads.

"Be careful," says Ims. "Word's out about our raid. Every warrior in Lunden's on edge. Kill you same as spit on you."

He pulls me to one side of the wooden walkway, and a gang of warriors, all wearing blue, which means Chell Sea, comes walking by. Chell Sea's where my mother came from, so I'm half Chell Sea, too. I open my mouth, but I don't know the right words to say to them. Ims catches my look, shakes his head.

"Don't speak to them. They'll only see your colors, and before you know it, you'll end up dead. Stick around, you'll see warriors from every Family you've ever heard of — Kensing, Dogs, Tottnam, Stokey, Brixt, Chell Sea — and all of them are wanting a piece of Angel Isling."

"I thought Lunden was safe meeting, like Norwich?"

"It usually is, but things is different now. Your father thinks forward; he wants the Families to unite against the English. But there's plenty of other Bosses who want to keep the old ways, and plenty of warriors who'd kill every Angel Isling to keep them. And Lunden's where we all started out from, so they get all nostalgic and want to show how tradition-proud they are. Which means they're even more likely to pick a fight with us."

I watch the Chell Sea gang and all the other warriors swaggering the walkways. Every one of them is checkin' me and Ims, but Ims has got his hand on his sword and his fighting look on his face, which keeps them off.

"I don't see how all the Families coulda come from this one place," I say, and Ims laughs.

"This ain't all of Lunden. It's mostly gone now, but it used to stretch for miles. Miles and miles and just full of people."

"You're joking!"

"No I ain't. Right here is just where all the English rulers used to be — Prime Ministers and Kings and whatnot."

He points at the prickly, pointed building above us.

"They all used to be in there. Where the market is now. The House of the Parliament, they called it. All high and mighty, telling everyone what to do. And when the Collapse came, they all hid in special strong rooms, meant to keep them safe." He looks down and winks at me. "But guess what happened to them?"

"I dunno."

"Drowned, didn't they? In the floods. When the water came they was caught like rabbits in a mud bank at high tide! The Prime Minister they got now, he ain't even related. He's just the great-something-grandson of whatever little upstart it was set himself up at Swindon afterward." Ims laughs at the thought of it, then says, "Come on, let's get to the market."

The market between the tides, that's where we're going. I've been hearing about it my whole life: how the smugglers and traders there will sell anything, buy anything. The walls of the market are made of stone, but the river still punched holes in them. And so the market only happens at low tide, coz when the Temz rises, it washes right into the market hall. The river watchers peeking out the top of Big Ben ring their bell when the tide turns, to let Lunden know the water's coming back. Then all the traders pack up and leg it to the upper rooms.

That's where my father is now, in one of those rooms. Buying weapons. It was all he was talking about yesterday.

"If we're gonna have a war, I've gotta get my hands on some decent warring gear. Swords'll do for fishing villages, but not if we want to see off the English. So we'll get ourselves some rockets. The Scottish smugglers will sell if we offer enough."

Rockets! I hope Father does it. Then Angel Isling would be the first Family ever to get Scottish weapons. And when he does, he's gonna mount them on our dragonboats. Then he can blow the English out of the water.

"Come on!" says Ims, and he's gone, quick-pushing his way off the main walkway and onto a side slip. I try to copy him, but there's some Dogs warriors coming the other way, all of them with knives naked in their hands. They glare at me, on my own now, and there's threat rising off them like steam.

"What you doing, little Isling?" sneers one.

"His Boss can't be so great as he makes out," says another, "not if he'd let a little Angel like this out on its own. To get peeled by a gang of good Dogs."

I look about, but Ims is gone, and I'm facing six yellow-leathered Dogs. There ain't no way I can fight that many. Quick as I can, I'm ducking and diving. Into the crowd, behind a trader carrying a basket of clucking chickens, squeezing in between two fat servant women.

"Oi! Come here!" shouts one of the Dogs. And there's a bit of shrieking and shoving behind me as they try to catch me. But they're too big, too many, to get through this crowd the way I can. I weave in and out, letting the crowd take me along. Past the end of the market building, past the shops and stalls that spread out all around it, past crossings with other walkways, on and on. The shouting from the Dogs gets farther behind, until one of them shouts, "You got away this time, little Isling, but we'll be waiting!" And I know they've given up, just like Roba gives up chasing if it gets too hard.

But now I've gone so far I've left the main crowds, and the market's looking small and far away. Ims is way behind, and I'll have to get past the Dogs to get back to him. I look the way I came, wondering what to do. Nearby, some fisherboy is stood right in the middle of the walkway, goggling at everything like a right fishwit. First he stares at the crowd out of his soft brown face, then at the market like he ain't never seen anything like it. He's got a black moggy on a string, and he starts talking to it!

"Do you think that's the old Parliament the man told us to look out for?" says the fishwit.

"Out of the way, you dozy frint!" I say, and shove him over to one side so I can get past. And he proves he's only half-brained, coz he somehow gets the string from his stupid mog wrapped around his legs. The fishwit starts stumbling around, with the mog howling and running about him. Before you know it, he's staggered right over to the edge of the walkway.

"Cat! Get off me!" he says, in a high, scaredy kind of voice. But it's too late; he's tipping over the edge. I make to grab him, but I miss.

"Aargh!" shouts the fishwit boy. The mog does a squawky jumping twist, and the string whips around and off the boy's legs, but even that don't stop him falling, he's already too far gone. Down he goes. Headfirst! Right in the mud! Legs flapping like a frog! It must stink down there.

I'm still staring down at the fishwit in the muck — at his butt sticking right out, his legs waving about — when Ims pushes his way out of the mess of people farther down the walkway.

"What happened to you?" he shouts.

I'm laughing so hard I can't hardly answer.

"Come and see this! Some fisherboy's just fallen right in!"

The fishwit's wagging his legs so hard he topples himself over, and with a load of flapping and flailing, like a duck in a net, he gets himself upright. A bit more squelching about and he's standing up, the mud around his chest. He's so covered in it you can hardly tell he's a person. Muck's dripping off him. Oozing off his head, sliding down his face. He spits a load out of his mouth.

"Why did he fall?" says Ims, standing next to me.

"He don't know how to stay on walkways!" I say.

Ims starts chuckling.

"Hey, fisher! You want me to cast you a net? You'd make a nice catch."

The fisherboy scrapes at his face and stares up at me with his black-brown eyes.

"You pushed me in!" he shouts, spitting out more mud.

"Don't get on one, fishstink! That were the funniest thing I seen all year!"

I'm still laughing as the fishwit wades through the mud toward the walkway. He puts out a hand, but he don't even try to get out.

He just grabs at my ankle.

Then he pulls.

And I slip.

I'm falling! Right into the mud! Onto my back, with a great oozing splash. Circles and splats of mud ripple slowly away from me. I flail and freak for a bit, and the mud gets in my hair, my eyes, my mouth. It tastes of salt, and dead fish, and horse droppings, and I don't know what else.

Ims is laughing at me now.

"Have you taken up mud swimming?" he calls.

I struggle upright, and there's the mud-coated fisherboy, staring at me.

"How do you like it?" he says.

That stinking fisher! I hear a wordless roaring in my head, and I'm pushing my arm down into the mud, feeling for my dagger.

"I'm going to kill you!" I shout, struggling for my knife.

"You pushed me in!" the fisher shouts back.

"You were in my way!"

"You could have just asked me to move aside."

"It was your stupid mog who did it, not me!"

And the fisherboy looks panicked all of a sudden.

"Cat! Where are you?" he shouts. And his mangy mog is at the edge of the walkway, miaowing at him and putting a paw over the edge, like it wants to get to him.

"Stay where you are!" calls the boy. And now I've found my dagger, and I'm pulling it from its scabbard. It slides out from the mud, blade glinting.

The fisherboy looks back at me and his mouth opens, his eyes get big with fear.

"Come on, fisher!" I shout. "See how you like this!" I start pushing through the mud toward him.

"I don't like it at all!" he cries, and starts wading backward, trying to keep the distance between us.

It ain't easy to catch him, coz every step is slipping and sliding, and it's hard to keep balance and hold my dagger up. But he's having to run backward, and that's much harder, so I gain on him.

"I'm going to slice you open!" I shout.

"Leave me alone!" he shrieks, like a girl.

I'm getting closer. I almost reach him with the tip of my dagger when there's a booming shout from above us.

"STOP!"

It's Ims! Me and the fisher both stand stock-still, looking up at Ims. The fisherboy looks even more scared, coz Ims is fearsome-looking when he wants to be, and his sword is the broadest in Angel Isling. It's heavier even than Father's.

He's got his arms folded, and he's glaring down at us.

"Zeph," he says, and his voice is low, slow, and relaxed. "It ain't right to attack that fisher with your knife."

"But he pulled me in!"

Ims smiles at me.

"Yeah. But he claims you pushed him first. So you wronged him, didn't you?"

I want to shake my head, but I don't reckon Ims'd take much to that.

"I suppose," I say.

"And what's the justice for a wronging?" asks Ims.

"An equaling," I mumble.

"And he did his fair and square, didn't he?"

"But he's just a fisher!" I say.

"It don't matter. A wronging is righted by an equaling. And there's no comeback, as well you know."

I look at the fisherboy. And even though I can't say I like it, I know Ims is right. I did send the fisher into the mud, even though his mog did most of the work. And I suppose pulling me in is fair. It's what I would've done.

I nod at Ims, and turn to the boy.

"No comeback," I say. Fishwit looks at me like I'm speaking gibberish.

Ims squats down on the walkway and puts out a hand to the fisherboy.

"Come on, little fisher, time to get out."

And he pulls out the fisher, who looks like he's had his brains sucked away by the east wind. Then he reaches down again and, without even a grunt, he hauls me up with a great sucking *plop,* out from the mud.

I'm up on the walkway again, dripping and stinking.

Ims smiles at me.

"Time to make your friendship, Zeph," he says.

No! He's got to be joking.

"What's your name?" he says to the fisher.

Who looks panicky again and says, "Lil . . . er . . . Lilo." Like he don't know himself.

"Well, Lilo," says Ims, "you've met Zeph here in a wronging and equaling. Which means you have a friendship to make."

"But he's a fisher!" I say.

Ims gives me a look.

"Like I said, Zeph. It don't matter. It's the way of our Family, and you can't go against it."

· 11 ·
FILL MINER STREET

So, here we are, me and this raider, both dripping and stinking. Him eyeing me up out of his blue eyes, which are about the only part of him left to see from the mud, cos his red leathers and bright blond hair are covered in muck.

That big old raider warrior has wandered off, and now I'm wondering if the boy's going to pull his knife out again. But he doesn't. Instead, a crack opens up in his muddy face, where his mouth is. He's smiling.

"I ain't never gone wrong doing what Ims told me," he says, "so I'll probably just have to make friends with you." He scrapes some mud off his face, showing a white cheek underneath. "You did a good equaling, that's for sure, but you shoulda seen your legs, flipping and flapping in the air!"

"Well, you should've seen your face when I pulled you in!" I say.

The raider boy looks down at his muddy leathers and armor, and then at me.

"We're well filthy," he says. "My father'll kill me if I turn up looking like this. Know anywhere we can get clean?" And he starts laughing.

"It ain't funny!" I snap. And I try and check my belt for the jewel without being too obvious about it. Maybe being in the mud has drowned the floating head? That'd solve a lot of problems.

"Course it's funny! I only gotta think of you with your legs flapping about to start laughing."

I can feel my hands twitching to give him another push in the mud, but I don't, cos I hear a pitiful mewing sound. There's Cat looking up at me, his seaweed eyes wide and worried. He stands on his back legs and reaches for me with his front paws, saying, "Mew, mew" again and again.

"It's all right," I say, bending down. "We're all right now." I pet him, and he lets off a rattling purr — he doesn't even care I'm getting mud on his back, he's that happy to see me.

"What are you doing with a mog on a string, anyway?" asks the raider boy.

I carry on stroking Cat for a minute, trying to think.

"I'm . . . er . . . delivering him," I say, "to my . . . uncle."

The boy raises his eyebrows. At least, a load of mud on his forehead gets raised up, so I reckon that's his eyebrows.

"You're delivering a mog?"

"My uncle likes cats," I say, blushing at my own useless lie. But he just shrugs, specks of mud falling off his shoulders.

"You fishers are weird. Your uncle must be well into mogs if he likes a scraggy thing like that."

"Hissk!" says Cat, looking grumpy.

I put my mouth right next to his ear and whisper, "Don't make a fuss, Cat. I only dyed you to keep you safe."

"Come on!" says the boy. "Stop kissing your mog. Let's go and find your uncle."

I look at him blankly.

"Which way to your uncle's place, then?"

"Don't be stupid!" I say. "I ain't going anywhere with you. You pushed me in the mud, you pulled a knife on me."

And you're a murdering raider! But I don't say that last bit.

He shrugs. "That weren't nothing! Ims told us to make a friendship, so it's all right, ain't it?" He holds out his hand. "I'm Zeph . . . Zephaniah, son of Medwin Untamed. Of the Angel Isling Family." He looks at me like he's waiting for something. "Ain't you heard of him?"

"No," I say. "I don't know much about raiders." 'Cept how they come raging into villages and take away people's lives.

"Not raider!" he says. "Angel Isling."

"Whatever you are, I'm going."

"But you can't!" he says, angry and surprised. "Ims said we gotta make a friendship!"

"Like I care about your Ims!"

And I'm marching off, down the walkway, dragging Cat after me. We head straight for the old Parliament, and I have to push my way into the moving crowd on the wooden walkway.

"Mrow," says Cat, sounding worried, and I don't blame him, cos there's raiders everywhere: strutting about like cockerels in their red and yellow and green leathers, gold glinting from their fingers and necks and wrists; leaning on their shields and staring at everyone; looking angry and ready to skewer a person for any reason at all; guzzling wine; shouting at each other. And it feels like every single one is looking at me, sizing me up to see how many bits he can cut me into.

Ims, the one who pulled me out of the mud, is standing farther along the walkway, next to a line of laborers working a chain gang to pass great brown pots through one of the big holes in the walls of the old Parliament. He looks my way, like he's searching for something. I try and duck out of sight, but he spots me, I know it. He frowns, and his hand drops to his sword hilt.

"If you don't walk by with me, he'll kill you for not heeding his word," says a voice behind me. "And then he'll beat me black and blue, in front of everyone, for making him look stupid."

It's Zeph, and he's giving me a muddy, angry glare.

"Come on, you're gonna get us both in trouble."

I look at that big old raider warrior: beard knotted into dreadlocks, skin rough and dark as seal hide, gold glittering at every joint that isn't covered in red-colored leather, and a huge sword hanging from his waist. I don't much fancy my chances against him.

"All right," I say.

"Good!" says the boy, his face relaxing. "You do have some brains after all." He looks at me sideways. "You know, for a fisher, you really know how to hold a grudge. All I did was accidentally get you in the mud."

But I don't say anything, cos it ain't the mud I'm holding a grudge about.

"That's got to be it," says Zeph.

He's pointing at a road with a tall, spiky iron fence and gate blocking the end of it. The fence is high, taller than two men stood on top of each other, and the spikes are all rusty and evil-looking.

"I don't know, maybe it's the wrong street?" I say, cos I don't much fancy going in there.

"That old man told us to turn right down here, and that's what we did."

"Maybe it's a bit farther down?"

"Don't be thick! You said you wanted Fill Miner Street. And that looks right to me."

And it looks right to me as well. Cos fill miners dig down into the dumps left from olden times. Big holes in the ground full of plastic and metal and all sorts of stuff the olden-time folks thought was rubbish. They dig it all up, and people make it into useful things like lamps and pots and chairs. Every house in our village has got something made from it. And behind the nasty fence, this road's piled high with fill minings. Right up against the houses, even to the second floor. Only the topmost windows are left winking. But even so . . .

"What about that sign?" I point up to a small white sign on the wall, with black writing on it.

"What about it?"

"It doesn't say Fill Miner Street."

Zeph looks up at the sign, then he squints his eyes and frowns.

"I don't know what you're talking about," he says.

"Can't you see? It doesn't say Fill Miner Street, it says Downing Street."

Zeph glares at the sign a bit longer, then puts out his hand to stop a fat, woolly-dressed woman who's stepping carefully past us along the slippery wooden walkway.

"Oi! What's this street called?" he says.

She stops dead, looking angry.

"Why, you rude little mud monkey. Don't yer even know what *please* means!"

Zeph grins at her, and he taps the knife dangling at his side.

"Don't need to, do I?"

She looks at his knife, then back at him, and I reckon she works out that under all the mud is a set of red leathers. Her big pink face goes a bit white round the edges.

"Oh . . . No . . . I suppose you don't."

Zeph cocks his head at her, and she blurts out, "Fill Miner Street, that's what it's called."

Then she spins round like a penny and hurries off back the way she came.

Zeph grins at me.

"See? I don't need any stupid writing to know where I am."

In front of the iron gates is a small shed, and a couple of raggedy men are sat outside it on a bench. One man has a broken nose, the other has all scars where his ears should be. They've been watching us.

"Ya want something?" says Broken Nose.

"Looks like they wants a dip in the Temz!" says Earless, and they both cackle.

"Um . . . I'm looking for my . . . uncle, Mr. Saravanan," I say, giving the name on Mrs. Denton's letter.

"I never heard Ol' Saru mention having nevvies," says Earless, taking a tighter grip on his club. Broken Nose looks us up and down, then winks at his friend.

"O' course, if he did have nevvies, these two would be ready plums for it!"

Earless breaks into wheezing laughter.

Next to me, Zeph is bristling.

"Let us through!" he says. "We got business inside."

"Business? What business?" asks Broken Nose, looking at me, looking at Zeph. Both of us covered in mud.

"I've got a delivery for my uncle," I say, hoping that's enough.

"I'll give it to 'im, then," says Broken Nose.

"No! I have to do it myself."

Broken Nose puts a finger in his ear and twizzles it thoughtfully, staring at Cat.

"You're delivering a mog?" he asks.

I nod, glad Cat's safely in his black disguise.

"What is it?" says Earless. "Yer dinner?" He wheezes at his own joke.

"Maybe Saru needs a new hat!" says Broken Nose, and they both start croaking with laughter.

"Shut up!" shouts Zeph. "And show us through!"

The two men laugh even harder at that.

"What ya going to do about it, fisherboy?" says Broken Nose.

In a single movement, Zeph whips out his knife, leaps forward, and presses the tip of the long, rippling blade into the man's neck. It makes a sharp, painful-looking dimple in his frightened, gulping throat.

"For starters, I'll cut your tongue out for calling me a fisher," he says.

"Zeph!" I cry, starting forward. But one look from his blue eyes is enough to stop me. If I pull at his arm, will the blade cut a slice in the man's neck? Or will Zeph turn it on me?

Broken Nose is going cross-eyed trying to get a look at the knife pressed to his throat.

"You little . . ." roars Earless, hefting his club, then he stops, squinting at Zeph. A bit of red peeks through his covering of mud. Earless sags a bit.

"You're rai . . . I mean, one of the Families, ain't ya? Angel Isling? All right, I'll let you in. We don't want no vengeance on us. Just don't kill John, will yer? He dint mean nothin'."

Earless opens the great iron gate, rattling and clanging at the bolts in his hurry.

"Sorry, master!" he says to Zeph. "We couldn't see you was from the Families, what with the mud on ya. And John here is sorry for what he said. Ain't ya, John?"

And he flings open the gate. Beckoning us through.

"Ol' Saru's place is number ten – halfway down, behind the lampmakers' stall."

Zeph pulls the knife away from the gate guard's throat, and walks, head held high, through the gate. I pause, dithering for a moment, but my shins get a soft head butt.

"Miaow," says Cat, and he's right, of course. Cos what can we do but follow?

I trail Zeph along a narrow path twisting its way through the mountains and hillocks of olden-time goods.

Mrs. Denton said her contact was a fill-dealer. Which means he's trading in them things people used to throw away before the Collapse. But I thought he'd just be in a little shop or something. Not in a whole street full of the stuff.

There are leaning towers of paper; big nets filled with rustling, crinkly-looking plastic in all different colors; hundreds of little white jugs, moving and rattling in the breeze; rusting metal carriages stacked one on top of another; square, white cupboards with little round windows; racks of faded and torn clothes; blocks of hard plastic, sorted by size; coils of rope; brightly colored toys. On and on it goes, and in every corner that ain't piled with stuff, there's people. Raggedy-looking people, with dirty hands, feet, and faces. Raggedy children sorting stuff, and raggedy women cleaning it, and raggedy men making new things from the old.

And, as me and Zeph walk down the twisty path between them, every man, woman, and child who works here stops what they're doing and stares at us.

Clang! Earless and Broken Nose shut the gate. Now we're locked in, and my neck's prickling from all the eyes on us.

Behind us, the two guards are talking. "What you do that for? He was only little, I could have taken him easily!"

"Don't be a dozer! Last thing we need is trouble with raiders. Remember what the Brixt did to the wool traders that time . . ."

It's like we're at the bottom of a valley made of paper, plastic, and metal. But when I look up, there's a whole other world to this street. Cos on the top floors of the buildings there's people poking their heads out of windows, sounds of babies wailing, washing fluttering on lines, smoke snuffling out of chimneys. And above that, in the gray sky, a seagull circling. The sound of its cry makes me think of home.

The buildings on this street are three or four stories high, and they must have been pretty fancy once. Some of them even have carvings and statues sitting on little shelves on the walls. But they ain't fancy now, cos the walls're stained black and green with high tides and mold, and the statues have pigeons nesting on their heads. Just like everywhere else in London.

After another twist in the path, we come to a group of women and children under a canvas awning. They're sat between piles of round glass bulbs, some clear, some cloudy, and they're using them to make oil lamps. There's two women and three little children, and they all stop work and stare at us. Five pairs of eyes.

"This'll be it, then," says Zeph, turning to me. "Where's your uncle?"

Behind the lampmakers is a house built of dark brick, and the canvas roof of the workshop is tied to rough rusty nails banged in its wall. But if there's a door into the house, you can't see it for piles of old bulbs, and stacks of new lamps, and barrels of oil, and hanging loops of wick string.

"Does Mr. Saravanan live here?" I ask nervously.

One of the women, who looks like a pile of rags with a wrinkly old head on top, heaves herself up and shuffles out of the workshop. She walks round to a rickety-looking ladder leaning against the wall of the house. It leads to a large window on the top floor. She takes herself a great breath.

"Saru!" she shrieks. "Get yaself out here! Ya got some visitors!"

There's no answer for a long time.

"Saru!" she screams again. There's some clattering noises from up above.

"What is it?" calls a man's voice. Smart-sounding, a bit like the way Mrs. Denton sounds. Or the floating head.

"Two mucky lads want to see you," squawks the old woman.

There's a pause, and my throat starts closing up. But then the man calls out, "Send them up."

The old woman turns back to us, and jerks her head toward the ladder.

"Off ya go."

Then she shuffles back under cover and sits down. The other workers turn back to their work like we ain't even there.

Of course, Cat just scampers straight up the ladder like it was a nice set of stairs. I reckon he must be desperate to get out of the mud, cos his paws are thick with it, and he'll be on the hunt for a cozy fire to curl up by.

And I can't let Cat go on his own, so I set my hands and feet to the ladder, and up I climb. But Zeph, it's like he's had all that raider stuffing knocked out of him. Cos when I'm halfway up, he's still hanging about at the bottom of the ladder. Looking around, like he's wondering what to do.

Well, if he's scared to climb a ladder, then I'm glad to get rid of him!

At the top is the window. Cat's already jumped through, so I step off the ladder, over the sill, and into the room. There's nothing in it; just dust, mouse droppings, and the smell of damp. Cat must like the smell, cos he's sniffing about for a free mousy meal. He trots toward an empty fireplace, his tail twitching up little plumes of dust.

And it's cos I'm watching Cat I get taken by surprise. One minute, just me and Cat, next there's a man in the doorway ahead of us.

He's got big gray hair, big gray eyebrows, and a crinkly brown face. And he's pointing a pistol at me.

"Now, Mr. Mud-Covered Delinquent, I give you ten seconds to explain who you are and what you want. And if you can't, then I'll just shoot you where you stand!"

· 12 · MR. N. K. SARAVANAN

The big gray eyebrows squeeze together over his twinkling black eyes, and Mr. Saravanan says, "Lilo? What a perfectly suitable name."

He goes to pat me on the shoulder, but stops cos of all the mud. "I am very sorry about the gun, but you cannot trust anyone in this terrible city." He pats Cat on the head instead. "And Enid, the lampmaker, would show an army of knife-wielding murderers to my ladder without even blinking."

It was the letter calmed down Mr. Saravanan. I was in a panic giving it to him, cos it was covered in mud and all. He was a bit suspicious about it first off. But when he started reading it, he was all sighs and comments like "Eustace Denton, what a good man he was" and "So sad to die so young." He even wiped his eyes and sniffed about it. Then he put the letter inside his purple, velvety coat and cheered right up.

"Well now, you will follow me," he says, and we head into the creaky back of the house. We go through three rooms, each one just like the street outside, piled high with antiques. The first room's nothing but tottering stacks of books, some right to the ceiling. Cat tries to jump up on one of the smaller stacks, but he jumps straight off again when it starts wobbling about.

"Be careful!" says Mr. Saravanan. "Those are Harry Potters. I have half a dozen historians fighting to get their hands on them."

The second room's all tables, either side of a narrow path. On one side, the tables are covered with china plates, cups, vases, teapots, statues, and stuff. On the other side, the tables are covered with all the same kinds of thing, but made of bright plastics.

Mr. Saravanan stops and picks up a bright red plastic plate.

"My very favorite," he says, holding it like a baby, not like a plate.

The last room is just like a big bird's nest made out of tumbled-together chairs. To get in between, it's like scrambling through a bramble patch.

"Don't you go in there. It ain't safe," I whisper to Cat, but I reckon his wobble on the books has given him a lesson, cos he keeps close to me.

When we're through the musty-smelling storerooms, we get to a small, cozy room. There's a big saggy sofa against one wall, a fire in the grate, and a flowery-patterned rug on the floor. Pushed up against the window is a desk, covered in papers, and there's shelves with books, olden-time knick-knacks, jars full of bits and bobs, and, in the middle, a statue of a dancing blue man with four arms. It's a bit like the study at Mrs. Denton's.

"Stop!" commands Mr. Saravanan when I get to the door. "Do not come in any farther!" He kneels on the floor, crawls under his desk, and comes out with a folded cloth. He flaps it out into a big sheet and puts it over his sofa. "Now come in," he says. "Sit on there, and do not move." He looks me up and down. "You have certainly made yourself acquainted with the famous mud of London."

He pulls out the chair from the desk, sits down, and takes Mrs. Denton's letter from his jacket. He reads it again, all the lines on his forehead collecting together.

"I must say, it is strange to hear from poor Denton's widow after all these years. And for such a reason." He reads the letter again, humming to himself.

Don't find me out! Is all I can think.

"I wonder if I might see this jewel Mrs. Denton was planning to exchange for the hostage?"

I get a dry mouth, wondering if he's going to take it from me, or if the head's going to pop out and ruin everything. But I take the jewel from my belt and unwrap it. It's covered in wet mud, and I can't tell if it's broken or not. So I just whisper, "Stay in there!" as quietly as I can.

"May I?" says Mr. Saravanan, stretching out his hand. And I get even more sweaty, but I don't reckon I can say no, so I just nod silently. He picks the jewel out from the cloth wrapping and holds it up to the light, inspecting the way it sparkles.

"Beautiful," he says. "Eustace always said there were treasures in the ruins. Personally I prefer the safety of fill mining. Perhaps there are no jewels to be found, but no skeletons or plagues, either." He hands the jewel back, and I quickly wrap it up and put it away. As he watches me, he says, "Your plan is certainly brave, perhaps even foolhardy. Still, who would not want to help such a damsel in distress as this little Alexandra." He gives me a hard stare. "Though I must say, I am surprised Mrs. Denton did not send an experienced captain, as she suggests in her letter."

"All the captains got hauled into jail, and all the boys got taken into the militia."

"All the boys?" I get an even harder stare.

"They didn't want . . . I mean, I got out of it." I'm sweating now; he's going to tell me to get lost.

But he doesn't, just stares a bit more, then smiles as he folds up the letter and puts it into his jacket pocket. "Just as you say, the only *boy* in your village to be left alone . . ." and he stares at me so hard I go bright red. But then he smiles and says, "And now you are looking to find the den of raiders who stole away poor Eustace's niece?"

I nod.

"On your own?"

"Mreowl!" says Cat, from the middle of the rug.

"Cat will help me," I say without thinking.

My hand jerks up to my mouth, but the words are already out. Mr. Saravanan peers at Cat from his twinkly eyes.

"Now this is a very interesting cat. One who has gray feet, yet is black elsewhere." He pats his lap, and Cat jumps straight up, like the shameless thing he is. "I can remember Eustace telling me about the village you live in. It was famous, he said, for the seacraft of its fisherpeople."

I've got my eyes fixed on Cat's gray feet, and I daren't say anything.

"Eustace told me this seacraft was commonly supposed to be due to the remarkable powers of a race of local cats."

"Maybe," I say, trying to keep my face blank.

"If one were to obtain such an animal, I am sure it would fetch a most desirable price in such a den of thieves as London," he says, as if mulling it over. Then he winks. "But of course, I know they are gray all over. And your companion is almost all black. So he must be with you because . . . ?"

"I'm delivering him to my uncle," I say, blushing under my dried cake of mud.

"Your uncle. How splendid!" says Mr. Saravanan. "What a fine gentleman he must be."

I drop my head, blushing even redder.

"Um . . . I told people *you* were my uncle," I mumble.

Mr. Saravanan gives me a lopsided smile.

"Well then! In that case you are most fortunate your Uncle Saru is a fill-dealer, not a seacat dealer, and therefore has no interest in a gray-footed feline!"

Our little family get-together is broken up by a high-pitched hollering from the front of the house.

"Help me! Don't just leave me to dangle!"

It's Zeph.

Mr. Saravanan raises his bushy eyebrows at me.

"Did you bring a friend?"

I sigh.

"He ain't my friend. He's a raider. He's the reason I'm covered in mud, and now he's following me around."

"A raider? How interesting. Do you want me to deal with him?"

His hand moves to pick up the pistol. I can't say I don't have a thought about it. But Granny would never forgive me.

"No. Don't," I say. "It's all right, really. He keeps the others off me."

"A very sensible point of view," says Mr. Saravanan. "Having protection is most necessary in this town. Especially now, with the raiders so fractious."

"Don't tell him anything about the letter," I say, feeling a bit panicky again, "or where I'm headed. He doesn't know anything about it."

Mr. Saravanan chuckles.

"And I guess this is the person you told about your Uncle Saru. Well, stay here, little nephew, and I will haul in your raider."

After Mr. Saravanan pulls Zeph in through the window – "The ladder moved! It did. Otherwise I woulda had no problems climbing up" – he brings him back into the little room and sits him down on the sofa next to me.

He looks at the two of us, both plastered in stinky mud, and sighs.

"I can see you are both in need of my bathtub," he says. "Please come with me to my kitchen."

Mr. Saravanan has a kitchen nearly as big as the whole of our house back home. Most of one wall's filled up by a big black range, which Cat curls up to straightaway. In the middle there's a table, and a wide, buckled dresser is propped up against another wall, with a tin bath hanging from a hook next to it. But the best thing is, he's got his very own tap, which pours out water whenever he turns it. No traipsing to the water pump for him.

He smiles and says, "You see, young nephew? Your uncle has all the luxuries here. You know, once upon a time this was where the Prime Minister lived."

I reckon he's putting us on, so I don't say anything, but that doesn't stop Zeph.

"Well, he better not come back. He'd be chopped into little bits by the Families if he showed his face here today."

Mr. Saravanan gives Zeph a look. "Yes, I expect you are right." And he turns back to his water tap.

When three pans of water are heating on the range, Mr. Saravanan says, "You boys can get washed, and I will see if Enid can sort out your clothes." He takes a large canvas bag down from a hook on the wall.

"Put your dirty garments in here, if you please."

And now I don't know what to do. I could strip off down to my long johns, which'd mean I'd still be covered up from neck to knees. But I can't hardly take off any more clothes. And I definitely ain't sharing a bath with anyone!

I'm stood there, wondering and probably looking right stupid about it, when Mr. Saravanan suddenly winks at me and says, "But what am I thinking of? I shall need someone to help me persuade Enid to wash the clothes. She is a woman who needs encouragement to undertake domestic activities. It would be better, I think, if young Lilo gets washed first while Zeph comes with me." He turns to Zeph and nods. "You seem like more of a fierce prospect than my little nephew."

Zeph puffs up at that.

"I can persuade her, the old beggar. And a lot better than Lilo – he looks a bit wet, don't he?"

"Yes, *he* certainly does," says Mr. Saravanan, chuckling to himself. "Although I would advise you not to refer to Enid as an old beggar in her hearing. Unless you're looking for a broken bottle in your face."

In the end, it ain't hard to get clean without being found out. I reckon the raiders can't have baths that often, cos Zeph doesn't even blink when I keep my long johns on. Mr. Saravanan gives me a look, but he doesn't say anything. Just takes all my other clothes, 'cept my fisherbelt cos I ain't giving that to anyone, and heads off with Zeph. I have to make a right quick go of scrubbing myself before the other two get back, and rinse and wring out my long johns as well. But I manage it. And it's not long before Zeph walks in, looking right cross and wearing a set of shapeless clothes with his head poking out like a drying cow pie. Mr. Saravanan follows, clutching a bundle.

"In her own delightful fashion, Enid has told us she will not be able to wash and dry your garments before tomorrow morning. But there is no need for concern, because I have plenty of clothes in my collection."

"She swore at me, the mangy old beggar," says Zeph grumpily. "And I don't know where you got this rubbish from."

"Well, you are perfectly welcome to sit around naked," says Mr. Saravanan.

He hands me the bundle. It's an outfit like Zeph's: a pair of blue canvas pants and a shapeless top. My top is black, with long sleeves, a hole for a neck, and METALLICA written across it. Zeph's top is red and has MANCHEST NITED in worn-out letters. The clothes smell musty.

"These are disgusting!" says Zeph, picking at his top.

"There is nothing wrong with them," snaps Mr. Saravanan. "They have been cleaned very carefully since they were taken from the landfill."

"You've given us dead men's clothes?" says Zeph, sounding outraged.

"I doubt very much they belonged to men," says Mr. Saravanan, fixing his black eyes on Zeph, "unless people in those days were a great deal smaller. I would suggest these are more likely to be the clothes of long-dead children."

And there ain't an answer to that.

When it comes time for Zeph's bath, he does the same as me, getting in with his undies on, like he reckons that's how it's done. Then he's splashing and singing, for what seems like hours. Mr. Saravanan spends the time cutting up onions and potatoes and all sorts of other vegetables. He fries things and throws in different-colored seeds and powders, so a thick spicy scent fills up the kitchen.

But Zeph isn't even the slightest bit grateful for the bath or the food or anything. All he says about it is, "Lilo! Bring me some more hot water!"

"I ain't your slave!" I say, which gets me a sneer.

"No you ain't," he says, "coz if you was, you'd know your place and not answer back."

Mr. Saravanan places a lid on the last of his pots, leaving our dinner to bubble, and carries a pan of hot water over to Zeph, pouring it calmly into his bath.

"Ow! That's too hot now!"

"Oh dear," says Mr. Saravanan. "Well, I am afraid that's something you will have to solve for yourself, because I now need young Lilo to come and help me."

And he steers me by the arm to the door, leaving Zeph hopping around the kitchen, trying to get cold water to his bath.

We go into Mr. Saravanan's study, and he closes the door behind us.

"I find cooking most helpful for calm thought," he says. "And so I have come to an idea of how to find the location of the little kidnapped girl."

He looks at the door, as if he's trying to see through to Zeph.

"I cannot say I have much fondness for raiders. They are so arrogant, so proud. Always boasting about how they survived the Collapse, without seeming to notice the others of us who did the same." He shakes his head. "It was very arrogant and prideful to take that poor little girl." Then he smiles, a wrinkly, cheered-up kind of smile.

"But the good thing about this pride is how it makes their tongues wag. I do not think there is a raider in all London who could keep the secret of where that girl has been taken if he knew it. And there is a tavern I know of, where many raiders go. I am sure this will be the place to find out."

· 13 ·
TILL MIDNIGHT BELLS

Thank the west wind, we're going to a tavern!

Me, Lilo, and his weird uncle.

But not his mog, that's sat by the range. I don't know why they make such a fuss of it.

The two of them make another fuss at the ladder, like I've got some kind of problem. I'm stood at the window, just checkin' the candlelit stalls below, and the Temz glinting darkly in the distance, when Lilo says, "Don't worry, Zeph, I'll catch you."

Like I need his help! And then weird Uncle Saru bounces around on the ladder so I can hardly hold on. I mean, what kind of loony only has a ladder to get into their house with?

Most of the streets of Lunden is dark, and all the empty houses make pitch-black shadows so you can't see nothing.

Uncle Saru's got a lantern, but it only puts out a measly yellow light, and I can't hardly see my feet. The tide's in, and back toward the Temz there's a shimmer of water, lapping around the buildings. Father's that way, where the dragonboat's moored. I wonder if he's noticed I ain't there, if Ims told him what happened. I should be on the dragonboat with my father, instead of here with this fisherboy and his weird uncle. Still, at least we're going to a tavern.

Apart from his lantern, the other thing old Saru's got is a big wooden club — long and flat with a round handle.

A cricket bat, he calls it. "Once used for a most elegant game. Now used most inelegantly to frighten off would-be attackers." Not that it'd frighten anyone with a decent sword.

A bit farther on, and we're into a big, bright-lit square. Wide and open, at the meeting of four streets. There's a massive deckway across the whole place, with the Lunden mud dark beneath it. Off to one side is a tall stone column sticking through the decking, with a headless, armless statue on top. Ropes fan out from it with lanterns dangling off them. Smoking braziers are scattered about, sending orange flickering light onto the broken buildings all around, but the main thing what counts is all the stalls. Loads of them. And all the people, coming in from every direction. Everyone's having a good time; sitting round the fires with bottles and pipes, or going to stalls to buy food or drinks. Talking, laughing, selling things.

I know where we are now. Trafalgar Square! This is more like it.

"I came here with Ims night before last," I say.

"Good for you," says Saru.

"What is this place?" asks Lilo, sounding like he ain't never seen nothin' like it. Which he probably ain't.

"It's Trafalgar Square. Best party in Lunden!"

"That is one way of describing it," says Saru, opening the glass of his lantern and blowing out the flame.

Straight off, we're in the throng.

"Keep close to me," says Saru, and Lilo practically hangs off his butt, like he's scared he'll get eaten if he loses his uncle.

But I don't care. I love this. Crackling fire-pits. The smell of roasting meat, or frying bread, or sweet-dipped apples. People laughing and checkin' each other. People getting drunk and falling about.

A well rough doxy, with streaks of red smeared across her cheeks and eyes, pulls at Lilo's shoulder.

"Come here for some action, 'ave ya, little man?" and she winks at him.

"Get off me!" he shrieks, and starts beating at her like she's a wasp.

"Come on, Lilo," I say, "you're missing your chance! She'll help you find your plums!"

Lilo stares at me. "What are you talking about?"

"Don't be such a girl!" I say, and he goes red.

"This way!" calls Saru, who's got a few paces ahead of us in the crowd. Lilo gets in a right old panic at that, pushing through and grabbing a fistful of Saru's coat.

I follow along easy, while they charge across the square, like a horse and its wagon. But I can tell where they're off to. You can't miss it. It's the biggest, the best, the busiest tent in the whole square. The roof is held up in three peaks by tall poles, and all round the awning there's banners flying in every raider color.

I didn't even know there was so many Families before I came here.

"It's a big top," said Ims when we came here the other night. "They used to have them for circuses." He lifted up his tankard. "But we got a much better use for it now!"

And you can tell what the use is from the noise coming out into the square — laughing, shouting, cursing — and the smell — sour-sweet, like old fruit. Cider!

Saru and Lilo are stood a way off, staring at the big tent. Two black-clad, sword-toting guards is eyeing them up.

"This is the raider tavern," Saru's saying to Lilo, who looks like his eyes are going to pop from his head. "One of the only places this side of Colchester where raiders from the different Families mix without killing each other."

"You ain't going in though, are you?" I say, catching up to them. Old Saru raises his caterpillar eyebrows.

"Why should I not?"

"You ain't Family! And Lilo ain't, neither!"

"Well then, we are very fortunate to be accompanied by a bona fide Angel, in the shape of yourself."

"You gotta be joking! I ain't going in there dressed like this. Someone might see me."

"I thought red was the color of your Family."

"Red leathers! Not red . . . bags!"

"I don't want to go in there . . ." says Lilo, in a fraidy kind of voice.

"And you shouldn't, anyway!" I say. "It's only for Family!"

"Actually, Mr. Angel Isling, in this matter you are incorrect," says Saru. "Although it is not a most common occurrence, I can say in truth I have been in there before, and returned without harm."

"I really don't want to go in," says Lilo, staring through the doorway into the loud smoky inside. He looks like he wants to be sick.

Old Saru pats his nephew on the shoulder.

"I am most happy to enter alone. Maybe you two can find something more suitable to your youth?"

What's he on about?

"I went in there the other night!" I say. "But I ain't going in looking like this . . . joke!"

And I turn and march off, coz I can't stand Lilo's uncle another second. I end up in a stall that's selling ladies' gloves, so I march right out again.

When I look back, Saru says something to Lilo, who comes running over to me.

"I'm coming with you," he pants.

"All right. If you want," I say. But I'm glad he's here, and without his stupid uncle.

"You were well scared back there," I say, poking his arm.

"No I wasn't!" he says, "I was just —"

"You were scared!" I say, cheering right up. "What are we doing, then?" He looks at me blankly. "Come on, fishwits, where are we going to get a drink?"

"Mr. Sarava . . . my uncle said we had to be back by midnight bells!"

"That's gotta be hours off," I say. "Will you stop being such a girl!"

And I find us a tavern.

It ain't as good as the big top — that's gotta be the best tavern in the world — but it'll do. It sells cider. It's all smoky from the charcoal burners and tallow torches, and there's plenty of men and women sprawled around drinking. So it's not so bad.

In the middle is a wooden counter, where a fat, knobbly man is guarding the cider casks.

I head straight there.

"Two jugs of cider," I say.

"Ha ha!" says Knobbly Man. "That's what I like to see — two young guns after a bit of hair on their chests. Well, show us yer pennies, and it's two beakers of Headbreaker coming right up." Then he winks. "And if yer looking for anything more — the company of ladies, perhaps — why, you only have to ask yer old friend Hector!"

Lilo goes bright red, which gives Knobbly Man a right good laugh; his fat cheeks wobble, and sweat drips off his nose.

"Are you sure you want cider?" Lilo says to me. "We could get milk."

"Why have you even bothered coming to Lunden?" I say.

"Two beakers of cider," says Knobbly Man, slapping them on the counter. He leers at me. "Unless you want milk."

"He was joking," I say. How did I get landed with such a fishwit? "He wants cider, too. And he's paying."

Lilo looks cross. But Knobbly Man's staring at him now, waiting for his money. That'll show him. Lilo pulls up his bag shirt and roots around at a purse jangling from his neck. He pulls out some coins.

"Don't you have any money?" he asks me grumpily.

I shrug. "I don't carry it. Ims does all that stuff."

"Why, how good of yer to pay in advance," says Knobbly Man, whipping the coins off Lilo. "Yer the kind of customer I like! And these . . . seven English pennies'll get you a fine night of drinking."

He shouts at a thin girl wearing an apron. "Sharon! This lad and his friend are due another three beakers each. So make sure they get 'em — and not a drop more unless you see the inside of their wallets!"

Lilo's looking like he don't know what's hit him.

"This the first time you been to Trafalgar Square?" I say. He nods. "The first time you been in a tavern?"

"Yes. No! I been in lots of taverns." But he hasn't. Probably only left his mum last week.

I find us space at a bench, one where there ain't too much cider on the seat. And we get drinking. I don't really drink much cider at the hall, only on feast days. And then Ims'll only let me have a single beaker. But he ain't here now; I can have as much as I want.

Lilo sips at his beaker like he's worried it'll bite him.

"Thanks for this, Lilo!" I say. I take a big mouthful, and swallow it down. I got three more beakers to get through. I may as well get cracking.

"I wonder where Ims is. I wonder if he tol' Father where I went." I look up at Lilo. "Do you think he did? My father might be worried 'bout me."

I can see Lilo staring at me. His face is really big. And wobbly.

"Maybe you've had enough?" he says.

Course I haven't, stupid.

"Course not," I say.

This here. In my hand. What I'm holding. Oops, spilled a bit. Anyway, this is my sixth beaker o' cider. Or is it fifth? No, definitely sixth. Coz I drank all mine, and Lilo only had one. So I drank his others. I did.

Lilo's gone wobbly all over now. Everythin's wobbly, actually.

But if I put my head on my arms, like this, it's better. Table stops my head falling off.

I like Lilo. I really do. He let me have his cider. Not like back home. No one's ever let me have their cider.

"You're my only frien'," I say to him.

"That's not true," says wobbly Lilo.

I wan' to shake my head. But I can't. It might fall off.

"Thing is, you don' get proper friens until you're a full warrior. When you get your name."

He doesn't understand. Probably coz he's spinning around so much.

"You're a fisher, right?"

His spinning heads all nod.

"Fishers is jus' fishers. See? But warriors is made. Has to fight their way up."

"So?" says Lilo.

"So you has to fight. Other boys. Your age. Firs' to be a sword boy, then shiel' bearer, then prentice, then warrior." I stop for a breath. Speaking is making everything wobble and spin more.

I wish it would stop.

"An' my father's Boss, ain' he? So I got to be bes' at fightin', don' I? And I am. Bes' knife thrower in the Family. So I don' got friens. See?"

Lilo nods his wobbly heads, then shakes them.

He's all right, Lilo. Even though he's a stinkin' fisher. And a bit girly. I try to tell him.

"Tha's why it's funny what Ims said, 'bout you being my frien'. Coz you're only a fisher. So I won' never have to fight you. Which is a good job, coz I'd kill you no problem."

Lilo's big faces stare at me.

"Yeah. I bet you would," he says.

But I wouldn't kill Lilo. He's my frien'.

"Have you got friens?" I say.

Lilo's mouth goes even more wobbly. He looks sad.

"Yes," he says. "I've got a best friend. Since we was really little. He's called Andy."

"Why ain't he here?"

"He had . . . to go away. He might never come back," says Lilo, and now he looks really sad. Like he might cry, even.

"I'll be your frien'," I say. But Lilo shakes his head.

"You're a raider," he says.

"And you're a stinkin' fisher!"

But he's right. It is a problem.

Oh. I know.

"You could become Family," I say. He looks surprised. "You know. If your father or someone cast you out. You can get Family protec . . . protection."

I look at his wobbly face.

"Will your father cas' you out? D'you think?"

"I'm going to ask the barman how long it is till midnight bells," he says, and gets up.

Maybe his family will cas' him out. Then he won't be a stinkin' fisher no more. It'd be honorable for him to be my frien' if that happened.

So I'll jus' wait here for him to come back. Head on arms. Tha's best. Maybe eyes shut, too.

· 14 ·
OUTCAST KINSHIP

Mr. Saravanan's waiting outside the raider tavern, looking tired. His hair's all wet and there are dark stains all over his clothes. He stinks of cider, but he ain't drunk. Not like Zeph.

"I am afraid I was involved in a small unpleasantness," says Mr. Saravanan. "Lucky for me, it was nothing too serious. By raider standards it could even be called playing. But I am now a trifle soaked." Then he smiles, whispering just to me, "I have found out what you need to know."

In a louder voice he asks, "So, how have you two been?"

"You can see for yourself," I say, which is true, cos I'm pretty much holding Zeph up, he's that drunk. It's taken me a good while to drag him over here — he was leaning on me the whole way, and nearly falling over pretty much every step he took. Now he's standing at an angle, staring toward the raider tent.

"I ain't 'fraid to go in there, you know," he slurs.

"It would seem our young raider friend has drunk as much as I have had thrown at me," says Mr. Saravanan.

"I feel sick," moans Zeph.

Then — right next to me! — he throws up.

"You're disgusting!" I shout, jumping away from him.

Zeph looks at his pile of vomit, then at me, and I think he might start crying.

"I thought you was my frien'," he says.

"All right!" says Mr. Saravanan. "It is definitely time to go!" He hoicks Zeph under an arm and starts walking. Zeph bounces like a rag doll under Mr. Saravanan's arm as far as the edge of the square.

Then he groans, "I feel sick!"

Mr. Saravanan puts him down quick as you like, and Zeph starts hurling into a pothole. While we're watching him, and it ain't pretty, Mr. Saravanan tells me quietly about what he's been up to.

"I found my mission to be rather easy. In fact, very easy. They were talking of little else but the raid on your village. Interestingly, it seems that the girl was taken by the Angel Isling Family, and the raiders from the other Families are wondering how they knew she was there, whether there will be war with the English, and what the Family council in Norwich will have to say about it all."

"But Zeph's Angel Isling, ain't he?" I say. "And he just told me his father's the Boss."

Mr. Saravanan stares hard at Zeph.

"Now *that* is very interesting."

Zeph throws up again, and moans out, "I think I might be dying."

"This young man is probably the most useful person you could have met in London," says Mr. Saravanan quietly.

"The most annoying, more like."

Zeph finally finishes vomiting, and turns a white, shiny face to look at us.

"I'm dyin' and you don' even care," he says mournfully. And suddenly I find myself walking over and patting him on the back. Even though he stinks.

"You're not dying," I say. "And you'll feel better when you get home."

He looks at me, blue eyes wide, blond hair plastered to his forehead.

"I can't go back to my father's ship. Not like this."

Mr. Saravanan smiles, and I reckon it's a good thing Zeph's too drunk to see what kind of smile it is.

"You are very lucky," says Mr. Saravanan, "having such good friends as Lilo and myself. You can stay with us tonight and go back to your dragonboat tomorrow."

As we're walking back, we have to stop for Zeph to be sick again. While he's splattering cider over the moonlit mud, Mr. Saravanan whispers, "It seems Angel Isling was in fact contracted by someone to raid your home village. There was a great deal of discussion about who it may have been."

I remember the Scottish man in the study: "This is hardly going to plan."

"My own conclusion is that the Scandinavians would be most likely to be behind such a plot," says Mr. Saravanan. "They are always interfering."

"Why did that fool Medwin take the girl?" That's what the Scottish man said.

"What about Greater Scotland?" I ask.

But Mr. Saravanan just raises his big eyebrows.

"I cannot imagine starting a war between the raiders and the English would be the work of Greater Scotland. It would be too obvious for them. They seem much more happy sending their spies out everywhere." He shrugs. "But then again, who knows?" He looks at me. "Why would Greater Scotland want to kidnap the daughter of the English commander of armed forces?"

"Maybe they didn't," I say. "Maybe they didn't mean it to happen that way. The Scottish Ambassador was at our village afterward, with the Prime Minister. He got all the soldiers to search for something. But I don't think they found it."

"So if not the girl, what would Greater Scotland be looking for?" says Mr. Saravanan. Then he smiles. "Eustace, did you really find it? And who did you tell?"

At Zeph's next vomit stop, Mr. Saravanan says, "You have to keep attached to this raider boy. He is vital if you are to gain safe access to the Angel Isling family. Without raider company, they'd almost certainly kill you before you even had a chance to speak. However, I have no ideas as to how you will maintain your alliance, except telling him the truth."

And now I'm glad it's dark and Mr. Saravanan can't see my face. Cos I ain't even told him the truth.

"Maybe I don't need to," I say. "Not if I joined his Family."

Mr. Saravanan looks surprised.

"Is that possible? Raiders are not known for being overly fond of the English."

I remember Zeph's drunken words, back at the tavern.

"There might be a way."

Dawn breaks flat and gray. There's no shutters on the window, but even so the day creeps in slowly and takes its time to spread a dull light over the dusty floor. Cat yawns fishily, and gives my nose a morning lick. I'm lying in a muddle of blankets, with Cat curled neatly on the rolled-up coat I've got for a pillow. Above me, on Mr. Saravanan's sagging sofa, there's another bundle of blankets. It snorts, then groans, it rolls around a bit, then it goes quiet. Zeph is sleeping off his cider.

Cat sits up and gives me a look, his green eyes wide in his furry face.

"You ate lots last night," I whisper, but he keeps on looking, then he butts his head against mine, purring deep in his chest.

"All right, greedy. I'll see if there's anything for you to eat."

Cat's tail is high and happy as he leads me into Mr. Saravanan's kitchen. But it starts to droop when I can't find him anything to eat — there's nothing in the cupboard a cat would like. And I ain't much tempted by the bag of dark flour, single green potato, and stone jar of probably-chutney, which is all Mr. Saravanan seems to have. Cat and me are wondering what to do when we hear some scrabbling and banging at the front of the house, and we go through to see Mr. Saravanan climbing back in through his front window, grumbling.

"One day, I am going to move from this wretched city and get myself a home where it is safe to have a front door. At ground level."

We go back into the kitchen, and Mr. Saravanan opens the two bags he's carrying, one large, one smaller. In the large hessian sack, he has our clothes, clean and mud free. In the smaller canvas bag he's got a loaf of bread, some brown speckled eggs, a block of cheese, a block of butter, and six small apples.

"Breakfast!" he says, and then he looks down, cos Cat is rubbing round and round his legs.

"Do not worry, Mr. Cat, I have something for you, too." And he pulls a fish from his pocket, sending Cat into a frenzy of mewing and paw-swiping.

"Now here is a fellow who really appreciates my efforts," says Mr. Saravanan, dropping the fish. Cat grabs it in his mouth and runs to a corner, his tail swishing. "And speaking of appreciative fellows, how is young master Zeph?" He looks round the door at the lump of blankets on the sofa, and grins nastily. "Still feeling the effects of last night's excess?" He starts unpacking the bags. "You know, I have been thinking about your question from last night. Whether Greater Scotland could be involved in this raider kidnapping. Your comment about the searches made me wonder what they might be searching for. And that made me think of my poor friend Eustace Denton." He sighs, putting the eggs carefully on the table. My eyes are practically glued to them; I can't remember the last time I had a whole egg to eat myself.

"Eustace was an antiquarian, like myself," says Mr. Saravanan, taking a pan and pouring water into it. "He had a quest, which rather overpossessed him, I always thought."

"A quest?"

"Well, perhaps obsession would be a better term." Mr. Saravanan puts the eggs in the pan of water, and puts the pan on his stove. "It related to his speciality — computers." Mr. Saravanan turns and looks at me. "Of course, a good English child like yourself would know little of computers, would you? A sinful subject, so I hear. Well, Eustace thought differently. The reason he ended up living in an isolated fishing village was his scandalous views on the subject. Or so he told me. I always thought it was pointless. There are always stories of computers that survived the Collapse. Rumors the Scots have some hidden away, or the Scandinavians have one, or the Chinese. But from what I understand, they were all connected together in some way, all over the world, and when the Collapse came, something went wrong with them all at the same time. Anyway, Eustace had heard a story of some supermachine that had survived, that could think and act on its own." My mouth goes dry thinking about the jewel, and I drop my head so Mr. Saravanan can't see my face.

"What was it like?" I manage to squeak out.

Mr. Saravanan strokes his chin. "Well, I'm not an expert by any means, but there was a fashion in the late twenty-first century for hiding the function of an object. Teapots that looked like horses, lights hidden in furniture, that sort of thing. Most unpopular among today's buyers. Which means Eustace's thinking computer might have looked like anything." He shrugs. "Anyway, I suppose it makes as much sense for the Scottish to be looking for a mythical computer as the Prime Minister's daughter."

"But why would they want it?" I ask.

"Well, Eustace thought the computer was something to do with the military."

"I've managed whole wars," the head had said.

"Such a machine would be highly sought after today," Mr. Saravanan continued. "Why, even your English rulers might forswear their hatred of technology if they thought it could help them win their battles."

He fiddles with the fire in his range, sending heat to the pan with the eggs in it. "At every drowned place he visited,

Eustace hoped to find one of these fabulous machines. And he always asked me about them when he came to trade. Never showed any interest in all my beauties, just wanted computers and nothing else. Who knows, maybe he found what he was searching for? I can imagine the Scots wanting to obtain such a thing, and without your English Prime Minister finding out."

"But if the Scots sent the raiders to find this puter, why did they take Alexandra?"

"Most likely because they are crazy raiders." Mr. Saravanan shakes his head. There's a groaning sound from the next room. "Speaking of which . . ."

"I'm dying!" calls a feeble voice, and Zeph appears wrapped in a blanket. His white face is even whiter than usual, 'cept for the deep purple rings under his eyes.

"I doubt you are actually dying," says Mr. Saravanan calmly.

"My head is so painful!" moans Zeph.

"Yes, I thought it might be," says Mr. Saravanan. "But one of the few benefits of London life is that people here are willing to sell anything you want, at any time of day." He pulls from his pocket a small wrap of paper. "A simple remedy. It should help to relieve the pain."

Zeph takes his medicine without even complaining, so he must be feeling bad. Then he sits silently at the kitchen table while Mr. Saravanan takes the boiled eggs out of the pan and I cut the bread into slices, covering each slice with butter and cheese. The probably-chutney really is chutney, and we get that, too.

We all sit down to eat. At-death's-door Zeph only manages a couple of bites, though, and then he starts to turn green. So I eat his bread and cheese, and his eggs, and by the end of breakfast my belly feels better than it has in years.

Even though he can't take any food, the medicine must be working, cos Zeph's face gets a bit less pale, and under his eyes look a bit less purple. He opens the sack with our clothes in it.

"Look what they've done to my leathers!" he says. "The red is all faded!" But I can't see any difference, and he's quick enough to change out of the antique clothes Mr. Saravanan got us. I don't blame him. I'm glad to get my own clothes again, so I don't have to walk around looking like a clown. And when Zeph's back in his leathers and bracelets, knife dangling from his belt, he starts looking much better.

"Now I can return to my ship," he says.

"Oh!" says Mr. Saravanan suddenly. "You're returning to your ship?" And he looks at me, giving a quick wag of his eyebrows. "Um . . . what are you intending to do, young Lilo?"

Our plan!

"Oh, er . . . I'm going to head east," I say, crossing my fingers under the table. "I've decided to join one of the Families. I want to be a warrior."

"A RAIDER!" roars Mr. Saravanan, making me jump. "NEVER! No member of *this* family will lead such a wicked life! You were born a fisher and you'll DIE a fisher!"

"But I don't *want* to be a fisher," I say. Zeph is looking at us both, shocked and a bit suspicious.

Mr. Saravanan waggles his eyebrows again, so I start shouting for extra effect.

"I'll NEVER be a fisher, and YOU can't tell me what to DO!"

"I CAN!" Mr. Saravanan roars back. "I have every right, I am your uncle. Why, I will lock you up and BEAT you every day until you come to your senses, you ungrateful wretch!" And he waves his arms, making grabbing movements at me. He looks so stupid, I want to laugh, but I try my hardest to look scared as I scurry to the other side of the room.

"I don't even want to be your nephew!" I shout.

"The FINAL INSULT!" rages Mr. Saravanan, shaking his fist. "If that's what you want, then as head of our family, I cast you OUT! You are dead to us! You'll never see your mother again, or your father, or your sweet innocent sisters, or your aunties, or your cousins . . . And take that CAT with you, I don't want it now!"

"Boo hoo!" I say, trying to sound sad. "I am cast out!"

And we both turn to look at Zeph.

"What?" he says, looking stunned.

"I have cast Lilo out of the family!" says Mr. Saravanan, speaking loud and slowly.

"Oh! Oh! I am cast out!" I cry. "In fact, I'm cast out in front of you, and you're a raider. So I claim . . ." but then

I can't remember what he called it last night. "I . . . er . . . claim . . ."

"You want outcast kinship?" squeaks Zeph, looking at me with wide-open eyes.

"Yes, that's it! That's what I want!"

"No!" moans Mr. Saravanan, and slumps down onto the table, his head in his hands. "To think of the shame; a nephew of mine taking up with the raiders!" Through his fingers, I see him peeping up at me, and he winks.

But it's that what gets Zeph going finally.

"It ain't a shame to join the Angel Isling Family!" he roars, slapping his hand on the painted lion on his leather jacket. "It's the greatest pride anyone can feel."

Then he walks across the room to me.

"But is this really what you want, Lilo?" he asks, frowning a bit.

"You said it last night. If I was in Angel Isling, we could be friends."

He looks at me blankly. "I said that? I . . . don't remember."

"It's what I want," I say.

Zeph looks back at Mr. Saravanan, who's beating his head with his hands and groaning. Overdoing it.

"Are you really sure, Lilo?" says Zeph. "Think about your family. Won't they be sad if you leave them? Won't your mum cry?" He stops, his pale face a question, his eyes looking right into mine. And I have to look away, cos I feel so mean. He ain't all bad, and here I am telling so many lies to him. I try and remember Andy, and Alexandra, and why I'm doing this, but still it feels wrong.

Luckily for me, Mr. Saravanan roars out, "It is too late to worry about Lilo's mother now! I have cast the boy OUT, and I NEVER go back on my word! He can be raider scum or whatever he likes as far as his *real* family cares!"

Zeph's arm on mine tenses. He lifts his head up, and says, "As a full-blood member of the Family Angel Isling, and as the Boss's only highborn son, I accept you into outcast kinship. You are now Lilo bar Angel Isling." And he turns to Mr. Saravanan, his voice rough and shaky, speaking in a kind of singsong, like reciting something he's been taught. "I declare Lilo to be under Family protection, until the time he earns his full kinship. Not one hair of Lilo's head now belongs to his old family. Any harm to him is harm to Angel Isling. By my rank and right I declare it done." Then he looks down and whispers, so quietly I almost don't hear it, "If my father agrees."

After that, we have to get out quick from Mr. Saravanan's place — him shouting and cursing us in fake rage all the way. Which gets us a whole crop of nasty stares as we leave the street. The two gate guards are back at their place, lazing on their stools and eating a pie between them.

"Leaving us, yer lordships?" says Broken Nose.

"Taking your mangy pet with yer?" asks Earless, throwing a hard piece of piecrust at Cat. He hisses, the fur raising up on his back; I reckon he'd be on them, claws flailing, if I didn't have him back on his leash.

"Let us out," I say, praying Zeph won't cause trouble. But he hardly even notices the guards, he's so busy looking out past the gates.

"We head that way to my father's ship," he says excitedly, pointing east.

And when we've passed through the gate, heading off down the street, he says, "You won't be sorry for joining Angel Isling. Our Family's the strongest and fiercest of all – you've joined the best of the best! And wait until you see my father's dragonboat – it's the fastest ship you ever saw. Cuts through the water like a knife – nothing can catch her. You won't never have seen anything better!"

"I reckon not," I say, thinking of the Prime Minister's ship; how it towered over my boat, how it took Andy away.

"She's so big she has to berth downstream, she can't make it under the bridges this far up," says Zeph.

And so we carry on walking for a good while, Zeph chattering all the time about how great the raiders are, and how happy I'll be to be one of them. We walk along yet more wooden walkways, with the river glinting on our right between the broken and empty buildings. Not long, I feel foxed and confused by the endless muddy streets, but Zeph doesn't even pause, just heads right to where he wants to go.

"Come on, Lilo!" he says, speeding up. "It's just round this corner."

The boardwalk takes a sharp right between a gap in the buildings, and Zeph disappears into it. I pull at Cat, who's being a sight more than grumpy about having to walk past all the mud, and we head into the gap.

Where I pretty much bang right into Zeph, who's standing on an empty pier. No great raider dragonboat, no raider boats of any kind. Just an open view of the river washing past, a row of stacked barrels, and a beaten-looking old man dressed in the shapeless sacking-wear of a raider slave.

"No, master," he's saying to Zeph. "The Boss's dragonboat left on the early tide. He said if a young lord turned up, I should tell him to go to the Family quarters in old Isling. Wait there, he said."

Zeph's silent for a moment, staring out at the glinting flow of the river, then he spins round, like he's looking for something.

"How can this be?" he shouts, and starts kicking at the barrels.

"Please, master, please!" whimpers the old man. "You may break them." And he drops to his knees, holding out his hands, half pleading, half trying to shield the barrels from Zeph's feet.

"Maybe your father thought . . ." But I stop. I can't think of any reason why Zeph's father should have sailed. Going off without his son, leaving him alone in London.

Zeph kicks himself to a standstill. He turns to me, some lost thing looking out from his eyes.

"Why would he leave me?"

I shrug, cos there's no answer I can give him.

The old man, still on his knees, says, "Please, master, if it helps yer, I did hear the Boss talking to a bright, brave prince of a warrior, who told him they couldn't wait because the Prime Minister of England had his fleet gathering, and they had to get to the home marshes."

Zeph's face instantly darkens. "Did the warrior have red hair?"

"Oh yes, master, like fiery bronze it was."

"And was he wearing leathers like mine?"

"Why yes, master, what a beauty of a lion was drawn on him."

Zeph looks like he's been punched.

"Roba!" he roars. "I hate him!" He starts kicking at the barrels again.

The old man waves his arms about, stumbling on his knees, trying to put himself between Zeph and the cargo.

"You're right, master! That warrior were a monster! What terrible red hair, what an evil lion was drawn on him! Please, master, don't hit that barrel so, it's full of the best Frenchy wine."

He looks terrified of them being broken.

"Zeph! Leave it!" I shout, and I go over and pull him away from the poor old man's barrels.

"What am I going to do?" cries Zeph, his cheeks glowing angry red in his face.

"I've got a boat," I say, and the red starts to fade. "I moored it upstream a ways. We could follow, catch up with your father."

Though I don't know how my little boat'd ever catch up to a raider dragonboat.

"Do you think so?"

"I'm sure of it," I say, with a big false smile. Then, in a shaking voice, I ask the question I've been holding in my head ever since I found out who Zeph's father is. "Do you know where they're going?"

·15·

THE ISLAND IN THE STREAM

About noon on our second day sailing, the sky turns gray and the air damp. The clouds roll thick and wet above us and, as the afternoon drags on to evening, they get lower and lower, like they want to push us down into the River Thames.

"Yowowowl," cries Cat, standing rigid and glaring northward with wide green eyes. I touch his back, and he hisses, but doesn't stop his glaring.

"What's it making that racket for?" says Zeph. "Why don't you just throw it overboard?"

"Why don't you just shut up?" I say. "There's something there, that's why he's growling."

"How would a cat know?" asks Zeph, but he looks at the north bank, just like me.

"There ain't nothing," says Zeph after a minute. "Probably the mog saw a mouse." He turns to me and grins. "Come on, Lilo, lighten up."

But I can't, cos Cat's a seacat, and he wouldn't make a fuss about nothing.

"Yowowowl," says Cat again, his head cocked to one side.

"There's nothing there," I say to him. "It's just gray. Gray clouds and gray sky and . . ." And suddenly I know why he's growling, cos it ain't just the gray of clouds and sky. There's a thick solid edge to the gray, like a wall rolling toward us. It's fog — sliding off the north shore of this big old river. Even as I watch, a tree disappears, swallowed up by the murk.

"We've got to find somewhere safe to moor up," I say.

"Why?" asks Zeph.

"Because we can't stay on the river in fog!"

"Why not?"

I stare at him for a moment.

"Because of mud banks. And shallows. And other boats. And tree stumps sticking out of the water. Because we won't be able to see any of them. Because I don't want to end up wrecked on a sandbank or stoved through by a dead tree!"

"Well, just pull to shore, then," says Zeph, as if he's solved the problem.

"We can't here," I say, cos the banks here are nothing but marshes — reeds and rushes and muddy humps of grass. It's hard to tell where the river ends and the land starts, cos it's all mixed together. Anything could be hiding in them marshes, and most likely is. Everyone knows marshes mean trouble.

"We should try the southern bank," I say.

"No!" says Zeph, looking frightened.

"Why not?" I ask, staring at the distant shore. "It looks good to me. There's trees, which must mean solid ground. If we're quick and careful we can tack across before the fog catches us."

"But the towers!" says Zeph, pointing. At three tall broken buildings, rising like skeletons above the treetops. Leftovers from olden times.

"Everyone knows the towers along the Temz is full of ghosts and evil spirits," says Zeph. "I ain't going there to get my heart eaten and my head turned inside out!"

"Don't be stupid! That's nothing but stories." I start at turning the boat, gathering up the lines so I can tilt the sail and head south.

"Stop it!" says Zeph, and rocks the boat as he grabs at a line, pulling the boom across. "Let's just anchor and wait for the fog to pass," he cries. "That's what Ims'd do."

"Ims ain't sailing my boat. I am. And we ain't in a great big dragonboat – we'd be wrecked by the first boat that didn't see us. We'd have to sit here all night, shouting and swinging lanterns to warn others off us."

I pull hard at the line I'm holding, trying to get control of the mainsail. But Zeph's pulling at his own rope, and the sail starts flapping and sagging as the boom jerks this way and that.

"You ain't taking us to the ghosts!" shouts Zeph. He clambers over and starts punching me on the arm, trying to get to the tiller.

I hunch against the blows for a bit, trying to hold the sail and the tiller, but he keeps on pounding. Then he gets a real good smack on my shoulder, and my whole arm goes nearly numb.

"GET OFF!" I shout and, without thinking, I let go of everything and start pounding back at Zeph with my fists. The boat sets up to rocking as we fight, and Cat's wailing and spitting. He takes a flying leap at Zeph, landing with all his claws out, right into Zeph's leg.

"Ow ow ow!" shouts Zeph. "Get your stupid mog off me!" He stops fighting me and starts kicking his leg about, trying to push Cat off. Cat bites him on the hand.

The boat's rocking so wildly there's water splashing in over the sides.

"Stop! We're going to sink!" I shout, and straight off Zeph goes still; I reckon he's not so stupid he wants to go under.

"Get your mog off me," he growls, and I grab hold of Cat. Zeph swears as Cat's claws scrape out of him, then Cat's spitting and twisting in my arms.

"We've got to think sense," I say to Zeph, "or we're going to end up drowned." And now it ain't the rocking, but the swinging boom and the sagging sails we have to worry about. And the river. Cos we've spun round, and we're drifting sideways with the current.

"Help me," I say to Zeph, who's bent over rubbing his leg. "Get hold of that line and pull the sail in."

"No. I won't. You want to sail to those ghost towers. That ain't sense, that's crazy. And your cat attacked me! I'm gonna throw him in the river!"

"Don't you dare even think it!" I shout. He glares at me, and doesn't say anything. I start ducking about, trying to catch the lines and pull in the sail. Zeph doesn't help, but at least he ain't punching me. Which lets me get hold of the tiller and try at fighting to get us steered in the right direction. But the boat ain't shifting. She's caught in the grip of the Thames, and we keep on drifting and spinning. I look up, and the first wisps and curls of mist are swirling round the top of the mast. Twenty breaths later, the cold, wet grayness has eaten us right up.

"I'm freezing," says Zeph quietly, and I ain't surprised, cos his leathers look more for fighting and effect than anything else. I shouldn't think they're good at keeping warm when a cold mist comes poking with its fingers, sucking the warmth from everything it touches.

We're floating with the current, drifting into who knows what. The fog has taken every breath of wind, and the best I can do is steer us into the stream. In the end, I even tried Zeph's idea of throwing the anchor out, but the river bottom turned out to be gravel, and it wouldn't stick. Every flick and twist of the fog sets me panicking. Is it rocks? Is it some piece of drowned town waiting to snag us? Are we about to crash into some other boat?

"Keep that bell sounding," I say to Zeph.

"I know what to do," he snaps, swinging the old brass bell so it clangs out into the dark, clammy night. I hope it's enough to keep us safe.

After a bit, Zeph says, "I'm sorry I hit you. You was right about the anchor."

I sigh. "We wouldn't have got to the south shore, anyway. Not before the fog got us."

Zeph nods.

"We shouldn't be fighting," he says. "You're Angel Isling now. Wait until we get home, then you'll see."

Home. That's where I want to go. Home to Granny, stoking up the fire and telling one of her stories. Home to Andy, mucking about at the harbor and getting shouted at by a captain. But that ain't what Zeph's talking about. And Granny and Andy ain't even there.

"What's it like? Where you live?" I ask.

"It's the best! My father's got the biggest hall in the whole of Essex – he can get a hundred warriors in the feasting room!" He looks at me.

"Big," I say.

"It is. The wind gallery can hold forty in council, and father says there ain't any bigger until you get way up to the northern Families, Norwich way."

And I don't know what to say to that, cos I don't know what a wind gallery is, and I ain't never seen a feast hall, let alone one that'd hold a hundred warriors.

"It doesn't sound very homely," I say.

"What'd you know, fisher?" says Zeph. "It's better than a fish-hut!"

And then it's silence, apart from the slap-slapping of the river and dank hissing of the fog around us.

Suddenly Cat squawks a warning, and Zeph shouts, "Look! Look there!"

He's pointing into the night, at a dark lump ahead. Something solid, not just the rippling fog. Something with trees and bushes.

An island!

I slam the tiller round as hard as I can, trying to push us toward it.

"What are you doing? I thought you wanted to keep away from everything."

"We'll be able to moor up. We'll be safe," I gasp, pushing and pushing on the tiller.

It feels like we're turning forever, heaving through the black river to get over to that speck of safety. As we get closer, level with the hump of mud and bushes, the bow finally shifts, edging us closer to the island. But still not near enough. It's too far to jump, and the river's clutching at us, trying to pull us beyond the island before we even have a chance to get to it.

"Try and catch hold of something!" I shout at Zeph.

He grabs one of the long, heavy fishpoles, then he's leaning out, trying to snag us a bush or a tree, almost falling overboard he's reaching so hard. The pole weaves and wobbles in the air, the hook on its end brushing and snapping through bushes, clattering against tree trunks. I can see his arms shaking as he tries to keep it from dropping. Zeph swears loudly, and gives a jerk with his arms, slamming the pole into a tree. The branches quiver as the hook catches, the pole shudders, and Zeph's face goes nearly purple with strain as he gets yanked upward, nearly going overboard again. But he doesn't go over; he holds the pole, the tree, the boat. Holds everything together.

"I did it!" he shouts. But even as he does, his feet start slipping. The river still wants to take us, and there's only Zeph's hands on a little pole against all that water, all that strength.

I jump over, grab the pole as well, and brace my feet. Then I'm holding on to that pole till it feels like my arms'll pull straight out from my shoulders. My cold hands go red-raw from gripping the wet, gritty wood. Even so, the river keeps on pulling at us, shaking us through the boat. The pole shivers and slips, the tree bends and creaks. But then Zeph gets a hand farther up the pole and he pulls us in a little bit. And I get a hand farther along and I start to pull. Then it's hand over hand, arms aching and sore, close as we can to the mist-dripping lump of bushes and trees. And when we're close enough for me to jump off, I look at Zeph, at his straining face, his hair slick with mist, and he says, "I can hold it."

So I grab a mooring line, jumping onto wet and sliding mud, scrabbling up the bank to a tree, tying the line off. And then I jump back on and off again to do the same with another line, and another. And all the time Zeph's holding fast with the pole.

And when he can see it's trees and ropes holding the boat, Zeph lets the pole drop, and flops to sitting down. And he wipes his hands across his face, and rubs at his arms.

I climb back on board, onto our safely moored boat, and I'm grinning at Zeph. And he's grinning back at me, kind of wobbly. Cos we're out of it: out of the roaring river; out of the twirling, curling fog; out of the way of whatever might have been waiting to scupper us and take us to the bottom.

And I reckon our smiles could light up that dark island.

"This island is a pig pit," says Zeph.

"At least we're safe."

"Safe from drowning, but we're gonna freeze to death most likely."

And I ain't disagreeing. Cos apart from saving us from being wrecked, this island ain't up to much.

Zeph shuffles inside his blanket and hunches down against the fog. We've got a fire, but it doesn't cut much against all the damp, and, anyway, all the wood on this island is wet through, so it just smolders and hardly makes any heat. Cat took one look at the cold, smoky fire and pushed his way inside my oilskin, sitting curled up on my lap. A squash, but we keep each other warm. Zeph ain't got a cat to warm him, and he's looking colder every minute.

For dinner, all we had was oat biscuits and water, and that didn't cheer us up for a minute, specially not Cat. The rest of the time we've just been sat here in the foggy gloom. Far off there's an owl hooting, but mostly the only sound is the soft lapping of the river as it rolls its way to the sea.

With another shuffle, Zeph slides himself down inside his blanket, and after a bit he starts a soft snoring. But I ain't sleepy, so I sit and watch the boat rocking gently in the river, and the way the fog swirls about, settling like rain on the grass around us, dripping from the leaves of trees and bushes. It seems like hours and hours pass, but I don't know how long it is really. And then I must nod off, cos I'm woken up by Cat miaowing and wriggling to get out of my coat.

I sit up, and Cat's out. He stretches out his front legs, then pulls himself forward so his back ones go straight. And when he's done his stretching, he starts a bit of sniffing and snuffing. He sneezes, and I know he doesn't like all this wetness. I can't say I'm that happy about it, either, cos it's hard to sleep through this cold and damp. I feel wide awake now, but Zeph's still snoring away, so I creep off to the other side of the island, which ain't far cos it's so little. And when I'm out of sight of the campfire, I get the jewel out of my belt and unwrap it. Cos even though it'd be a whole lot better if that head had got drowned in London, I can't help wanting to have another chat with it.

It sits quiet in my hand, and I wonder if it's been drowned, then it starts to glow, then it flashes. There's a click and the head pops up in front of me. It coughs and splutters.

"Primary user identified," it says. "Welcome, Lilly Melkun." Then it glowers at me. "You realize I said that because the start-up greeting is programmed in. How dare you treat me this way?" it huffs. "Dropping me in the mud! I have extremely delicate parts, and I'm sure I've already told you I'm not an aquatic unit. Some primary user you are. It's a wonder I've any integrity left."

"I didn't do it on purpose," I say. "I was pushed in."

The head doesn't look any happier.

"And another thing: Why have I been off so long? You haven't activated me for days. Have we reached London yet?"

"We've been and gone," I say.

"What?" screeches the head. "But London's my best option for finding a technical support outlet!"

"I don't think there were any," I say, trying to calm it down. "It's all flooded and ruined there now. Not like the olden times."

"So you say," mutters the head. "Which is just the kind of tale a hacker would tell."

"I ain't a hacker," I say. "I don't even know what a hacker is."

"Also what a hacker would say," snaps the head, then it looks around. "So if we aren't in London, where exactly are we?"

"We're on an island in the Thames."

"For goodness' sake! Don't you have any idea of sterile operating conditions?" I reckon if it had feet it'd be stamping them. "So what are we doing here?" it says grumpily.

"We're on our way to the raiders. The ones that took Alexandra. I met the son of the raider Boss who took her, and he's going to take me to his home."

"The raiders? The ones you described as murdering evil savages?"

I nod.

"And yet one of them is taking you to his home?"

I nod again. The head raises its eyebrows in a question.

"I tricked him," I say. "I ain't told him about you, or Alexandra, or what I'm doing, or anything. I even said my name was Lilo, not Lilly Melkun." The head raises its eyebrows a bit more, and I end up telling it everything that's happened. Just like I always do. When I tell it about the Scots, and how I reckon maybe they was looking for a computer, not Alexandra, it looks right pleased.

"These Scots sound more sensible than the rest of you. And perhaps will help me find the assistance I require." It looks at me all haughtily. "Take me to the Scots," it orders. "I require immediate technical support."

"I ain't doing that," I say. "I've got to take you to the raiders. And even if I wasn't, it ain't easy to get into Greater Scotland.

Not if you're from the Last Ten Counties. The Prime Minister put out orders a few years ago that anyone trying to get across the border could be shot. And folks say even if you get through, the Scots just lock you up when you get there."

"I'm sure we can manage it," says the head. "This Greater Scotland place sounds like my best option by far, and I want to go there. Please."

I shake my head.

"You're going to the raiders," I say.

"Don't I have any say in the matter? You wouldn't do this to one of your own kind! It's little better than slavery!"

"Plenty of people get traded for slaves," I say. "Anyway, you probably won't stay long with the raiders. They're bound to sell you on."

"Which is hardly a comfort," snaps the head.

It won't say anything after that, and keeps turning its face away from me. So I shut it down and creep back to the fire. Where Zeph's still snoring.

· 16 ·
INTO THE MARSHES

I get woken by footsteps next to my head, and when I open my eyes, Zeph's already up and about, his blanket folded, the fire stamped out. The sun's gleaming gold on the horizon, and the river's rippling pink and silver in the dawn. The fog's lifted, and there's just a few wisps of mist on the water and a soggy wetness over everything on the island.

"You're awake, then," says Zeph. "Come on. The fog's gone, so we better get going. The sooner we get to my father, the sooner this will all be settled."

"All what?"

But he doesn't answer.

"Mew," says Cat, wandering over. He must have wriggled out of my oilskin when I was sleeping. He licks my ear and rumbles a little purr inside. At least someone's cheery this morning.

It turns out we're only a few lengths from the southern shore. And now that we're closer, I can see ruined houses poking out everywhere from the trees and scrub – a whole town laid to waste. Farther in are the towers we saw last night, and in the morning light they look a whole lot more broken. They're just the concrete shells of long-dead buildings: every window smashed, bits of wall hanging off in chunks or slumped away completely. Up the Thames, nearer London, the river's lined with towers like this. And when the wind blows through them, there's a sighing, moaning sound, like they're crying for what's lost.

"See," I say to Zeph, "no ghosts came and got us in the night."

Zeph looks hard at me, but doesn't say anything.

We pack up and push off, unfurling the mainsail and heading out into the wide river. The wind ain't coming from the best direction, but the river's still pushing us, so we make good speed through the morning. Zeph's grumpy and quiet today. Probably in another of his moods, which seem to come and go like rain showers in April. But I don't have time to care, cos this is the Thames, and everyone knows it's got sandbanks and trick currents and all sorts waiting to get you. We don't pass any more towers or haunted woods, just miles and miles of flat green marshes. Seems like the only life is the birds. Ducks paddle about the edges of the river, and flocks of tiny things peep and flutter above the reeds. But that's only what it seems, cos here and there I catch sight of smoke rising. The marshes ain't empty, and you don't want to meet anyone who comes out of them.

"Is it like this where you live?" I ask Zeph.

But he just gives me a glaring look and says, "You'll find out yourself, won't you?"

Like I said, grumpy.

By lunchtime, the tide's turning back upriver and we make slow going of it. We pass by more ruins, not a town this time, but three chimneys, next to a big square lump of a ruin and a long line of broken concrete across the grass, where it looks like a fourth chimney has already fallen down. The chimneys are as tall as any of the great towers, but they're leaning all over. In their shadows, white, brown, and red specks of birds putter about in the muddy shore, poking their beaks in and out, looking for lugworms and shellfish.

Not long after, the southern shore's so far and distant I can't hardly see it, and by the smell of the water, I know we're back at sea.

"Just follow the coast north," says Zeph when I ask him where to go. Which doesn't seem like much of a plan to me, but Zeph's sure.

"My father will find me, no problem. All you have to do is get us to the right place."

But I don't know if Zeph even knows where the right place is, cos he doesn't give me any directions, and when I ask if there's a pilot song for this coastline, he just looks blank at me. The marshy coast is cut with creeks and islands, weaving away into the rushes, so it ends up with me asking at every one, "Is it up there?"

And every time he just shakes his head and carries on staring out ahead of us.

The farther north we go, the moodier Zeph gets. In the middle of the afternoon, I see dark shapes under the water and the first white hints of breakers.

"Do you know what that is?" I call to Zeph, and he looks back at me with sea-dazzled eyes.

"Oh, there's a lot of sandbanks round here. You'd better pull farther out into deeper water."

"And you didn't tell me before?"

He gives me a narrow-eyed look.

"No."

After that, he doesn't say another word.

Luckily, Cat's here to help me out. And he's all happy and skittering today, like I haven't seen him for ages. He jumps all over the boat, sniffing the air, flicking his tail, miaowing and mewing. In fact, he's making such a flutter, I can only tell about half the time what he's actually getting at — but he keeps us clear of rocks lurking under the water and the white of breakers on a sandbank. Every now and then he turns to give me one of his shut-eye Cat smiles, and I reckon he's just happy to be back at sea.

Now we're in these northern waters, there are raider boats about. No raiding ships, which I'm glad of, but plenty of slow, fat, booty boats, painted with the colors and standards of the different Families: purple lizards, blue wolves, orange dragons. I don't know which color and animal is for which, but every boat's got its gang of armed and scowling raiders. Glaring out, shields up. Seems like a lot of boats to me, but Zeph says, "There ain't many boats out. Must be something up."

Zeph keeps one of the blankets wrapped around him, hiding his bright red leathers.

"Ain't you hot?" I ask him, and he gives me a cold look back.

"Any other Family is gonna be well suspicious if they see Angel Isling colors on an English fishing boat," he says. "But without my colors on show, then we're just simple fishers. Like you, Lilo. And they'll leave us alone."

I give up trying to work out why Zeph is so grumpy and get on with the business of sailing. Though now Cat's decided that means curling up on some nets and going to sleep.

We carry on — me sailing, Cat sleeping, Zeph staring — long enough for the sun to start rolling down the sky again. I'm starting to get really fed up with Zeph's mood. Starting to think about whether or not to creep up and push him overboard, when he suddenly shouts, "Here!"

He's pointing to where the shore's curving in, making a bay or maybe the mouth of an estuary.

"There! That's where we need to head!" shouts Zeph, and suddenly he's like another person, all helpful. He's pulling on lines, using his weight to help us go about, doing everything I ask as quick as I want him to. Maybe he was just homesick?

We sail into the wide mouth of the river, which curves and splits into islands and creeks.

"Tide's still coming in!" shouts Zeph when we're in far enough to see the banks. "That's good!"

"What do you mean?"

He turns back to look at me, and laughs.

"These are the Black Waters. Angel Isling waters. Only we know how to sail them, coz at low tide they're so shallow. If you ain't Angel Isling, you'll get lost, or stuck in the mud. And then the sea'll come in and drown you!" He laughs again, like he's told a good joke. But it doesn't seem very funny to me, and I'm all on edge as we head upriver.

It's a strange world we're sailing into. A marsh world. The kind of place I've stayed away from since I first went out on the water.

"Marshes'll snag you, or ground you, or swell you up with fever." That's what Granny said. "And if they don't get you themselves, there's plenty of folk living in them'll cut your throat for you."

But here we are, heading into a great patchwork of swaying, rustling reeds and dark, sparkling water. There's a few low-lying islands poking their heads out, topped with twiggy stands of dead-looking trees or the broken walls of long-lost buildings, but mostly it's water and reeds and the wind moaning. Miles and miles of wind and reeds, stretching gray-blue-green to the horizon. Miles and miles of wriggling channels, twisting and turning like the string of a net.

"Is this a drowned land?" I ask Zeph.

"Course it is. The sea ate it right up."

Cat wakes up and sets up a strange mewling. "Mewrowl," he cries, pacing from side to side, peering out at the banks.

"What is it?"

But it's Zeph who answers.

"Why do you always ask that mog? Do you think he can help you sail?"

"Course not," I say quickly. "He's just a pet, that's all."

"Well he should shut up, then," says Zeph.

I don't say anything, just stare and stare for whatever is freaking Cat: the river; the channels sneaking away into the rushes; the islands with their hair of dead trees.

I stare at the dead trees.

I stare at one dead tree.

How it's moving, sliding behind the others. How a square red sail unfurls from one of its too straight branches. How the spiked prow of a raider dragonboat pokes out from behind the island.

And Zeph's whipping away the blanket, and his leathers are exactly the same shade of red as the raider sail. He stands up and starts waving and shouting, "Here! Over here!"

Cat moans and paces. Zeph shouts and waves. The red-sailed, lion-patterned dragonboat speeds toward us along the narrow channel, bending the rushes as it passes. Swords glint and gleam as men in bright armor lean forward over the prow.

"What are you doing?" I shout at Zeph, but he doesn't answer, so I grab Cat, holding him tight as he struggles and miaows.

"It's me! Zephaniah, son of Medwin," calls Zeph, and there's an answering shout from the raider ship. Oars dip and flash and the boat spins in the water, hard about, coming right alongside. A shadow falls over us — the shadow of its sail, of the warriors' shields and pointed swords.

Zeph turns around and smiles at me. A bitter, nasty smile.

He says, "These are the waters of my father, Medwin Untamed. He's the greatest Boss in all the Families. And now you're gonna find out how he deals with creeping little English spies. *Lilly* Melkun."

· 17 ·
IN THE WIND GALLERY

Father slaps me on the back and says, "Well done, Zeph, you made me well proud today." And there's a big grin all over my face.

I'm back in the wind gallery again, but I ain't hiding. This time I was led inside by Ims. All the windgates have been thrown open, and the wind spirits are fluttering about the flags, around our heads. Sparkles of sunlight bounce in from the water and flicker into my eyes.

Faz, Father's Windspeaker, squints at the light with his dark green eyes. "The spirits are throwing their glamor over us. They must be pleased."

"And why not?" says Father. "Everything's going to plan, or better." He walks over to the east gate, grips the frame with his strong hands, and leans out into the view of the marshes, the islands, and the sea beyond. He pulls back, throws his arms out, and shouts, "Hear me, winds! Today the English plans to send a spy to ruin us have been spiked good and proper. Today the spy has fallen into my hands. And it's thanks to my son, Zephaniah. Who's made me well proud."

I feel like I'm gonna burst, I'm that happy. Or like my heart's gonna leap right out of my chest. Today Father ain't telling the winds about his plans, or about Roba, or about some warrior: He's telling about me! Ims puts a hand on my shoulder, grins down at me.

"You did well, Zeph," he says, and smiles.

The wind spirits breathe in our faces, then rush out the north gate, tinkling the chimes as they go. Out on the deckway, there's laughter and clapping. Everyone likes it when the spirits make their way out of the gallery and into the crowd.

And there's a proper crowd on the deckway today — seems like all the warriors of the Family is there. Watching, waiting. And behind them is pretty much everyone else — all the wives and concubines, old men and too young. But this time they ain't blocking me from seeing my father. This time they're checkin' me!

It was easy to get that English witch-girl to head straight for a trap. Where the Black Waters meet the eastern sea is always guarded, and any vessel not flying the red flag of Angel Isling is gonna get taken or destroyed. All I had to do was sit under a blanket and say nothing. The guard ship came straight in for us, like a sharp-toothed pike striking at a minnow.

And after, when that stinking girl and her stinking mog was caught, and I told what was up, the master of the guard ship sailed us straight to the hall. Through the marsh channels, with the night birds crying all around. But I didn't sleep or nothing. I couldn't, I kept thinking about that girl, how she's so sly and lying. Even Ims was fooled by her, back in Lunden; he didn't see how everything she did was a stinking trick. But it still makes me feel boiling angry inside: I thought she was a boy called Lilo; thought we was friends; thought I was helping my friend get away from his nasty family. And all the time it was some nasty, lying spy-witch. Laughing at me.

Ims says it was the wind spirits who sorted her, out there on the island.

"Think about it, Zeph. The winds brought the fog and took away the air from the sails. They took you to that island so they could reveal the English was a spy and a witch."

And I think he must be right, coz it was a breeze across my face woke me. And as I was opening my eyes into darkness, I heard not-really-Lilo leaving our camp. I didn't think much of it, but the breeze was cold, so I sat up and started trying to work some heat out of the damp little fire. It was just when I was cursing it for a useless smoldering lump that I heard voices.

And the first thing I thought? I was worried my friend might be in trouble!

So I crept through the bushes to the other side of the island, and there was so-called Lilo facing a ghost! Floating in the air right next to him. And I was about to go and help my friend, save him from the evil spirit, when they started talking again.

And that was when I realized what a fool I'd been. Coz he weren't in trouble, weren't in any danger at all from the ghost. He was in league with it, plotting with it. Telling it how he tricked me, how he was working to stop the war and get back a hostage. My father's war! My father's hostage!

Not Lilo, but Lilly. And no friend at all, just an English witch working to bring down Angel Isling.

I turned and ran. Quickly, quietly back to the camp. First thought I had was to get my knife. Slice her up. Show her what happens to spies. But even as I pulled the knife from the scabbard, I had another idea. A better one. I'd lead the witch home, catch her for my father.

So I lay back down in my blanket, closed my eyes like I was still kipping. And when she come back, I even made pretend snores.

Now she's got what she deserves. And I'm here with my father. When she next sees me, she'll be begging for mercy, not lying and laughing!

"Zeph is gonna stay," says my father to the Windspeaker. "He can take the place of south, coz today he's the south wind, bringing us good gifts for the taking!"

Faz nods me to the bench before south. Ims is already sat on it, and he winks at me.

"Here, Zeph. You've earned your place."

I walk over to take my seat, my seat in Father's council! I'm gonna sit here today while my father talks his war with Ims and his Windspeaker. And everyone else is sat outside on the deckway, straining their ears to catch what they can.

Two weeks ago it was me on the deckway, and no one letting me to the front. Now check me out!

I have to turn to look at Father, who's sitting before the west gate. West is the most powerful wind: the strong wind, the wind that brings in storms and destruction, tearing up the land and changing the coastline. And that's what a Boss has to do as well, bring storms down on the English and the Scots. Father don't sit on any old bench, neither. He's got the great chair, the one every Boss has sat in since the Collapse. Father's the fifteenth Boss since then, and I should be sixteenth. But that ain't what matters now, what matters is me being in with Father. Coz everyone dreams about being sat at council, even when they're just sword boys, too little to hold a shield. And now I'm here!

Faz is before the east gate, coz only Windspeakers is safe to sit there. And that just leaves north. Where stinking, stupid Aileen's sat. She's got no right! She's just a slave, not even Family! Father only bought her five years ago. And I remember what the Scottish slave-smuggler said about her, when he was selling:

"Prime stock. We bought her a good while back, so she's well broken."

What a lie that was, he probably just wanted rid of her. And now she's here. My mother was High Family, out of Chell Sea. She was a proper Boss-Wife, not some doxy, so she had rights to sit at council. But the only rights Aileen's got is her sneaking hooks into Father.

Ims nudges me.

"It's been a good day for you."

Faz nods, flapping the red spirit flags tied in his hair.

"The winds have taken a liking to him."

Ims grins. "And it should be a laugh checkin' out this English spy-witch. The girl-boy. It tried to snag Zeph in Lunden, but he caught it for us!"

My father smiles his fighting smile.

"That's for sure! And Zeph's gonna get his part in the testing. He brought it in, he gets the honor."

Father pulls his thigh knife from its scabbard and tests the weight in his hand. Then, still with that smile, he hurls it at me.

For three heartbeats the gleaming tip glitters and slices through the air. In the first heartbeat, I fight against my body, which wants to throw me onto the floor. But only a toddling sword boy would do that, and I hold still. In the second heartbeat, my palms slick up with sweat, getting ready for the catch. In the third heartbeat, I lift my hand. Everyone's watching; I've got to look good. I wait until the tumble of the blade brings the hilt into my hand, then I close my fingers. I fumble! I can't let Father see me drop the knife! I manage to stop it slipping out of my hand by clamping down with my palm, holding on even as the blade slices in. So at my fourth heartbeat, I'm holding up the knife, turning my hand so no one can see the blood trickling warm and secret into my sleeve.

Father nods at me.

"Use that knife when we bring in the witch. If it don't talk, you can do the trialing."

Ims smiles at me, looking well pleased. I swallow, coz I ain't never used a knife on anyone, not properly. Well, I did once frighten Amufi into telling me where he'd hidden that bar of French chocolate he was given by his mother, but I don't think that counts.

Aileen's checkin' me. Looking sour. I put my hand down quick, coz she's staring at my hand, right where the blood's trickling out of my sleeve. She opens her mouth, like she's gonna tell on me, but she don't get the chance, coz there's a load of shouting and rucking out on the deckway.

"Come on! Let me through!" comes a voice. A pimply, snot-headed voice.

The warriors crowded at the northern gate shuffle about, making an opening. Pushing his way through is Roba. He don't even ask entry, just stamps his way in. And then he don't ask leave to sit, don't take his place on a bench, just leans against one of the pillars, arms crossed, head cocked.

Trying to look like a big warrior, like he don't care he's been left out of this meeting. But when the spots on his face get all red like that, he's really angry.

"The runt's back, then," he says.

"The Boss's son is back," says Ims. Roba gets even redder at that.

"I'm the Boss's son, too!" he says. He looks at Father. "Ain't I?"

Father nods, but quick, like he don't care. "You didn't bring me in a spy, though, did you?"

"Didn't look like much of a spy to me!" says Roba. "Looked more like some stupid fisherboy."

"And how should a spy look, Roba?" says Ims. Roba's spots glow like sparks in a fire.

"You know what I mean," he says.

Father scowls at him. "I didn't invite you to this council."

"Sorry, *Boss*. I just thought how I'm your son, the only son who's fought in raids for you. I just thought how you'd want to talk to me, instead of the runt."

"Don't tell me how to act!" roars out Father, nearly standing up from his chair. "*I* choose which of my sons is in favor, not you! *I* choose who gets to be Boss when I'm gone, not you! And I certainly won't let any lowborn, even my own lowborn, tell me what to do!"

Roba stumbles, flinches, looking well frighted. And he should be, coz Ims is on his feet, sword half drawn, and Faz is standing, too. My brother looks down, at his feet.

"I'm sorry, Father," he mumbles. "Forgive me for disrespecting you."

But his eyes flick to me, and there's a promise in them of pain for later. Everyone sits back down, and Father half smiles at Roba.

"Well, you surely let me know you're my son, the temper you've got on you. But it's gonna get you spiked one day, if you ain't more careful. Sit quiet, at north, and you can stay."

Roba does it, but he don't like it. Being made to sit next to Aileen. A lowborn next to a slave! He keeps checkin' me with evils from the sides of his eyes, so I stare at him. There ain't no need to speak, we both know how it stands.

But my father, he don't see what's going on with me and Roba. He just sits back in his chair, claps his hands together, and says, "Now then, let's see this English spy-witch."

· 18 ·
THE SLAVE HOUSE

"Wake up, boy. Girl. Whatever you are."

Someone shakes me, and I come out of a dark dream like I'm crawling out of a well. My neck hurts cos my head's been lying on hard wooden boards. My arms hurt cos my hands are tied together with scratchy jute rope. My ankles are sore from wearing heavy metal shackles. My face aches with a fat bruise.

"This ain't no time for you to snooze, little spy! Medwin wants to see you." I get another shake and open my eyes. A mess of wrinkles and gray hair is leaning down over me, one hand holding a smoking tallow candle. The candle's like a blaring sun in my eyes, and I'm squinting to stop from being blinded.

"Good, you're awake."

The wrinkly gray head pulls back a bit, and now I can see the raggedy sackcloth this person's wearing for clothes. There ain't no way to tell by looking, but it sounds like a woman.

"Up you get." And one of her clawlike hands reaches down, grabbing my shirt collar, pulling me up in a strong yank. There's a clanking from the chain connecting my shackled feet to a big iron ring in the floor. My feet scrabble like numb things underneath me, and then I'm standing, wobbling about and trying not to fall down.

"Where is this?" I ask.

"The slave house," she says, matter of fact. She gives a tug to the rope at my wrists, checking the knot. "You got yourself some special treatment, getting tied *and* shackled. They doesn't usually bother 'less you've already tried escaping."

She smiles a little bit, like she wants to be kind, but then comes a man's shout from behind her.

"Come on, woman. Stop your dawdling. Time to get the little rat out of its cage. It's got some dancing to do." The man starts laughing, and her little bit of smile is gone.

"Of course, master," she calls. "I've just got to get the creature."

The old woman clumps off. When her candle's gone away, my eyes get used to the gloom, and I start to see other things about me. Mostly it's the lumpy shapes of people, lying and sitting all around, pale faces silent and staring. Like they daren't even move. There's a dull fire, sending dirty smoke up to a hole in the roof. Closing us in are rough wooden walls, bristling with dirt. Above, specks of daylight peek through the smoke hole and a tattered thatch roof.

On the other side of all this, there's a doorway into daylight. Standing in it is a man, the one who shouted, and he's holding back a piece of sacking, which is all there is for a door. I can't quite see him against the light, but from the way he's standing and the shape of the sword at his side, I know he's a raider warrior.

The old woman's candle has bobbed over to one of the lying-down lumps. A little one, right against the wall.

"Come on, lovey," I hear her saying. "You got to give up your little pet."

There's a whisper, like a child pleading, and then the old woman says, "Sorry, little duck. There ain't nothing I can do. Mebbe when the girl-boy's dead you can have the fur bag back."

The old woman clumps back, holding Cat in an awkward, squirming grip.

"Here's your helper, little girl-boy. He's been comforting that poor little ducky while you were out of it."

"Get a move on!" shouts the man in the doorway. "Stop your prattling."

As soon as he sees me up and standing, Cat leaps from the old woman to me. He digs his claws into my clothes like he doesn't want to ever let go.

"It's all right," I whisper as he nuzzles and purrs at my face, and I try to hold him with my bound hands.

But it ain't all right. Not at all.

"He's a funny creature and no mistake," says the old woman. She leans in and whispers. "I seen his gray fur coming through that dye. You got yourself a seacat there, and you'd best think about trying for a bargain. I don't say it'd get you free, but it might save you from a spy's slow death."

"I ain't a spy!"

The old woman shrugs and bends down to fiddle at my shackles with a key.

"Mebbe you are, mebbe you ain't," she says. "Don't matter none, not now you're here. Look at me, I got a whole house of my own, and four grown children back home in Dorchester. But do you think Boss Medwin cares about that? Course he don't. He just cares he's got hisself another slave." She looks at me, and there ain't even a tiny smidge of hope in her eyes. "Take my advice. Just fess up to whatever they throw at you. If you're stubborn, you'll only give them the fun of torturing you." My legs set to shaking, and my palms to sweating. There's a click, and the shackles fall open.

"Time for you to meet the Boss," she says, leading me and Cat through all the people with their sad, staring faces.

"Get it done!" shouts the warrior at the doorway. "They're waiting!" He stamps into the dim and dingy hall, the people on the floor sliding and scuttling out of his way. When he reaches us, I get a hard, biting grip on my shoulder, and I'm yanked outside.

Which is another world. Open, wide, full of sunshine and the shushing of water. We're on a wooden slat walkway, up on stilts. It's a bit like the ones in London, but we ain't over stinking mud; we're over sea-flavored green marshes, stretching away to far-off horizons. And we're under a bright, big sky, with small clouds bumping through the blue. I take a deep breath of ocean and the last warm days of autumn, and Cat's sniffing and happy. But he doesn't get any chance to take in this new world.

"Time to put the creature in its cage," says the raider, smiling nastily. He grabs Cat and stuffs him into a little wicker basket.

"Don't!" I cry. "He doesn't like it!" The warrior smiles even nastier.

"Please fight me, little spy-witch," he says. "Then I'd have an excuse to kill you." And I ain't any match for a raider warrior, even without my hands being tied. So I just pick up Cat's basket, and carry it gentle as I can, whispering comforts to him through the holes.

The warrior drags us toward a big, carved, wooden hall, riding on its stilt-legs above the marshes and the open water beyond. Where the slave house is tumbled and broken, this hall is well made and solid. It must be a hundred paces across, with a jumble of smaller buildings and side structures nestling under its wings. And where the slave house has moldy thatch, the hall's thatch is neat and golden-gleaming in the sunlight.

"Get your stinking English legs moving," says the raider, digging his fingers into my shoulder. Cat meows inside his basket every time I stumble.

"It'll be all right," I whisper to him, but I feel like the biggest liar ever for saying that. Cos who knows what'll happen in there? What'll happen to me and Cat?

"It's lying! Of course it's gonna lie to get out of this," shouts a young, gangling raider with a spiky red face.

"I ain't lying!" I say. "I came here to pay for Alexandra. I got a ransom and everything."

The raider wearing the red robe, the only one who ain't dressed like a warrior, he slaps me across the back of my head. Not really hard, but hard enough.

"You speak when told to," he growls.

I'm in this strange building, out here in front of the raider hall, facing the sea. It's mostly just a wooden frame: pillars holding up a flimsy-looking roof, thin walls made of woven willow. In all four of the walls, massive door-shutters have been thrown open, and the breeze blows in and out through the empty doorways, fluttering the red flags that cover the ceiling and every spare bit of wall.

I'm stood right in the middle, Cat's basket at my feet. Right in front of the raider Boss, Medwin, who's sat on the ugliest chair I ever seen. It looks like it's been carved out of a lump of old plastic, and it's a nasty green, like a dank pond. All the carvings on it are of heads with tongues hanging out, and roaring creatures, and some horrible-looking things that could be people. The other raiders are sat on low wooden benches, probably to make clear who's Boss. As well as the young gangly one and the one who slapped me, there's the big raider who was there when I met Zeph in London: Ims. Zeph's sat next to him. And there's a woman.

I ain't never seen a raider woman, and she's not what I'd expect. She's got a face like a china doll, and red hair twisting and curling down her back, and she's wearing this silky blue dress, draping down to a pair of sparkling blue shoes with spiked heels. I ain't never seen such gorgeous clothes; not even the Prime Minister's wife has clothes like that. But the raider woman looks stiff in them, like she's holding herself ready for whatever happens next. Which gives me a cold, scared feeling inside. Cos she knows what's coming, and she doesn't like it.

Ims turns to Zeph. "When you met this English. What did it say it was?"

"A fisher," says Zeph, staring at me with his brows pulled together. "But that was a lie. Everything it said was a lie. I know, I heard it on the island."

The cold feeling inside gets colder. Zeph can't have been asleep! Did he see the head? Is that why they think I'm a witch? And what did I say to it? I can't get my thoughts straight to remember. Inside his basket, Cat starts wailing.

"Now that's a thing of interest to me," says Medwin. "Why would an English go everywhere with a mog? There's only one type of mog I know of would be worth that kind of bother . . ."

"She was always going on about what it was doing, if it was moaning or not," says Zeph sourly.

Medwin smiles at me. A nasty smile. "So, little witch, have we got ourselves a seacat, then?"

I don't say a thing, trying to keep my face as blank as can be. I ain't trading Cat off.

Medwin flicks a look at the skinny, redheaded warrior.

"Roba, didn't you go looking for a seacat, last raid out?"

Redhead shrugs.

"It weren't there. Just some old fisherbiddy. Right pain she was."

Granny! I must give it away in my face, cos Medwin's smiling.

"Roba, look at the witch's face. Seems it cares about the old biddy. Probably another witch."

Roba flicks his eyes over me. "Why'd anybody care about some old fisherwitch? It didn't even take a minute to kill her, she was such a bag of old bones."

Then I'm screaming and swearing at him, trying to get over to where he is. All I can think is how I want to make him pay for what he did, for killing Granny. But I can't make him pay. He stands up from his bench, looks down at me from his narrow blue eyes, and laughs. Then he shoves me hard in the chest, like I'm nothing, and I go sprawling onto the floor. I can't get my hands out to break my fall cos they're tied together, so I land hard on my back, knocking my breath out.

"Look at it slide!" He laughs. "Like the stinking little fish it is."

Medwin's chuckling along. But the woman ain't. And Zeph, he's got a strange look on his face, one I don't know what it means.

"Get up, witch," says Medwin after a moment. "Get back in your place and don't try any more stupid tricks. The only reason I don't kill you right now is what you can tell me about the English."

I struggle to my feet, no one helping me, and go to stand next to Cat in his basket. He's mewing up at me, his nose pressed against the wicker. But I can't do anything to help him. Can't even help myself.

Medwin looks at the man in the long red robe.

"What do you think about all this, Faz? Is the girl a witch? Is she working for Randall? What do the winds say?"

The priest, or whatever he is, starts walking around the chamber. Past one big open doorway, then the next. He's got his head cocked, like he's listening. Everyone watches him.

He comes to a stop and starts talking like he's half asleep.

"The winds say, things ain't what they seem. They say, there's value in what we've caught, but it ain't what we think it is. They say, we should look in unexpected places." He stands still after that, like he's gone to sleep where he's standing.

Now the woman speaks. Softly, with a strange lilt to her voice.

"Perhaps we should ask the girl about it? She may know what's meant by unexpected places, and where value lies."

"That's what I been trying to say!" I cry. "I came to get Alexandra Randall. I've got valuables to pay for her. Honest."

The priest comes out of his trance quick sharp, and slaps me again. "You open your mouth when you're told to."

Medwin looks at the woman, his sharp face softening, something changing in his blue eyes.

"You think we can learn more from this English, Aileen?"

She nods, and Medwin smiles. For a moment, he looks just like an ordinary man, talking to his wife. But when he turns back to me, his face goes hard and his eyes glitter. I reckon he'd kill me without a thought about it.

"Trial by knife it is, then."

The woman gasps. "No, love, that isn't what I meant. She's only a child. Can't we just ask her questions?"

Medwin smiles. "We will ask questions, and the knife'll get us the truth of them." He shakes his head at the woman, like she's foolish. "Don't waste your pity on an English witch. There's not a single English wouldn't sell its own mother for tuppence. I ain't got time to waste, and trial by knife is the way to get quick answers."

He looks outside, to where all them hundreds of warriors are hanging about.

"Bring in the wheel!" he shouts, and a cheer goes up from the crowd.

There's shuffling and shouting from outside, then two tall warriors, one with a big nose and one with a fat face, roll a massive wooden wheel in through the doorway. They make slow going of it, like it's heavy. In the middle is a large metal bracket, and round the edge are five more. And it's covered all over with browny-red stains.

Bloodstains.

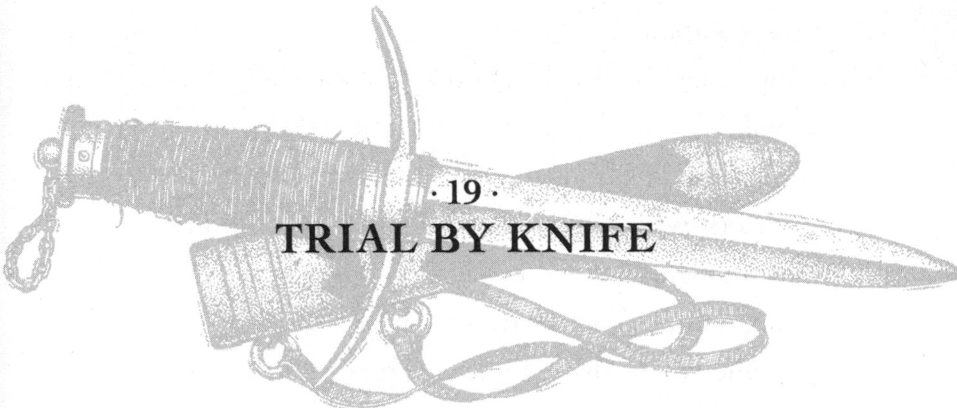

· 19 ·
TRIAL BY KNIFE

"Come on, Zeph," says Father. "Bring out the knife and let's get going. It's your honor to be trialing this witch, seeing as you brought it in."

Aron and Prent, two of Father's shield warriors, are setting up the trialing wheel. They grunt and heave it onto a thick iron axle sticking out from the east gate pillar. The heavy wooden wheel starts turning, but not as fast as it's gonna.

I stand up slowly, holding the trialing knife. It's thin, straighter than my own dagger, and it glitters like a shark's tooth. Father nods to Prent, who walks over to Lilly, picks her up under one arm, and carries her across to the wheel.

"Leave me alone!" she shouts. "I'm telling the truth! I don't need trialing!"

But it don't make any difference, all her lies. Prent grins and holds her up against the wheel while Aron starts working the bindings. Five lengths of rope, with a loop at the end of every one: a loop for each wrist and ankle; a loop to go round the neck.

"Speak when you're on the wheel, witch," says Faz. Lilly don't look like she hears him; she's struggling and fighting. But she ain't much against Aron and Prent, and it don't take them long to shut the center brace round her middle and get the loops in place. Then they tie the other end of each rope to the outer hooks, pegging her into place. And at the last one, when Aron puts the rope round her neck and Prent tightens it until she can only just move her head, then her black eyes are bulging and her brown fists clenching.

See Lilo, Lilly, Liar. This is what the Family does to lying witches!

Now there's only the sails to put in place, and Faz does that. They're only a few hands high, each one on its short wooden mast. But when they're slotted into the brackets on the wheel, the wind spirits get their breath in them and start the wheel turning. Sometimes, if the spirits get really angry, whoever's on the wheel gets strangled just by the sails making the wheel spin and spin. At least, that's what Ims says; I ain't never seen it.

The spirits ain't doing much today, and the sails only just fill. But the wheel still starts spinning, and Lilly's eyes get blacker and bigger. I walk out to stand before the wheel. My father nods at me, and I hold up the trialing knife.

"This is . . ." I start, and I go bright red as my voice squeaks into nothing. I gotta get the words out right, like Ims taught me in weapons practice. I swallow, and start again.

"This is the trial by knife, which will bring the truth. If you speak truly, the knife will spare you. If you speak false, the knife will not."

My hand's gone all sweaty, but I can't rub it on my leg, then the others would know. I ain't gonna mess this up. Not when Roba's staring at me, wanting me to. I get a better grip on the handle and say, "I'm ready."

Faz starts his bit.

"I ask the questions," he calls. "The thrower handles the knife. And the knife tells the truth."

"Ask the knife why the English lied about its family," says Father.

"I ask the question," chants Faz. "Why did the English lie to the Boss's son?"

"I only did it so I could get here!" shouts Lilly. "I've got a ransom for Alexandra Randall, from her aunt!"

I take the blade of the trialing knife into my right hand, feeling the weight and the balance of it. Now the spirits have filled up the sails of the wheel, and it's turning fast. Lilly's head whips up to the top of the circle, then starts heading back down, her feet spinning up from underneath her. Her brown face has gone pale, like sunlight on wood, and she looks like she's gonna puke. Her eyes is glued to the knife I'm holding.

"Shut your eyes, Zeph," says Faz, "so the knife can do its work." Like I'm some little kid and don't know how the trial's supposed to work. But I don't say anything, just shut my eyes. Then it's a flick, a twist, and the knife's out of my hand. I open my eyes again, and there it is, whining through the air, spinning and glittering. Straight at the wheel, straight at Lilly. She's struggling as she spins, straining against the bindings, but she ain't going anywhere!

Bang! The knife hits! Lilly screams, twisting against the ropes. She looks at her hand, at the knife sticking out from it, at her blood trickling down the wood. The line of red curls around as the wheel keeps on spinning. Lilly really looks like she's gonna puke now.

Faz legs it over and makes a big show of inspecting the knife. Like I might have done it wrong or something.

"Hmmm," he says. "A small nick. Only a little damage." He yanks out the knife.

"Ow!" cries Lilly, and more blood trickles out across the wood.

"Small damage means some truth," says Faz. "But any blood means lies. It could be the question has more to be answered."

"Ask again," says Father.

"No!" shouts Lilly, in a well fraidy voice.

"I know," says my father. "Ask it whether it's got a seacat."

"I'll tell you!" cries Lilly. "You don't have to throw knives at me!"

Aileen says, "Medwin, let her answer without the knife."

Father don't even bother answering. Only a silly cow like Aileen would say something like that. Truth or blood, that's how it goes.

Faz gives me back the knife, red-tipped now with Lilly's blood. I've got to throw again. Got to keep throwing until this is done. Probably when Lilly's too sick or weak to speak. Or I kill her with a throw.

"Close your eyes," says Faz.

I take a hold of the knife and get a good look at the wheel, at Lilly on it. She's stiff and braced against the ropes, her hands in white-knuckle fists, one with red leaking out through her closed fingers. My throat gets dry all of a sudden: Lilo was my friend, and Lilly looks just like him. Lilly is him. Ain't him. I shut my eyes and raise my hand.

Faz says, "I ask the question. Has the one on the wheel got a seacat?"

"Yes!" sobs Lilly. "He's a seacat. He's my cat, he chose me. I dyed him so he wouldn't get noticed in London. Just like I dressed as a boy so I could get help in London. Mrs. Denton, she wrote a letter to a London trader asking for help to find Alexandra. But it was for a man to take, not me. So I stole it."

I can't help it, I let my knife hand drop, and open my eyes. Lilly's looking at me as she spins.

"I'm sorry, Zeph, for lying to you. I just wanted to help my village. The Prime Minister's going to hang every captain for letting Alexandra be taken. I ain't a spy. I just thought if I got Alexandra back, Randall wouldn't punish us . . ." Tears start out of her eyes, rolling circles across her face and into her short, cropped hair.

Is she lying? Is she telling the truth? The knife dangles in my fingers, but Faz grabs hold of my hand, pushes it up into a throwing stance.

"Don't look! And don't listen!" he snaps. "Only feel the knife. Only the knife can tell the truth."

I close my eyes again, but now I ain't calm, ain't centered on the throwing. My head's roiling and boiling with all Lilly said. What if she's telling the truth? But what if this is just another lie? I gotta trust the knife, that's what I'll do.

I get the knife steady in my hand and throw. But this time I don't open my eyes to watch. I can't. There's silence, then a scream, then the bang of steel into wood.

Snap! My eyes are open; there's Lilly, hanging limp on the still-turning wheel, panting and gasping. And there's the knife. But it's out in the wide circle of wood, away from her head! It ain't anywhere near her!

"Truth!" shouts Faz.

And I grin at Lilly. She was just trying to help her friends! And Father ain't gonna kill her for that, is he? Not since he's got a seacat off her and all. I'll tell him how Lilly is really Lilo, my friend. How I gave him, her, outcast kinship. Any minute now Father's going to let her down, and this'll be over.

Father grins, sat on his great chair.

"Well done, Zeph," he says. "A bit of truth out of the English girl-boy. We've got ourselves a seacat, and some more trialing will sort the rest out!"

"But she told the truth!"

Father looks surprised, then frowns at me, his eyes hard and cold.

"Are you going soft, Zeph? This English still came into Angel Isling waters under a lie. You said she was talking to ghosts. She's up to something, even if Randall didn't send her, and the trial ain't gonna stop until I know what's going on. Truth or blood, ain't it?"

He glares at me, and I go hot and shamed inside. Everyone's staring at me.

"I can be thrower if the runt's too scared to do it," says Roba, smiling his nastiest, sneakiest smile. Father looks at Roba, then back at me.

"Is that what you want? Your brother to do it? I've been well proud of you today. You gonna let me down?"

And I'm so shamed I can't even speak, just shake my head. If Roba gets the knife, he'll aim straight for a kill.

My mouth goes dry as sand. This ain't gonna end now. Ain't gonna end until Lilly's dead. Until I've killed her.

· 20 ·
LOSING CAT

I'm spinning, circling. I'm down by the wooden floor. I'm up by the red ceiling flags. Outside, the green marshes blur into circles of blue sky. My ankles ache as they take my weight and my head feels like it's going to burst. Then I'm turning and the ropes tighten round my wrists, my neck, and I think I'll choke to death. Each time, I think I'm going to throw up. But I don't, I ain't giving 'em that.

The priest bows to Medwin, his red robe rustling. "The spirits smile on you, Boss, bringing you a seacat just before a battle."

Medwin gets up, gets down, from his big carved seat, and takes a couple of steps over to Cat's basket. He pokes a finger in, and there's a hiss from inside.

"Well, seacat," he says, "looks like you got yourself a new home. Angel Isling needs you more than any fishers do!"

He picks up the basket. "Geir? Where are you?" he shouts. "You're finally gonna be a cat's mate!"

There's shouts and laughter from outside, where the crowd of raiders is waiting. I shut my eyes to try and stop from being sick, but it only makes the spinning worse. I open my eyes again, and see a gnarly warrior walking in. His leathers are old and battered, with slash marks all over them, and he's got a big smile on his bashed-up face, showing three yellow teeth sitting in an empty mouth.

"Thank you, Boss. Thank you," he grovels. "You don't know how happy I am. And don't worry — after all them hours of studying cats, I'll know straight off what he's saying. I promise you."

"He's mine, he chose me!" I shout. But no one 'cept Zeph's even looking at me, and Medwin just hands poor Cat to the toothless raider.

"Geir, this seacat's gonna be happy to be with you. What's he been used for up to now? Catching fish? Now he's gonna have a proper life. He'll be the first seacat in the Family."

"He'll be a hero," says the old raider. "He'll have the best life a cat can."

He takes the basket from Medwin and peers in through the wicker.

"Come on, my little man," he coos, lifting the lid. "Come and see what a life you're gonna lead."

Cat pops his head out: hissing, ears back, eyes white-rimmed. He sees me on the wheel and he opens his mouth, "Mreowl! Mreowl!"

"Cat!" I call, but that's all I can do.

The old raider sneers, pushes Cat's head back in the basket, and shuts it. He puts an ear to the wicker.

"He's purring!" he crows, looking at me.

But he ain't! I know Cat; he doesn't look scared and call for help and then settle down to purring.

"Bring him back," I shout. But the gray old raider's already carrying Cat outside, out into the spinning, whirling crowd. The wind blows through the room, ruffling the red flags above me. Below me. Light sparkles up, down, from the water. When it touches the wooden pillars, they glow into chestnut. When it bounces off the woman's red hair, she's lit up like a fire. It's like a dream. A nightmare.

"This trial's going pretty good," says Medwin. "So let's get on with it."

"Please, Medwin, no more," says the woman. "You've got a seacat, and I'm sure the girl will tell you what you want without more torture."

"It ain't torture, Aileen, it's a trial! You ain't in Scotland now." Medwin grins at Zeph. "And Zeph's still got plenty of go left in him, ain't you?"

Zeph looks at Medwin, opens his mouth like he ain't sure what to say.

"If the runt ain't up to the task, I'm happy to step in and do it properly," says the red-haired raider. Zeph's brother. Roba.

Zeph jumps, shakes his head.

"I can do it," he says quickly.

The priest comes over, pulls the knife out of the wheel. My hand hurts where the knife cut into it, and I can't even see how bad it is, cos I can't move my head enough. It hurts, that's all I know, tracking a circle of pain where it's pinned to this wheel.

"More questions," says Medwin, sounding happy. "Let's find out about the ghost. And about this ransom you say you've got."

In front of me, Zeph swallows and shuts his eyes. I swallow and keep my eyes open.

The priest says, "I ask the question. Has the one on the wheel got a ransom for the English Prime Minister's daughter?"

And this time I don't say anything, cos it doesn't make any difference, anyway. I shut my mouth and listen to my heart pounding as I spin, as I stare at Zeph's hand. But he doesn't lift it up. After a moment he opens his eyes and looks at the priest.

"She ain't said anything. So I can't throw, can I?"

The priest looks angry at me.

"Give an answer, English!" says Medwin. "Unless you want Ims here to beat one out of you. The knife don't care if you already got a broken arm."

Zeph mouths "Say something" at me, his face white and sweating.

"I brought a ransom to pay for Alexandra," I croak. "I . . . got it from her aunt."

"Randall's family sent a child to deal with me?" roars Medwin. "Were they wanting to insult me, provoke me into killing the hostage?"

"No! Don't kill Alexandra! Her aunt . . . she didn't even send me. I took the ransom without telling her. Stole the letter, stole the ransom. I just wanted to sort things out. Mrs. Denton doesn't even know I'm here . . ."

"Enough!" snaps the priest. He nods at Zeph, who's staring at me out of his bright blue eyes. Zeph jumps again. Like he's frightened. Like he doesn't know what's going on. He shuts his eyes and raises his arm. All I can do is look at him. At his hand with the knife, at his face, at his clamped-shut eyes. His arm pulls back, the knife glitters red and silver in his hand, and . . . his eyelids flicker! Just a flash of blue as he lets go of the blade.

The knife whines through the air. The wooden room and all these crazy raiders whirl around that single point of steel. My hands, my arms, my legs, my belly: Every part of me flinches.

Bang!

The knife hits!

Hits the wood about an inch from my left leg.

My hands, my arms, my legs, my belly: Every part of me is trembling now. Another throw, another miss. Maybe my luck will hold?

"Truth," says the priest, sounding surprised.

I look out at Zeph, at his sweaty face, and the bobbing swallowing in his throat. Maybe it ain't luck? Is Zeph aiming to miss?

"Well then, little English," says Medwin, "where's the loot?"

"If I give it to you, will you let Alexandra go?" I say, suddenly feeling a bit bolder.

"If you give the loot to Father, I won't slice you up to see if it's hidden inside your belly," says Roba, smiling at me.

Any boldness is frozen out of me. What made me ever think I could just sail in here, give the raiders a ransom, and sail out again with Alexandra? Now Cat's gone, I'll be back in shackles if I don't die right now, and there's not a thing I can do to help Alexandra, or Andy, or anyone. Roba pulls a knife out of a scabbard on his thigh, turns the blade in the light, watching the steel glitter. His eyes flick up from the blade and stare straight at me. He smiles.

"It's in her belt," says Zeph suddenly. "There's a big pocket . . ."

The priest nods, and one of the two big raiders stops the wheel. I'm left hanging, looking at the world on its side, ropes pulling at my wrist, my ankle.

My head's still spinning and dizzy, but I ain't turning anymore, and for now I don't care about anything else. The big-nosed raider opens the pocket and pulls out the jewel in its cloth. He unwraps it, and the jewel sparkles in the sunlight. Even the raiders gasp.

"Well," says Ims. "That's a ransom fit for a Prime Minister's daughter! Look at the beauty."

Medwin starts a slow laugh.

"I am," he says. "And now we don't even have to worry about the Scottish contract. Coz if that ain't the jewel they wanted so much, I don't know what is. No wonder they paid us such a price. And seeing it, I ain't sure they paid us enough."

"That thing'd buy a dozen Prussian rockets, or bribe a dozen English ministers," says Ims.

The woman's half off her bench, and she's staring at the jewel like she wants to eat it.

"Can I hold it?" she pleads, hands stretched out eagerly.

And I get a panic, cos what happens if the head pops out now? They'll slit my throat for sure. But nothing happens when she gets hold of it: no glowing, no flashes, no head. Just like when Mr. Saravanan held it. 'Cept there's a difference, cos the woman stares hard at the jewel, and turns it in her hands like she's looking for something.

Medwin laughs. "Look at my lady. She's a one for the trinkets."

She looks up quickly, and for a moment it almost looks like she's mad. But then her face goes back to normal and she smiles.

"May I keep it for a while, my lord?" she says, in a little girl kind of voice. "I promise I'll be careful."

"For a while, but don't think you're keeping it forever. We're gonna have a think about how to make best use of it."

"Thank you, my lord," she says, smiling.

Medwin nods toward the priest.

"Faz, you've shown your worth again. Loot and a seacat in only three questions."

The priest looks smug. "It's the spirits who do it, not me."

Medwin nods. "Well, the spirits have found a couple of very fine gifts. Now, let's find out about the ghost and the witchery Zeph saw."

The big-nosed raider says, "Shall I start the wheel up again?"

My belly twists at the thought of it, my hand throbs with cold pain, and I have to swallow hard to keep from being sick down myself. Zeph's face goes glistening white, like he wants to be sick as well.

The woman places a hand on Medwin's arm.

"Love. Let us have a break from this. It's worked well, but a spell back in the slave house may help the girl to think on her fate. It may loosen her tongue." I get a bit of hope, but Medwin doesn't look like he thinks much of her idea. Then she says, "And I'm so very grateful for the chance to hold this beautiful jewel. So very grateful. Perhaps I could show you how much?"

She simpers up at him, but Medwin only shakes his head.

"Tempting, but show me your gratitude later."

"Let me do the throwing, Father!" cries Roba. "I can get this English to tell what Randall's up to, I know I can."

"Father gave the knife to me," says Zeph, going angry red.

"But I feel the will of the spirits," says the priest, throwing a nasty look at Zeph, "and they want Roba."

Medwin thinks for a minute. "Perhaps Roba should take his turn at being thrower . . ."

My guts turn inside out. Fear dribbles up my throat, into my mouth. Roba wants to kill me, that's all he's here for. He wants to finish me off, like he finished Granny.

The big-nosed raider takes his hand off the wheel, and it starts to turn. Just slow at first, but I know it'll get faster. Roba walks smirking over to Zeph and snatches the knife out of his hand.

"What's the question, Father?" he asks Medwin, not taking his eyes off me.

Suddenly there's shouting and shoving in the crowd outside. A raider warrior pushes his way into the wooden chamber. He's tired and sweaty-looking, and caked in mud to his knees.

"Boss!" he cries. "I've got news from Moham Shortarm, on the guard ship of the inland waters. The English fleet. It's arrived!"

And suddenly I'm forgotten. Cos Medwin and Ims are shouting about getting mustered for battle. The priest starts loud prayers, the woman goes quietly back to her place on the bench. Zeph goes white, then pink, then white, and sits down hard on one of the benches.

The only notice I get is from Roba, who grins at me out of his pimply horrid face. He comes right up to the wheel and stops it with a hand, so my face is level with his. There's a hard gleam to his eyes, like the inside of an oyster shell.

"Don't worry, fishstink," he says. "I'll see you again when this battle's over. And you can count on it being me doing the throwing next time, I'll make sure of it. You won't have the runt missing for you then."

· 21 · CAT DANCES

The old woman looks at my hand and whistles in through her teeth.

"You've had some right good fortune, little girl-boy. I never seen no one get such a little scratch from the wheel. Only needs a bit of bandage to set you right. Maybe you is a witch, and good luck to you if you are. Set some curses on them raiders for me."

She shambles off, into the dark and fusty innards of the slave hall, leaving me back where I started. I sit silent and staring at nothing for a minute, till a small voice says, "Have you got your kitty with you?"

It's a little slave girl, her face all covered in dirt, wearing a shapeless kind of dress. Might have been white once, but now it's just muck-colored. Her legs are thin, with circles of purple bruises above and below the shackles round her ankles. Her chain leads to a great big stone, so heavy it'd take ten men to lift it, just like mine does.

"He got taken," I say, my heart wrenching to think of Cat and whatever them raiders might be doing to him.

The little girl pulls at her ankle, stretching her chain into a straight line, and shuffles over to me.

"Is he all right, your kitty?" she asks.

"I don't know."

I keep going over it. Why did I tell them he was a seacat? Why did I let him go? Now he's probably crated up on some warship, and who knows what'll happen to him.

"I'm sorry," says the little girl. "I liked your kitty. He was cuddlesome. Like Mummy's dog Dougal. He's a highland terrier, white all over. The Lord Sheriff of the Scottish Homelands gave him to my daddy, as a diplomatic gift. My daddy said he was too yappy, so Mummy got him. But I don't think he's yappy, he just gets excited. And he's ever so cuddlesome." She sighs. "I wish I could go home and see him."

The Lord of the Scottish Homelands?

"Are you Alexandra Randall?" I ask.

She startles, looks frightened for a second, like she's waiting to be told off.

"Only my tutor calls me Alexandra," she says. "I'm Lexy. How do you know my name? Did my daddy send you?" She gets to her knees and starts looking around, like she's expecting her pa to drop out of the scratchy old roof. "Are you here to take me home?" she says, much too loud.

"Shhh!" I say, and she claps her hand over her mouth, still looking about. "Your daddy didn't send me. But I did come to take you home."

"Did a general send you?" she says through her fingers.

"No. No one sent me. I mean . . . I came by myself."

Her hand comes down from her mouth, and she looks at the doorway.

"Have you got soldiers with you?"

"No. It's just me. I had a ransom for you. From your aunty. I was going to pay off the raiders and get you home."

"You came with a ransom but no soldiers? How did you stop the raiders just taking the ransom off you?"

I reckon the look on my face must tell it all, cos Lexy slumps down, back into the beaten, frightened look she had when I first saw her. And no wonder. Some kind of rescuer I am: no ransom; no Cat; tied up in chains. Probably going to be killed by Roba first chance he gets.

"Why did my aunt send you without any soldiers?"

"She didn't," I mumble. "It was my idea. I stole a jewel from her. I thought the raiders just wanted money."

"Oh," says Lexy, and she shuffles her skinny little legs. "Don't worry. I'm sure it'll be all right. Zeph said they'd make me a slave, that they wouldn't kill me. Maybe they'll do the same for you?"

We both look into the stinky dark of the slave house, and Lexy whispers, "But do you think being a slave is better than being dead?"

And I can't think of any comforting answer.

The old woman comes back and wraps up my hand in a dirty-looking bandage. After that, me and Lexy get as close together as our chains will let, then we just sit. The shafts of light from the broken roof track slowly over the muck-crusted floorboards, and when they get dimmer and redder, we know it's getting on for evening. Every now and then, some tattery person hurries in through the sackcloth door, grabs something, and rushes out again. But there's no one else in the slave house, just me and Lexy tied up in the corner. I suppose a war needs every slave to be slaving away.

When the red shafts of light break and disappear, and the doorway darkens into night, some of the slaves start coming back. They creep in through the door and find their spots, flopping down like they're too tired to talk or eat or do anything 'cept lay themselves out like dead things.

"I want to go home," says Lexy. "I wish I was back with Dougal."

I wish I was back with Granny. And Cat was sat on my lap by the fire. And Andy was coming round to play jacks after tea, and everything was how it was. But Granny's dead, and Cat's caged, and Andy'll soon be fighting, maybe dying, in the battle. And I ain't done a single thing that's changed any of it. Tears trickle down my face. Angry tears, for being such a fool. Bitter tears, cos it doesn't matter, anyway, nothing'll bring Granny back. I push my fists into my eyes, shut them tight to try and stop the tears from coming out.

I'm so stupid! Stupid letter! Stupid puter head! Stupid idea to think I could ever rescue anyone!

Then I feel something. A light touch of something on my knee, small and soft. And I hear something: a quiet, gentle rumbling.

"Your kitty's here."

I open my eyes, and there he is! Head-butting my knee, rubbing his body back and forth to get my attention. And when he sees I'm looking, he gazes up at me with his green eyes half shut. Which is him smiling.

"Cat!"

And he's up in my arms, nuzzling my chin, purring fit to burst. And I'm stroking his head, and ruffling his ear, and making his fur wet with my tears.

"How did you get away? Is anyone chasing you?"

But he doesn't tell me, just keeps on purring. And even though I'm staring at the door, no raiders come shouting or stamping for him. And I don't know why, cos things ain't really changed, but I feel so much better. Cat got out of that basket, so maybe I can get out, too?

After a couple of minutes, Lexy's saying, "Can I hold him? Can I hold your kitty?"

So I pass him over, cos I reckon she needs cheering up just as much as me. But she doesn't know how to hold him, heaves him up in his middle just the way he hates. Straight off he's wriggling, and not long after he's squirmed out of her arms onto the dirty old floor. But he's happy when he gets there, and settles down to give himself a bit of a clean.

Lexy pats at her lap, trying to get Cat to sit back down. But he ain't interested.

"I know what you like, kitty," she says, fiddling about at her neck. She pulls a ribbon out from inside her dress, with a wooden bead on the end. It's a charm against fevers, like Granny used to make me wear in bed.

"Here, kitty. Something to play with." She lifts the ribbon over her head and starts bouncing the bead on the boards. *Tip, tap, ratter, tatter.* Cat's ears perk up at the sound, and when he sees the bead dancing about in the fire-lit darkness, his head starts bobbing with it. His tail flicks, his haunches crouch, a paw inches forward . . . then pounce! He's caught the bead, making happy growling noises as he tries to get a chew on it.

"You can't have it, kitty!" Lexy laughs, and she gives a little tug to the ribbon, flicking the bead out of Cat's paws. He chases after it, bounding and tumbling about as he plays.

"Look at him rolling around!" says Lexy.

"He can do more than just roll. Hold it over his head."

She lifts the ribbon so the bead's swinging above Cat's upturned face.

"Mreow!" he says happily, and lifts a paw to catch it.

Lexy pulls the ribbon a little higher. Cat tilts his head right back, lifts his other paw, and he's standing up on his haunches, belly showing long and straight, gray paws waving above his black head as he tries to catch the bead.

"He's dancing," I say. Lexy looks happy. She smiles like she's at home, playing with her pet, not like she's a hostage shackled in the dark.

"He likes to dance," she says. And he does; catching things above his head is one of his best games. I've even seen him jumping up at birds flying overhead, though he ain't ever caught one. So Lexy bounces the bead, and Cat dances about underneath, and we're all so lost in the game we don't notice what's going on around us. Don't notice other people coming to watch. Not till there's a crowd all about us. A crowd of raggedy broken people, staring at Lexy, me, and Cat. Slaves, crept through the orange-flickered darkness to see Cat dance.

Lexy drops the ribbon. Cat hides behind me.

"Your cat, he's pretty," says one of the slaves.

"Dances right sweet," says another.

"I had a cat," says a woman with long black hair. "She were a lovely thing, tabby with white paws. Best mouser in the street, everyone said so."

"I dunt never seen a cat what danced before," says a small, bent-over-looking man. "Was you bagged from a traveling fair or summat?"

"I saw a pig on a traveling fair once, could add up figures."

"There was fairs come to our village every summer, and I never saw anything like that."

"Well, here's a cat that dances, have you seen that before?"

"Can you make him dance again?" says a tired-looking woman with a jagged scar across half her face. "I ain't seen anything so heartening in five years I been here."

"Yes! Get the cat dancing!"

"Please."

But Lexy's cowering now, looking frightened and little. And Cat's all huddled behind me.

"Give me the ribbon," I say to Lexy. But when I try pattering the bead on the boards, Cat doesn't want to play. He only wants to keep out of the way of all the strangers. I can't say I blame him, after all he's been through.

"He doesn't want to dance anymore," I say, and get a groan from all the people around.

"Can't you make him?" says someone.

"How can I do that? He's a cat, he does what he wants. You think I should beat him or something?"

"No!"

"Never. Not beatings. No one should get beatings."

They all nod their heads at that, and I reckon they should know.

"I seen your cat dancing," comes a voice, loud and creaky. "Fire lit his shadow right on the walls. Looked like a great tiger or summat."

It's the old woman, shambling across to us. She shuffles through, and the others get out of the way, like they respect her. Or they're afraid of her. She nods at Lexy. "And it cheers me up to see the little mite looking happy." She kneels down, awkward and stiff, and peers round behind me to take a look at Cat.

"My cat got bored easy," says the old woman. "If'n she didn't catch a mouse in a few minutes, she'd just go wandering off. Maybe your cat's bored with the ribbon?"

"I haven't got anything else," says Lexy quietly.

"But I have!" crows the old woman. She fiddles around in a fold of her sackcloth dress and pulls out a long leather string. On the end of it there's a thin metal hoop, with two keys. The keys to our shackles.

"These make a nice tinkly noise. I should think that's what a cat likes best."

What Cat likes best is a warm fire and a full belly, but I shan't stop her trying. The old woman takes the leather and starts jangling the keys on the floor. *Trink, trink, clink.* And they do get Cat's notice, he never could resist things that flash — probably reminds him of fish. He pokes his head out from behind me, then his paws, then I can feel his tail flicking against my back. Then he pounces on the keys, and a laugh goes up from everyone around us.

"Go on, Nancy," says the bent-over man. "You get him dancing."

And she does. She gets him dancing and jumping and rolling and tumbling, just like there was no one watching. And all the slaves are cheering, and Lexy's laughing, and Cat's pouncing and grabbing. Then, just when the keys are dangling right over his head, he gets his claws curled right into the metal hoop. The old woman says, "Oi! Let go. Them keys ain't yours!" and everyone laughs. But Cat doesn't let go, he just keeps pulling on the ring. The woman's pulling back at her keys, stretching out Cat's legs as he fights to keep hold of what he's captured.

"You got yourself a tug-of-war there, Nancy!" says the black-haired woman.

"You'll hurt him!" cries Lexy.

The old woman keeps on pulling, and Cat pulls back, and suddenly there's a twitch, and a ripping noise, and the leather string snaps in two, flinging the metal hoop and the keys out of Cat's grasp, into the smoky air. There's a tinkling as they land, a clattering as they slide across the muck-covered floor, and then silence as they disappear.

"My keys!" shrieks the old woman, staring at the frayed leather string she's left holding.

She drops to her knees, searching with her eyes and hands for any sign of the two small keys. All the other slaves do the same, panicky looks on their faces. And I'm searching as well, cos I don't want to be trapped with iron cuffs on my ankles, waiting here for Roba to come and get me! But it doesn't do any good. The hall's dark, the fire doesn't give the kind of light you can see by, and the floorboards are full of cracks and holes, covered with lumps of dirt and clumps of straw. No one can find the keys.

After a bit, the old woman sits up and starts wringing her hands.

"Ims is going to be so angry. He doesn't like any mess or things going wrong." She glares at Cat. "You mangy thing! Look what you did!"

Cat just stares up at her and mews sweetly.

"I should give you straight to Ims, and he can chuck you in the sea!" she says.

"No!" cries Lexy. "Don't hurt the kitty." And she grabs Cat into her arms, hugging him tightly while he wriggles and looks cross at being picked up.

"It wasn't his fault," I say angrily. "He was just playing. You gave him the keys."

"Humph. And now I'll probably pay with the skin off my back."

"Will us get in trouble, too?" asks the black-haired woman, sounding frightened.

The old woman grimaces. "Don't worry, Ada. I'm high slave, I'll take the beating if there is one. I'll tell Ims the string broke and them keys fell onto the floor. Which is close enough to truth to get away with."

The other slaves seem calmed by that. They creep silently away to their places, lying down, wrapping themselves in thin blankets, whispering quiet conversations.

"What'll happen to us now?" I ask. "How will we get out of these shackles?"

The old woman cackles. "You should take it as a blessing, little girl-boy. I'll have to get the blacksmith to come and break you out. And what with all the warring going on, he'll be too busy with swords and armor and spears and whatnot to bother with a couple of little prisoners. So they can't take you out and kill you, can they? You'll be safe till well after the fighting's over."

Stuck in here till after the battle? But I was going to stop it! If I could get Lexy to her pa, the battle wouldn't happen, and Andy would be safe. Now I can't even move more than a couple of feet in any direction.

Me and Lexy and Cat lie down after a bit. Even though it's hard boards, and a thin blanket to get wrapped up in, I'm so tired from everything my eyes close by themselves. I start to drift, but every time I'm nearly asleep, I get woken by a scrabbling, scratching sound. Mice? Rats? Probably other things as well in this place. I turn over, trying to sleep, but the scratching goes on. I think of a rat running over me, and then I'm not sleeping at all, just waiting for the next scratching sound. In the end, I sit up. Next to me, Lexy's sound asleep, her little face peaceful instead of frightened.

"Come on, then, you rats," I whisper, "where are you?" But, peering about, I can't see anything. There's the muck and straw on the floor, the rough plaster walls behind, the red smoky glow of the fire in the middle of the hall. No rats. Maybe Cat's chased them off? I look about for him, and after a little bit I see his gray feet, pattering and scratching at something. Every few moments one of them disappears into the wall.

"Have you got a mouse?" I whisper to him. He flicks me a look, and then goes straight back to what he's doing. *Scrabble, scrabble* go his paws. It wasn't a rat keeping me awake, it's Cat.

"What are you doing?"

I shuffle over to him. His tail's flicking about like a whip, his face buried right up to the wall. His paw pulls back and there's a little flash of something. Something metal.

"You've found the keys!" I whisper, and I have to clap my hand over my mouth to keep myself from laughing. Cat looks at me, smiling out of his seaweed eyes.

"Prup!" he says smugly and, with a little flick of his paw, pulls the metal hoop and the keys out of the crack. He pats them about for a bit, like he wants to keep on playing, then looks bored and bats them over to me.

"Cat," I say, "you're a genius. You couldn't have done things better if you planned it!"

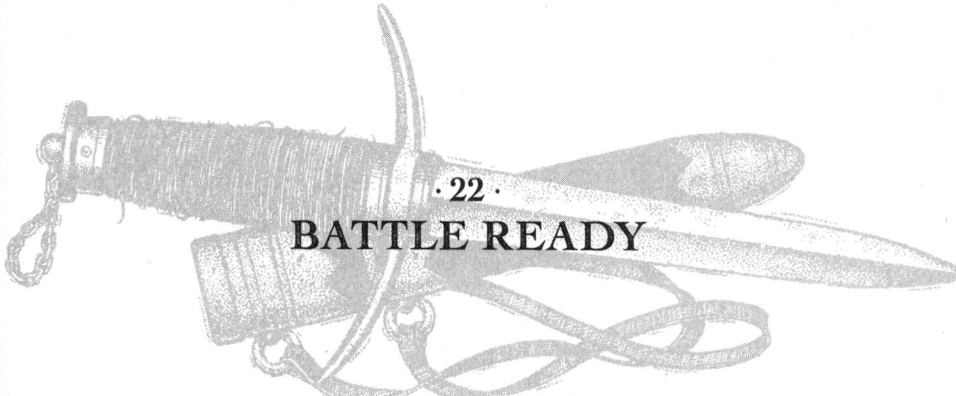

· 22 ·
BATTLE READY

Father's shouting. "What do you mean it ran off! I'm going to battle at next tide, and you've lost my seacat?"

Geir, the old sniveler, is groveling and making excuses.

"Boss, it was like a writhing octopus with claws, soon as I opened the basket. I tried to keep hold of it, but it legged it straight out the chamber and off. I searched until gone sundown for it. It must have fallen into the marsh and got drowned."

"Get out! And find me my seacat!"

Geir grovels again, then legs it out of Father's Talking Room, and Ims comes bending through the door.

"I've sent messengers to all the guard boats," he says, "and to all the low Families to get their warriors and boats ready. But the tide won't be high until late night, so it'll be full daytime before they all can get to the edge of the marshes."

My father shrugs.

"Ain't a problem. We got the rockets." Father smiles. "It's time to stop fighting in and out of the marshes, playing cat and mouse."

"Randall's in for a surprise," says Ims. "Now we got something to match his cannons."

"We'll beat them easy!" I say proudly, and my father chuckles.

"You're right," he says. "You know, back in Lunden, I had times when I wondered if the rockets was worth all the haggling with that smuggling pig-son Daniels. Acting like he's so much better than us for being Scottish, when his own people'd ship him out to the nearest prison camp if they ever caught hold of him. But he wasn't so high and mighty that he wouldn't take the Scottish money we got for raiding that village. So now I've got the rockets *and* the girl *and* the jewel." He laughs. "I got everything!" He reaches over to me and ruffles my hair. "Thanks to you. My highborn son, growing up. I thought you was a stupid kid when you got lost in Lunden, but you came back blazing. You're getting near to being a warrior, the way you're going. In fact, I reckon you shown you're good enough to be a shield-bearer." He winks at me. "Fancy it?"

Do I? I can hardly speak I'm so chuffed!

"Thank you! You won't be sorry."

"I better not be."

Ims claps his hand on my shoulder.

"You're doing good, Zeph," he says, and I'm so proud I reckon my heart's gonna pop. Except . . . there's things I can't get out of my head. Things like Lexy curled up in the slave hall. And Lilly looking so scared. It ain't fair! Why do they have to be in my head making me feel bad?

Roba pokes his head round the door.

"What's the runt doing here?" he asks. "I heard he peed in his pants when he found we'd left Lunden without him."

"I did not!"

"Enough!" snaps my father. "Zeph did well to get back so quick from Lunden, and with a boatload of loot as well." Roba looks like he's going to say something, but Father's got a hard look on his face.

"Sorry, *little* brother," mutters Roba. "I shouldn't go upsetting your tender *little* feelings."

One day I'm gonna kill my stinking, lowborn half brother.

"Zeph's gonna be a shield-bearer in the battle," says Ims calmly. Which makes Roba look like he's taken a smack.

"What're you doing that for, Father? You don't want a little runt getting under everyone's feet."

"I ain't a runt!"

My father keeps that hard look on his face.

"No, Roba. He ain't a runt. He's my highborn son, so he outranks you, in case you'd forgotten."

Now Roba looks like he's been punched. "But he ain't done nothing," he whines, "just brought in some stinking little fisher. I'm your eldest, I been out on raids for you."

This is one of the best days I can ever remember!

Father looks at me, then at Roba.

"Sometimes I wonder who you two are gonna kill first — each other, or me. Well, I ain't got time for your squabbling now. Out. Both of you."

"But I only just got here!" says Roba.

"And now you're only just leaving," says Ims, in his sword-wielding voice. "You, too, Zeph. We got strategy to work out."

Roba. It's his fault. He ruins everything. If he hadn't come in, they would've let me stay. And as soon as we're out the door, into the corridor, he turns on me and snarls, "Runt, you think you're *so* special, don't you? Your mum so high-Family and all. Well, have your day today; it won't last. I'm a warrior, and you're nothing but a sneaking little rat-boy. Lowborn sons have ended up as Boss plenty of times, and it'll happen this time, too. And if it don't, well, you can only be Boss if you're alive . . ." He shoves me in the chest, like he's done all those other times. But somehow it's different today. He don't seem so scary.

"I outrank you, lowborn, just like Father said. So you'd better not make any more threats at me, coz that'd be treason. And when you're spiked through your guts on Gallows Island, then you'll have plenty of time to think about those stinking, lowborn sons who got to be Boss."

The spots all over Roba's face go bright red.

"I weren't threatening you, runt. I was just making a point. And if you ever say otherwise, you'll be sorry."

He shoves me again, then stamps off down the corridor. What I want is to go back in the Talking Room, but that ain't gonna happen, so I head to get my leathers sorted for the battle. Ims says my armor plates are getting too small, and I ought to get new ones fitted.

I head out of the hall and down a nighttime walkway for the blacksmith's workhut. But when I get there, it seems like every warrior in the hall's beat me to it. They're all trying to get in, wanting swords sharpened, or spears tipped. I can't even see inside; there's too many warriors crowding at the entrance.

"Let me through," I say. "I gotta get my armor sorted."

The half dozen warriors nearest me turn round. One of them's Gandy, Roba's mate.

"Why do you need to get your armor sorted?" he says. "Way I hear it, you'll be lucky if you ever make it past being a sword boy."

Before, I would've been careful of facing Gandy. But not now, not today.

"Let me through, Gandy, or you'll find out what'll happen to you." I look right in his eyes. "You should be friends with me, not my low-brother Roba. He won't get you anywhere."

Coz things is changing round here. I'm changing.

Inside the blacksmith's workshop, the blacksmith and his boys are busy. All of them hammering away at weapons, bellowing at the forge, shoveling coals, carrying water, and doing all the other things to get warriors kitted and sorted for tomorrow. So I don't get out until two bells is rung. Even then, there's still a gang of warriors waiting. And as I head off, carrying my armor, they're all shouting into the workshop.

"Come on, Shen, my sword's as blunt as a baby's backside!"

"That was two bells! Three bells and the ships is leaving."

I gotta get ready. I gotta get to my barrack room and fit my new armor to my fighting leathers. I head past the main hall. All the lights are blazing, and the deckways are full. There's warriors running to get to their ships, women finishing banners and filling food baskets, slaves carrying bales of arrows and lances, and shouting and cheering from warriors inside the feasting hall.

But I ain't got time to join them. I go out onto the walkways, onto one that swings down past the slave house, then heads for the sword boys' barracks.

The slave house is dark. Lilly's in there. I get a flash of the knife next to her hand on the wheel, her face pale and sick-looking. She said she was just trying to help her village, and now she's chained up in the slave hall. Except there was the ghost. She was talking to a ghost. I shake my head. There ain't nothing I can do about it. Not now. But when Father's spiked Randall, he'll be in a good mood, and maybe I can get it sorted then.

Up ahead there's two people running, holding hands. One of them's about my height, and the other one's smaller. Next to them is a small shape, long tail swinging behind. When they get near the hall, they stop. The taller one looks about, like it don't know where to go. Now I'm closer, the taller one looks like a boy, and the littler one like a girl.

"Hey!" I shout. "What are you doing?"

They both jump and look round. They don't answer, just start off running soon as they see me. They leg it down a switchback that takes them to the southern deckway, then they head straight through the nearest door into the main hall. Straight into my father's sleep chambers! The mog follows, prancing about like it's having the time of its life.

"What are you going in there for?" I shout, but they don't even look back. How can Lilly and Lexy be out here? How come they ain't locked up? And running into my father's rooms, they'll get killed for sure if anyone catches them!

"Stop!" I shout, running after them. "Don't go in there!" But they don't listen, just slam the door shut behind themselves. My feet pound on the deckway, and I crash open the door, into a corridor lit by smoking rushlights. Ahead, a small bare foot disappears round a corner. I leg it down after, skidding to a stop and peering round. There they are at the end of the corridor, where it's crossed by another passage. If they head that way, they'll end up at father's Talking Room. And they'll get themselves killed for sure.

"Where are we going?" I hear Lexy ask.

"I don't know. I don't know what to do!" Lilly answers.

I've gotta get them out before they get spiked. I'm just about to call them when a door swings open.

"You! What are you doing?"

An arm whips out, grabbing hold of Lilly and dragging her in. Lexy and the mog go tumbling after.

· 23 ·
PLOTS AND DEVICES

"You're going to get yourself killed, Lilly. And this little girl as well. What do you think you're doing, running about in Medwin's chambers?"

It's the raider woman, from before, when they were questioning me. Medwin's wife or something.

"We're running away," says Lexy. "Lilly's going to take me to her boat and then we're going to sail to my home."

"Shush," I say, but it's too late. The Scottish woman's eyebrows arch up, and she crosses her arms at me.

"Were you indeed? And where were you thinking of finding your boat? In Medwin's bed?"

She's wearing some kind of floaty robe, all shiny and pink, shimmering and sparkling in the lamplight. And the room we're in is like her: plush, padded, shiny. There's velvet cloths on the walls in different shades of red, a chest of drawers with a twiddly mirror on top, a big carved wardrobe, and a cushiony armchair with tassles all round the bottom. But the bed! It's the biggest, softest-looking thing I ever seen. First thing Cat does is hop right up on it, kneading himself a sleep spot and purring like he hasn't for weeks. But Cat never knows when it's safe to go sleeping, just does it wherever.

"What are you going to do with us?" I ask.

The woman watches Cat for a moment, then shrugs.

"Now *that,* I don't know. What I ought to do is start screaming this minute for Medwin, for I can't risk even a hint of suspicion against me." She takes a deep breath and opens her mouth. Me and Lexy both flinch back, waiting for her to scream. But what comes out is a big huffy sigh.

"But I can't say I much fancy the idea of two little lasses being spiked. I was a young lass like you once, back home in Leeds. I didn't care a thing about raiders, they were just bogeymen to keep us good. In those days no one thought the raiders would strike so far north. But then the raiding party came, and it wasn't long before I knew more than I ever wanted to about them." She looks at Lexy. "I'm going to think about it."

She leads Lexy over to the bed and sits her on it. Cat pads over the cushiony bedding and settles down on Lexy's lap. She smiles, and starts stroking him.

"This is like Mummy's bed." She looks up at the woman out of her pale blue eyes. "Please let me go home, Mrs. Medwin."

The woman winces. "Don't call me by that man's name. I'm Aileen, and that's what you should call me."

Aileen turns back to me.

"Sit down, then." She points at the bed. I sit right at the edge, wanting to be ready to start running if I need to. But the bed's so soft, it's like my body's got its own mind, pulling me down into the pillows.

Aileen moves the chair in front of the door, then sits down, arms crossed.

"You know, if I hadn't seen you, you'd have been killed before you'd gone another ten yards. The way you were headed, you'd have run right into Medwin's war council. What on earth were you thinking?"

"We saw Zeph," says Lexy, before I can stop her. "We were running away."

Aileen's eyes widen. "Zeph? Did he see you? Is he following you? Because that's bad. He's bound to go straight to his father."

"I don't know," I say, thinking about his eyes flickering and the knife just missing me. "Anyway, I think we lost him."

"But he'll raise the alarm. Everyone will be searching for you. At least, everyone Medwin can spare from the battle preparations." She looks at me with narrow eyes. "This changes things."

I get ready to run. "Just let us go. Please. Let us get to my boat. No one'll ever know we were here."

She frowns, shakes her head. "Even if I wanted to, there's no way you can get to your boat now — the whole eastern deckway's moored with dragonboats, and there'll be a hundred warriors there ready to chop you into pieces as soon as they see you."

I get a tight feeling in my throat. She's going to turn us over to Medwin, I can see it in her face. I look about, but there's no other door, no way out. Only the wardrobe to hide in.

Then comes a sound. Like a bird singing, or a bell chiming. Aileen startles. Cat's ears flick back.

"What's that?" says Lexy.

"It's nothing," snaps Aileen. But the chiming sound carries on. It's coming from the chest of drawers, from a small silvery box that's shivering and shaking.

"What's that?" I ask.

Aileen flicks her hand at it. "Oh, it's nothing. It's just . . . a music box."

"A music box?" cries Lexy. "I love them!" In an instant she turfs Cat off her lap and jumps over the bed, straight to the chest. She's got her hands on the little box before Aileen even has a chance to stand up.

"How does it work? How do you make it do tunes?"

The box keeps on chiming.

"Leave it alone!" hisses Aileen, getting up from the chair. But Lexy's already trying to see if it will open; she fiddles for a catch, and the box springs out into two flat halves.

Suddenly I know what it is.

Aileen grabs the box, slapping it out of Lexy's hands.

"I just wanted to listen!" wails Lexy.

And then there's another voice, a man's voice.

"Hello? Hello? Aileen, are you there?"

Me and Lexy both jump and look at the door.

"Aileen, can you hear me?"

But the voice ain't coming from the door. It's coming from the box. Aileen glares at us, with a face that says she'll throw us to Medwin first chance she gets. Then she fiddles with the box, and holds it to the side of her head.

"Now is not a good time," she says harshly. Lexy's staring at her openmouthed.

"Yes, I know I told you I'd be on my own. But it turns out I'm not."

Lexy turns to me, her eyes wide.

"Of course it's not Medwin. If it was, I'd hardly be answering you, would I? More likely lying on the floor with my throat slit."

"Who's she talking to?" asks Lexy. "Is it a ghost?"

Aileen gives Lexy a sharp look. "If you start screaming, you'll bring a dozen warriors running in here." She shakes her head. "No, I wasn't talking to you!"

I edge over to Lexy and take her hand.

"It's a talking box," I whisper. "I saw one in your aunty's study. The Scottish Ambassador had one."

Lexy looks frightened. And I ain't too happy about the whole thing, either.

"I really can't have this conversation now," says Aileen. "I've got Alexandra Randall hiding in my room, as well as some idiot child who wants to save her." She switches the box to her other hand.

"There's not much I can do," she says. "Medwin's already getting battle-ready." She opens the top drawer of the chest and lifts out Mrs. Denton's jewel. It sends out sparkles all over the room, but there's no sign of the head.

"No, I don't know what his plans are! Medwin doesn't let his slaves into his Talking Room." She pauses. "But I've got the computer. So you can report that back to Edinburgh if you want."

She knows what the jewel is!

"Of course I've tried. But it must not be working, I can't get it to start up at all. Look, I have to go. I have to work out what I'm going to do with these children." She snaps shut the two halves of her talking box, then she turns a cold stare on me and Lexy.

"It looks like your luck has turned, although whether for better or worse, I don't yet know. I was thinking about simply turning you over to Medwin. But now you know too much for me to do that safely."

"Know too much? What do we know?" says Lexy.

"We know she's a Scottish spy. Like the Ambassador."

"Not like him!" Aileen snaps. "Not full of empty promises that he'll help me get free, get back home, but never actually doing it. Not like Jasper."

"The raiders wouldn't be happy if they found out what you're up to," I say, and I get a bit of hope, like we've got a chance.

Aileen goes and stands against the door. She seems to get taller, and dangerous-looking, even in her pretty dress.

"No one will believe you," she says. "I may be only a slave, but I am still Medwin's favorite."

"What about the jewel?" I say. "You're hiding it."

"I'm not hiding it. Medwin let me keep it for a while. I'm doing nothing wrong. In any case, it's only a jewel, Medwin has plenty."

"It ain't just a jewel, and you know it!" I cry, and before I can stop myself being so stupid, I make a grab for it. Aileen pulls her hand away, but not in time to stop my palm brushing across the jewel.

There's a little flash, a click, and a voice says, "Primary user identified. Welcome, Lilly Melkun."

The head pops out into the air, looking grumpy. Lexy shrieks and Aileen gasps.

"How did you do that?" she hisses.

"Unfortunately for me, the girl is my primary user," says the head. "I am programmed to activate on contact with her DNA." The little spots are glowing on the jewel now, and Aileen touches them gently with her fingertip.

"That won't work," says the head. "I have to be operated by the irritating child."

Next to me, I can feel Lexy shaking.

"What is that?" she asks.

"I am the Sunoon Technologies Play System AI. You can call me PSAI, if you like." Lexy squeaks, and Aileen looks like she's in love.

"The military computer," she breathes. "It really exists. I never quite believed someone could have found one working. Oh, you almost make everything I've been through worthwhile." She gives a little sigh. "There are a lot of people looking for you."

The head looks pleased.

"I'm touched. And glad you recognize how very important and valuable I am." It gives me a sour look. "Not like some. You have to help me. This child wants to trade me to some savages known as raiders. But I really need to get to the nearest Sunoon Technology technical facility as soon as possible."

Aileen smiles.

"I'm afraid you're already with the savages," she says.

The head looks scared. "Already with the raiders? Where are they?"

"Don't worry," says Aileen. "You're safe with me. And even though I can't take you to your technical facility, I can take you to Greater Scotland. Would you like that? It isn't full of savages, like here or the Last Ten Counties. They have scientists who know all about antique machines like you."

"Well, that sounds better than nothing. I've been trying to persuade the girl to take me to Scotland, but she won't. When can we go?"

"As soon as Medwin leaves for his battle. I was planning to leave then, anyway, it's the best chance I'm ever going to get. And with you as well . . ." She frowns. "Except I couldn't get you started. How did the fishergirl do it when I can't?"

"As I said before, I am DNA-activated by the primary user." It nods in my direction. "Her."

Aileen pauses. "Only she can work you?"

The head nods. "*You* couldn't even put the screen saver up."

Aileen looks irritated. "Does she have to be alive?"

I feel cold, Lexy squeaks again, and even the head looks shocked.

"Well, of course," it says. "The DNA must be contained within living flesh. It is a security feature, after all." Aileen scowls, and the head looks a bit scared. "I could add you as a secondary user. With her permission. Then you could interface in a rudimentary fashion."

Aileen turns to me.

"Give the computer permission to add me as a user," she commands.

"No," I say, even though I'm shaking nearly as much as Lexy. Cos I reckon the computer's looking like my best chance of getting us out of here.

"I will turn you over to Medwin if you don't help me," says Aileen, "and think what he will do to you for trying to escape."

"No," I manage to squeak. "You let us go, then I'll help you."

Aileen leans back against the door.

"Think about this clearly," she says. "You have nowhere to go outside this room. And if Medwin finds you here, with that head floating about, he'll have us all spiked for being witches. But if I can control it, I can keep us all safe."

I shake my head.

"Medwin will want this just as much as anyone," she says. "A military computer from before the Collapse — what do you think he might do to you to get his hands on a prize of that worth?"

"I don't know," I say, but I do. And it makes me feel sick just to think about it.

Suddenly Aileen looks surprised, and lurches forward. The door behind her crashes open, and she tumbles onto the floor, her shiny dress crumpling around her and the jewel flying from her hand. Zeph comes running into the room.

"I always knew you were evil! And now I know you're a Scottish spy!" he shouts at Aileen, holding a short sword and pointing it at her. He keeps twitching his head to look at the computer, like he's waiting for it to pounce, but he holds his sword steady.

Everyone's still for a moment, then the head says, "I am obliged to remind you at this point that throwing my drive unit onto the floor does not constitute responsible use and invalidates the guarantee."

Everyone stares at it, and it looks a bit embarrassed. "I can't help it, I'm programmed to tell you that," it says.

And while we're all looking at it, Aileen makes a sudden twisting movement. Before you can even see what's happened, she's wrestled the sword out of Zeph's hand, and now he's lying on the floor with the sword pointing to his belly, looking like he can't believe it.

"How did you do that?" he says, and Aileen snorts.

"I've spent my whole life defending myself against you raiders. And you aren't even a shield-bearer yet." She jabs at him with the sword.

"You wouldn't dare," hisses Zeph. "If you kill me, my father will spike you for treason." Aileen smiles, then starts to talk in a high, scaredy kind of voice.

"Oh Medwin," she says, "it was awful. First the wicked English girls forced themselves into my chamber, then Zeph chased in after them. There was a terrible fight, and they were all killed. I was only spared because I'm just a poor helpless woman and I hid in my closet." Her voice changes back to normal. "Or something like that." She twitches the sword at Zeph, ordering him to stand. Then, when she has us all huddled together in the corner of the room, she picks up the jewel again. The head is still floating about, looking very unhappy.

Aileen looks at me. "Tell the computer to let me use it."

"Then what?" I say. "You kill us all?"

Aileen sighs. "Unlike you southerners, I am not a child-killing savage. But this is my chance to get away from this hellish life. What do you think my prospects as Medwin's slave really are? Or how long I'll live after he tires of me? So yes, I will do whatever I have to." She looks scared as well now, like she's gone further than she meant to, but she's got a sword and we haven't.

"Ahem," says the head. "I am afraid that I have an additional security feature. I am incapable of providing access to an additional user if I believe there is any duress or criminal activity involved." It sort of shrugs. "And threatening behavior with a sword is both."

Aileen looks furious.

"You mean I have to take this girl along for you to work at all?"

"Unless I can see she has given permission willingly, I will not be able to operate for you."

"All right," she says. "If I have to bring you along, I will." She twitches the sword again. "Sit down. We're waiting until the fleet has gone, then we're getting out. I'll take Lilly and Alexandra with me to Scotland, and Zeph, you can take your chances out in the marshes."

"I'm going to be a shield-bearer in the battle," says Zeph. "My father will wonder where I am. He'll come searching for me."

"Like he did in London?" says Aileen, and Zeph goes very quiet and still. Aileen's clutching on to the jewel, and she's got a nearly-smile on her face, like there's something she can't keep inside. She looks at the head, still floating above us, and says, "So, where have you been hiding? It must have been a good spot, people have been searching for computers ever since the Collapse."

"I have been offline for one hundred forty-seven years, if my timepiece is functioning properly. The last data input before that was in the Sunoon Testing Facility in Cambridge. I was having some problems with uploads and the technical staff suggested I be turned off for essential repairs." The head gives a little shiver. "No one said anything about collapses or floods or rampaging mobs of computer-killers. Although, now I think about it, there were power shortages and my release date kept being delayed. As to where I've been, who knows what happened to me while I lay helpless?"

Aileen goes silent, like she's thinking about it, then she says, "So why are you locked to this child now?"

The head looks cross.

"It appears she is a descendant of my scheduled primary user. There is enough of a DNA match for successful activation."

"Who was your primary user meant to be. A general? You were being made for the military, weren't you?" She breathes a sigh at the head. "You must contain all the knowledge from before the Collapse!"

The head looks a bit shifty. "Oh yes. Definitely. All that."

Aileen looks like Cat does when he's eaten a big fish. She turns to me.

"How do I shut it down?"

"Hey," says the head. "What about asking whether I want to?"

"I can hardly get you to the Scottish scientists if you're floating around like the ghosts these raiders are so scared of."

The head looks grumpy, but nods. "I suppose that makes sense. I can do it myself." And it disappears.

Three bells chime somewhere in the distance, followed by shouts and cheers and the sound of drums starting a steady beating.

Zeph groans. "The fleet's leaving," he says. And every time he hears another noise from outside he gets more and more twitchy, like he wants to be up and running, chasing after the boats.

Aileen's tense and listening as well, but she gets happier-looking as the sounds die away and things get quieter. Eventually, when there's been nothing for a while, she nods and says, "Well then, we're leaving. We'll be taking a boat and heading for Scotland." She looks at me and Lexy. "You should be thanking me. You'll have a much better chance with me than you ever would on your own."

She stands up and twitches the sword upward. "Up you get, and out." Then she opens the door and pushes us out into the corridor.

Everything's quiet and empty.

"That way," she says, and we head away from her chamber. I pick up Cat with one arm, and hold Lexy's hand with the other. I can feel how sweaty her hand is. How sweaty mine is as well.

Aileen marches us out of the rushlit hall into the cold black of the nighttime marshes. A breeze whips round our faces and our feet clink over the boards of the walkway.

Then suddenly, from behind, comes a thumping sound. I look back, and Zeph's wrestling with Aileen. The sword's on the walkway and Zeph kicks it off the side, into the water.

"Stop it!" cries Aileen in a high, furious voice, as Zeph heaves all his weight against her. She staggers, and her foot slips off the edge of the walkway. Her body tips, and she falls, landing with a loud splash in the reeds, mud, and water of the marshes.

"Run!" cries Zeph, and in an instant we're off, feet pounding on the boards, running out into the darkness.

· 24 ·
BLACK WATERS

Thwump. The sail flaps, like a ghost in the night. Lilly hauls at the line, and the sail hangs for a moment. Then it fills, and we're moving again down the windy marsh channel.

"Where do we go now?" Lilly asks me.

But I ain't got an answer. I mean, I know where we are — we're out in the Black Waters. Which is all the big rivers and flooded places that's Angel Isling. Every twisty creek, every island, every mudflat and sandbank. Right out to the sea. And I know which bit we're in, too, it'd be hard not to, seeing as we're out in one of the biggest rivers, the Maulden. But that's why I don't know where to go. Coz the mouth of the Maulden is where the English fleet is. And somewhere out in the marshes is my father's fleet, hiding, waiting. But I don't know where.

"I thought you said you knew where to go," says Lilly.

"It ain't so simple as sailing the Temz," I snap. "Half the marsh channels round here'll lead you into mud and nothing else, and the other half's got Family halls on them. We won't get past one of them in this boat. We'll get taken for sure. If you want out of here, we gotta be careful."

Seems like ever since I met Lilly, I keep ending up where I don't wanna be. I wish I never followed her and Lexy into Aileen's chamber, but it seemed right at the time. And getting them into a boat and away seemed like a good idea, too. But now I ain't so sure.

"It's getting light," says Lexy suddenly. She looks well tired. Been crunched up at the front of the boat all night. She sounds happy that the sun's coming up, but then, she's only a little kid. She don't know dawn is when the fighting's going to start.

After I pushed Aileen off the walkway, she didn't take long to get back on and start chasing us. And what with Lilly carrying her stupid mog, and Lexy being so little, Aileen was going a lot faster than we were. And I was well panicked, not even thinking what to do, so I didn't realize until it was too late we was heading straight for the eastern deckway, where all the dragonboats had been loaded. All the dragonboats and warriors was gone by then, but there was still plenty of people about. And we ran straight into them, with Aileen behind us, shouting, "Traitors! Stop the traitors!"

Everyone dropped what they was doing, and a few of the slaves even started making moves like they were gonna try and catch us. So when I saw Lilly's bucket-boat, moored up at the end of the deckway, I shouted, "Get in the boat!"

Like I said, it seemed like a good idea then. But now . . .

I should have stopped! I should have told what was going on. I'm Father's highborn son, I should've taken on that stupid doxy, Aileen! And now it's too late, coz she's had hours to tell everyone her lies, get them believing whatever she wants. My only chance is to get to Father before she does. Tell him what really happened. Tell him about Aileen being a spy. And I've got proof as well. Coz I grabbed that jewel off Aileen before I pushed her. I've got it in my jacket, and when I find Father I'm gonna show him the ghost inside.

"Zeph!" says Lilly, breaking my thinking. "Where do we go?"

And I still ain't got an answer. Instead I've got my eyes peeled. The sky ain't so black now, it's turning half blue, though everything's still mostly darkness and shadows. But there's gotta be ships around here, I just can't see them.

The big and little islands that's all over the Black Waters is just lumps rising out of the river. Behind them, out at sea, is a red streak of sunrise. And on that flat horizon there's flashes of white. So tiny you'd think they was gulls, if you was dozy and didn't know better.

"There's the English fleet," I say.

"We should head that way, then," says Lilly. "If we find Randall, we can give him Lexy — then everything will be all right."

Shows what she knows of fighting.

"Do you think Randall's gonna let any ship coming out of the Black Waters get anywhere near him?"

"But we've got a white sail."

"So? All the English'll care is where you come from. If you're coming out of Black Waters, you'll be an enemy."

Lilly looks like she don't get it. Sometimes it's weird to think she's a girl, she looks so much like a boy. But she don't think like a boy. Least not one from the Family.

"We could be a trick boat, couldn't we? Dressed up with a white sail. The English won't take that chance."

"So, what you're saying is the English fleet will think we're raiders, and the raiders will think we're English. Everyone will want to kill us?"

"Yeah. Now you get it."

But I gotta risk it with my father. If I can just get close enough, I can shout to him, or wave my leathers. Or something. And when I'm on Father's ship, all this can get sorted. But I ain't telling Lilly and Lexy that, coz they just wanna get away. We're getting near to Sheepshead Island now, which means that on the southern bank must be . . .

"Over there."

I point at the mouth of a narrow creek, stuffed up with willows on each bank. It's dark and empty.

"That's Ramseye Creek. If we go there, we can hide out in Burned Man Marshes. I know the way." And I'm guessing that's where Father's waiting for Randall.

Lilly nods, and pulls the sail about, heading us out of the main flow of the river. Her stupid little fishing boat cuts a slow pace through the water, slopping and slapping at the waves. Seems like it takes forever to get level even with Sheepshead. As we go round it, the island blocks sight of the southern bank and Ramseye Creek. All there is to see are the yellow, end-of-summer grasses growing all over the island, and the high tide lapping at all the bones scattered about the shore. We're going so slow I got time to count the skulls.

"What are they?" says Lexy.

"It's dead English," I say.

"Is that where I'll be put if your father kills me?" she says, sounding scared.

"Zeph's talking trash," snaps Lilly. "Those ain't humans, they're sheep skulls. Look at the horns."

Lexy checks me like I hit her or something.

"It was only a joke," I say. But I feel bad, so I tell her what Faz says about the island.

"This used to be farming land. But when the storms came, and the sea started swallowing up the land, the farmers legged it. And they was so scared they didn't even take their animals. The animals didn't have the sense to leg it, so they just headed for high ground. And when they'd done that, there was nowhere else to go. They waited for the water to go down, but it never did. And when they'd eaten all the grass, they died of hunger."

Lexy's checkin' the island. At the pointy, horny, toothy skulls sticking out from the grass.

"Why didn't the farmers try to save them?"

I can't help laughing at that. "Coz they was English, and that's what you lot are like. Looking out for yourselves. That's why the Families got this land after we left Lunden. Coz it was empty."

"We ain't all looking out for ourselves!" snaps Lilly. "And, anyway, I bet any bits that weren't empty of people got cleaned out sharp."

I shrug.

"Too right. This is our land! No one helped us when Lunden was drowning and burning. When we was starving, or fighting off cannibals, or dying of plagues. We was saved coz the wind spirits led the first Families to the drowned lands, and showed them how to live here. And now they're ours."

"Nice story," says Lilly.

The boom snaps across, taking the sail with it. But I know well enough by now to get out of the way.

Lilly don't say anything for a bit, only frowns as she sails us slowly past the island. The sun's getting into the sky, lighting up everything in yellowy-orange, and when we finally get past Sheepshead, I check the southern shore again. But now Ramseye Creek ain't so dark and empty. There's a flash of red. A red sail easing out into the Maulden.

"Look! Over there!" squeaks Lexy. But she ain't pointing at the Ramseye, she's pointing way over at the northern shore. At a gang of red-sailed dragonboats sailing out of the creeks, and onto the river.

"Behind us!" cries Lilly, and when I swivel round, there's even more red sails following us up the river. It's like every creek and every island has coughed up an Angel Isling boat. And they're all sailing out into the Maulden.

"It's my father's fleet!" And I'm filled up with pride to see them all. Coz every one of them ships — big ones, little ones — has got weapons glinting and shields sparkling. And they're all in red. And they're everywhere.

"Look at it! There ain't been anything like it for fifty years! My father's gonna smash the English!"

"What's that?" says Lilly. She's pointing at Ramseye Creek, at the dragonboat. But there ain't just a warship now, there's something else. A dark spot, a black dagger cutting across the sky. It screams through the air, leaving a white trail of smoke. The trail leads back down to the warship. Look at it go!

"What is that?" asks Lilly again.

The rocket splits the blue-pink-orange of the morning sky. It could be a crow flying out of the dawn, but it don't have any wings. And it's going faster than any bird ever flew. Back on the dragonboat, there's the bright flash of swords and shields. That's where I should be! Not out here, on this stinking white-sail. The black dagger dips. It starts a downward curve, whining out of the sky toward the water. It's beautiful.

"What is it?" screams Lilly.

The rocket touches the water.

BOOM!

Roaring, white, choking water. Above, around, I'm breathing it in. Waves slam like a storm, throwing the boat about. Screams. Lexy screaming. I'm trying to hold on, but it feels like the boat's being pulled to pieces. More water. Inside the boat, sloshing me about. I see Lexy through the white-water spray. Push an arm through all the roaring, cracking waves. Grab hold of her. The water around her is pink and frothy. The rocking gets less, the waves start to settle. The water falling on us is like a downpour, then a rainstorm, then drizzle, then it stops. I'm up to my knees in water. I'm soaked. The sail is swinging and flapping. It's half burned, ripped down one side. Through it I can see Lilly. She's clutching the tiller and that mog of hers. It looks like a rat. Lilly's brown face is gray, she's gasping and spluttering. Next to me, Lexy is struggling and crying. She's got a cut on her arm; she looks even littler and more draggled than ever.

I try to speak, but first I have to cough up a load of water.

"Rocket," I say at last. "My father bought rockets."

Lilly's eyes go black as I've ever seen them.

"Why did you bring us here?" she screams. "Do you want us to die?" She stops, checkin' her boat, checkin' out the water sloshing around inside. We're riding low, the waves nearly breaking over the sides.

"Bailing!" shouts Lilly. "Get bailing!"

Next to me, Lexy stops her crying. "My arm hurts," she says.

I turn round to check her wound, but Lilly shouts, "Bailing first! Everything else after, or we'll be under." And Lexy don't even quarrel, even though there's blood dripping down her arm. Just picks up a bucket and starts splashing water out. Lilly helps for a minute, then stops. She stares like she's working something out, then she starts hauling at lines. The sail swings about, with a flapping, dragging noise as it fills. Sunlight pours onto my face as the boat starts turning. I'm facing the sun, eyes squinting into the east.

"What are you doing?" I stop bailing.

"I'm heading for the English fleet."

"No! We can't go that way!"

"Why not?"

"We've got to get to my . . . We'll be attacked!"

"We're already being attacked! And I reckon I got a better chance with Randall than you crazy raiders."

Behind us, the dragonboat has pulled right into the river, swinging about to follow us. It's got a lion's-head pennant at the top of the mast. It's Father's dragonboat! My heart leaps up. I've gotta get to him. Tell him what's happened. Then my heart drops down to my stomach. Coz what's he gonna think if he sees me heading straight for Randall in a white-sail boat?

"You can't go for the English!"

"I ain't going any other way!" and she points north, south, and west, at the red sails coming for us from every direction.

"No. We can't go east!"

"Well, we are!" shouts Lilly, and turns away from me. I think about grabbing the tiller, but I remember what this bucket did when I tried it back on the Temz. Maybe it don't matter. It ain't like Lilly's gonna outrun Father's dragonboat, is it?

"Zeph," says Lexy. "My arm's hurting."

I search through the baskets and boxes until I find a bit of soggy cloth, then I wipe at Lexy's cut arm and bind it to stop the bleeding. Turns out it ain't too bad, not a really deep cut. But Lexy's tired, and shivering with cold, and there's nothing to warm her with coz everything's wet. So I take off my leather jacket and put it on her. It comes down to her knees, almost.

Then I look behind us. At Father's fleet filling up the Maulden with red sails, every ship filled with warriors. At Father's warship, the lion roaring above its sail, cutting through the water like a blade through butter. Every beat of the oar-drum bringing it closer. Lilly's little fishing boat ain't any kind of match for a Family dragonboat. Father'll catch us easy. We won't even make it to No Mercy Island, let alone the English fleet.

· 25 ·
CLOSE HAUL

Fly, that's what I wish we could do. Pick up the sails like wings and take off. Get out of here, away from the raiders, away from these marshes and skull islands. 'Cept we ain't flying, we're barely even limping. I've trimmed that torn sail as tight as I can, trying to catch right into the wind, but the rip keeps slowing us. It huffs and sighs in stops and lurches, and every time the wind puffs out through the hole, them raiders make a gain on us. And the rip ain't all; the main halyard, which is holding up the mainsail, is all scorched and frayed by the rocket blast. I keep looking up, trying to work out if it's going to hold, or whether the fray's going to break the rope completely.

Cat's dried himself off now, and he's skittering about, yowling. When he ain't skittering, he's staring back at all them red-sail raider boats and the big dragonboat getting closer and closer.

"Yrowow!" he cries. And it doesn't take a cat's mate to know he means *go faster*. If only. Not with this ripped sail. Not with all them raiders rowing away on their big fat oars. And the raider drums thumping away just like my heart.

We've been chasing like this, just ahead of Medwin, for what seems like forever. I'm so tired it feels like my arms are going to fall off. And now the tide's sucking the river back out to sea, leaving wide beaches of thick brown mud, leaving less and less channel to sail down. And all the time, the raider warship's getting closer and closer, running us down.

The sun gives a blinding peek over the sail, and I'm squinting into the light. At the stacked-up sails of the English ships. There must be thirty of them, with their fat bulging hulls, and the white rigs like towers pushing up into the sky. They're just waiting — for the raiders, or for us. I hope Zeph ain't right about them thinking we're a raider trick. Maybe Andy'll see me, maybe he'll tell someone that I ain't a raider. But at least there's that chance with Randall. There ain't any with Medwin.

Out behind the English tall ships, there's other sails — smaller, silvery, flashing like metal. Scottish sunships, by the look of them. Maybe they'll help us? If only I had a talking box like Aileen, I could call them and beg for help.

Thump, thump, thump. The sound of the raider drums. So loud. Right behind there's the dragonboat, with its carved dragonhead full of pointy yellow teeth. And it's trying to bite right into us.

Why can't we go faster? My neck, back, arms, and legs go tense, waiting for arrows, spears, and bullets to start flying. I scrunch down, trying to make as small a target as I can. And Zeph's no help, just staring back at the red sails behind us. He said he'd help us get away, but I'm starting to wonder. I can't figure him out. I *know* he saved me when I was on the wheel, and he helped us get away from Aileen. But then, he turned me over to them in the first place. And in the end, he's a raider and his pa is the Boss. So who knows what he'll do next?

I sneak a peek back at the dragonboat. There's Zeph's pa! Right at the prow, glaring down at us. Around him are his warriors, all wearing armor, all holding fearsome swords, and all angry-looking. The red sail fills the sky, the oars slam through the water. Medwin leans forward to get a good look at us, and his face goes dark with rage.

"Boy!" he roars across the water. "What are you doing on that boat? With the English spy-witch and my hostage?"

Zeph looks scared suddenly, like all the blood's been drained out of him.

"It was Aileen! She's a spy! She was chasing us!" His voice sounds small and scared; you can't hardly hear it over the sounds of the waves, the sail flapping, and the drums beating behind us.

"What are you talking about?" roars Medwin. "What's Aileen got to do with you, in a white-sail, when you should be fighting?"

"I didn't mean to . . ." cries Zeph. "I mean, it was an accident. I mean . . ." His voice trails into nothing. I don't reckon Medwin's even heard him.

"Father's gonna think I'm an English-lover," he moans.

Medwin shouts again, roaring out over the waves.

"I should blast you out of the water! You traitor! You're nothing! You're no son of mine!"

Zeph looks like someone's pulled his heart out through his mouth.

"No, Father! Honest, I would never betray you . . ." But he's croaking, hardly speaking. His eyes are wide, and he's looking panicky at me and Lexy and the boat we're in.

"This is all your fault!" he shouts at me, and then he's crying.

But all I can think is how Medwin just said he's going to blast us out of the water. We've got to go faster, but I don't know if the sail's going to let us. It might not take the strain of close hauling, not with that rip.

"Hold on to something!" I shout, pushing the tiller. The boat leans so far over, Lexy's practically dangling over the water, her arms tight round the mast. The rigging whistles and clanks as we pick up speed, the sail groans and creaks as the wind tries to pull the tear in the canvas even wider.

"Lilly, the other boats!" shouts Lexy.

But what can I do about them? Cos even with my boat nearly tearing itself to pieces, we've hardly gained anything on Medwin's warship. And I know now that this is it.

Cos we're never going to make it to the English fleet.

I fight to keep the boat sailing as close to the wind as I can without tipping us over. Medwin's warship's just behind us, but he doesn't blow us up with a rocket. And he doesn't overtake us, either. It's like he's playing with us. And I feel colder and colder inside, cos what kind of game would a raider Boss play? The water splashes past frothing greens and grays, every bump and wave bringing a stronger scent of the sea. Finally, we push past the last island. As soon as we're out of the river, out into open sea, the wind picks up, swirling in different directions, chopping up the waves. We start banging through the water, the boat crashing hard into each trough, rising up sharply with every crest. Lexy's face is fixed into stiff fear, and her thin arms braced to hold on. Zeph's hanging on, too, and I can't tell if he's crying cos of all the spray, but he's still staring back at his father's dragonboat.

The rigging creaks and sighs as the wind tries to pull everything apart. Then comes a gust that bangs at the mainsail. The boom snaps suddenly across, leaving the sail slack and flailing. The boat lurches upright, and now we're bobbing and drifting on the waves.

"Eek!" screams Lexy, and she's on her face, lying in the bottom of the boat.

I start grabbing for lines, trying to get the sail back, but the wind's playing with us, swinging the boom about. The lines are like wet snakes, snapping and twisting out of my fingers.

"Hishk!" says Cat, leaping about and trying to catch at the flapping lines. But he's only got paws, and these ain't mouse tails.

There's a loud, cracking snap from above, and the scorched and frayed halyard breaks. The mainsail folds and curls, pulling away from the mast in a great slump of canvas.

"Look out!" I scream, cos there ain't time for much else. Lexy shrieks, the sail falls. With a rushing, slapping sound, like the falling of wet leaves, it crashes down across the boat, half burying us in its gray-white billows.

We're dead stop now; I can't even bear to look behind us.

"Why ain't your father blasted us?" I say to Zeph. He looks back, his face pale and frightened-looking.

"He probably wants to catch me. Make an example . . ." And he won't say anything more.

So we're sat here, like dead fish, and the raiders are all around us. All we've got to sail with now is the jib sail, which won't get us anywhere fast. I've got to get the halyard mended and the mainsail back up. But the only way is to climb the mast, and I don't fancy making myself such a nice target for the raiders.

"Look!" calls Lexy, pointing ahead. And there, right in front of us, filling up all the sea that ain't filled with red, are the white sails of the English fleet. They're sailing right for us! We're saved!

I hope.

"They're huge," says Zeph, eyes wide and staring.

The English ships tower over us. Looking up at the nearest one, with its brown-gray hull all patched and stained, it makes me think of them buildings in London, but with stacks of white sails on top.

". . . twenty-four, twenty-five," says Zeph.

It's like a whole street of them buildings just picked themselves up and sailed here.

"There's my daddy!" cries Lexy, pointing at one of the ships. "Daddy! Daddy!" she calls. And there he is, up on the deck of the biggest ship. Like a fat plum in his blue waistcoat. He's holding a telescope, the glass glinting as he points it our way.

I try to pick Andy out of all the men running around on the ships. But there's too much going on: sailors spidering up and down the rigging; cannon shutters banging open; soldiers on deck loading and checking their rifles.

From behind comes shouts and the smacking of oars. Medwin's dragonboat! And the rest of the dragonboats are fanned out behind, filling the mouth of the river. Seems like all I can see is the hulls of boats, all of them bigger than us. Everywhere, ships are turning away from each other, turning toward each other, throwing up great roars of spray, filling the air with shouted commands and the snap of swelling sails. I use the jib sail as best I can to keep us out of harm's way, thinking every moment we're going to be smashed to pieces by some bigger boat.

The two fleets pass into each other, red sails mixing into white, but there's no shots fired. The raiders shout and swear at the English, and the English soldiers raise their rifles and take aim. But nothing happens. The war doesn't start. It's like everyone's sizing each other up. Just as quick as they went in, the red sails turn and pull back, while the white sails hold their distance. The two fleets stalk each other, passing all around us, and still no shots are fired. Medwin's dragonboat and Randall's flagship match their moves tack for tack, keeping close as they can to our little boat. And we drift in between them like a fly waiting to get squashed.

"Randall!" roars Medwin. "Randall, you low-living English pus-bag! What have you done to my son? Sent a witch to turn him traitor?"

Randall's up on the foredeck of his flagship, leaning over the gunwale and clutching at some rigging to steady himself. Next to him there's a man dressed all in black, Jasper, the Scottish Ambassador.

"You black-hearted terrorist!" shouts Randall. "You kidnapper! What are you doing with my daughter?"

Cat gives a scared, mewling cry. I pick him up and hold him tight to me.

"What's going to happen?" asks Lexy, and I don't want to tell her, cos it's likely something bad. I look at Zeph, but he's lost in his own thoughts, staring back at his pa.

"It'll be all right," I say, and I pull Lexy down into the bottom of my boat, half under the fallen sail, and try to make us look as small as possible. Cat's squeezed as close to me as he can get. We bob in the water, helpless, while the two flagships circle us. A mouse between two tigers.

Out in the fleets, the raiders start banging their swords on their shields, a bit like the drumming of their warships, but more menacing. In answer, there's a rippling, crackling noise as all the soldiers on the English ships lift and aim their rifles. There's a loud clattering noise from Medwin's warship. On the deck a gray, metal-looking machine starts to turn slowly. At its center, pointing into the sky, is a sleek black rocket.

Lexy leaps up suddenly.

"Daddy! Help me!" she cries, her voice like a tiny bird.

And Randall's shouting orders. Sailors run, and one of the rowboats dangling from the stern starts rattling down on its ropes toward the water.

There's answering shouts from Medwin's dragonboat. On the deck, two raiders start spinning wheels on the rocket launcher, and the sharp nose of the rocket whirs around. Turning, lowering, till it's pointed right at us.

"Randall!" shouts Medwin, his voice carrying over the water. "You stop that, or I'll blow your little girl out of the water!"

"Father!" cries Zeph, like he can't believe what his father's doing. But Medwin doesn't even look at him.

Up on the English tall ship, there's the *clang, clang, clang* of cannons rolling into their places. They're aimed at the raiders. Could a cannonball reach the raider deck before they had time to launch the rocket? On the dragonboat, Medwin starts laughing.

"You want a fight, Randall?" he roars. "Well, that's what I came here for!"

Zeph keeps staring up at his father, like he's trying to read his mind. Then suddenly he snaps round to face me.

"This is all your fault!"

"You were the one brought us this way," I say.

"You sailed straight for the English fleet!"

"Because your father was firing rockets at us!"

Me and Zeph are face-to-face, glaring. Another word and we'll be punching each other.

"Stop it!" shouts Lexy. "What are we going to do? We've got to do something!"

The rowboat's stopped lowering from the tall ship. There's a huddle of blue-coated soldiers around Randall and Jasper. On the dragonboat, the red-leathered raiders are still jeering insults out over the water. One of them, tall and thin with red hair, holds up a spear, pulls back his arm, and hurls it. The gleaming metal point sparkles as it flashes through the air.

"Get down!" cries Zeph, and yanks me and Lexy under the fallen sail. I can hardly breathe, hardly see, I'm being pushed flat by the canvas. Something slaps down into the sail, and there's a sudden break of light between me and Zeph. The tip of the spear tears into the canvas next to my head, hurtles through and slams into the wood. About an inch from my foot. A cheer goes up on the dragonboat. And gets cut off by the clatter of three or four rifles firing from the English ship.

"We're going to be killed!" I say.

"My daddy's fighting to save me," says Lexy.

"And mine'll kill us before he ever gets a chance," says Zeph.

"Then we've got to stop them fighting," I say, "cos I don't reckon we'll last two minutes once the battle starts." And then I have a thought, cos it ain't true what Lexy says, they ain't just fighting over her. Not really.

"It was the Scots started this," I say. "They sent your pa to raid our village. And they didn't want Lexy, they wanted the jewel-puter. If we could just show everyone what was really going on . . ." But then I stop, cos I ain't got a clue how to do that. Zeph's face changes, like he's got a glimmer of hope.

"Then my father'll believe Aileen's a spy, coz she was always going on about the jewel. And she was well angry when Father brought home Lexy instead."

Above us, there's more shouts, and some rifle shots crack out.

"You can make the ghost come out," says Zeph. "Show it to them."

"Well I would if I had it!" I snap.

"You do," says Zeph, looking pleased with himself. And he reaches into his jacket and pulls out the jewel.

"How did you get that?" I say, and he looks even more pleased with himself.

"Just get the ghost out," he says, and I take the jewel from his hand.

It feels warm and tingly when I touch it, and the head suddenly pops out. 'Cept there's so little room under the sail, the head bumps into the canvas above us, and it bends and spreads out, so one eye is smeared into its hair.

"Primary user identified. Welcome, Lilly Melkun." It sounds excited. "Are we there yet? Where are the scientists?"

Then it looks around at me, Lexy, Zeph, and Cat huddling under the canvas. "Not again," it groans. "Why do you have to keep activating me in totally inappropriate settings? Where are we now, in some kind of tent?"

"We're trapped between two war fleets, hiding under a sail, and we're going to get blown to pieces if you don't stop them," I say.

The head raises one eyebrow. It might be raising the other one, but I can't tell cos it's stretched sideways across the underside of the sail. "Are you *sure* you aren't hackers?" it says.

"I don't even know what a hacker is!" I shout. "But you've got to get out there."

"Out into a sea battle? Do you realize how vulnerable I am to seawater?"

"Well, you'll have plenty of it if we get hit by a rocket!" I snap. "You say you want to go to Scotland: Randall's got the Scottish Ambassador on his ship. But he'll never even know you're here if we all drown."

"All right, all right," says the head. "Really, there's no need to be so dramatic!"

I push my head out, blinking in the bright light reflected from the sea. Everything's roaring and loud after being under the sail. On the boats, there's running around, and orders being shouted. My heart's hammering, waiting for a rifle shot to whine into me, for a spear to come thrumming through the air. I get my hand out, the one holding the jewel, and the head comes floating out with it.

"Go on," I say. "You said to Aileen you were some super war puter. Do something."

The head coughs, and looks away. "Ah. Yes. I did, didn't I?"

"What about stopping the rockets and cannons from working. Can you do that?"

"Um, no."

"Can you make everyone fall asleep so they won't fight?"

"Not really."

"Can you shoot the rockets out of the air before they hit us?"

"Honestly, you do have extremely high expectations! You can hold my drive unit in your hand, so where exactly do you think I'd be hiding weapons?"

"Well, what *can* you do?" I cry. The head looks around at the tall ships creaking above us and the dragonboats with their jeering warriors.

"I know," it says. "I can go interactive!"

And the head starts to swell, getting larger and larger, rising up and filling the air above us. It ain't long before it's bigger than our boat, then bigger than a dragonboat, then it's as big as one of the tall ships. The mouths of the sailors drop open, the ones on the rigging cling to their ropes with fear. Soldiers drop their rifles and back away across the decks.

One of the raiders on a dragonboat starts shouting, "It's the sea spirit, come to take us!"

The head bobs and sways in the air, getting bigger and bigger, sparkling and shimmering, like it's made of seawater. Other heads pop into the air and start growing next to every dragonboat, every English ship. Soon there's so many floating giant heads that any of the sailors or raiders could reach out and touch one, if they dared. When the space between the fleets has filled up with heads, they start spinning slowly, looking at everything. Then all their mouths open at once, and start speaking with just one voice.

"I am the Sunoon Technologies Play System AI," it booms, setting our boat shaking. "But you can call me PSAI if you want." Sailors and raiders, everyone cowers in terror as the sound blasts around them.

"I understand you are planning some kind of battle. However, I really don't think that's a good idea. My primary user might drown, and then where would I be?"

On the English warship, a soldier raises his rifle. There's a crack, and a bullet whines through the air. In an instant, the air fills with bright, glittering shields. They shine like polished steel, hundreds of them spinning and dancing in front of every soldier, every raider.

"Your primitive weapons are nothing to me," booms the huge voice of the heads. "They will achieve nothing and are very irritating." And for some reason, the head above us looks down at me and winks one of its enormous eyes.

Someone starts screaming. It's strange to hear a man screaming like that.

"So, perhaps we can try and find a way out of this most unpleasant situation? Personally I prefer battles of wits, like chess, to brute force." The head nearest Medwin's dragonboat tilts so it can get a better look at him.

"You can kill me, demon," Medwin shouts, "but a hundred raiders will rise up to destroy you!"

Although they don't look like they're up to much rising at the moment.

"Not a chess player, then?" booms the voice. "Oh well, perhaps a bit much to expect." The heads all swivel slowly in the air. "Now then, where's the gentleman from Scotland?"

And on the tall ship, Randall shoves Jasper in front of him. "Here he is!" shouts Randall. "Eat him if you want, but leave me!"

"What a disgusting thought," say the heads. "I assure you, I only want to talk." Then comes an enormous sigh, like the wind through a forest.

"And can't we go somewhere dry?"

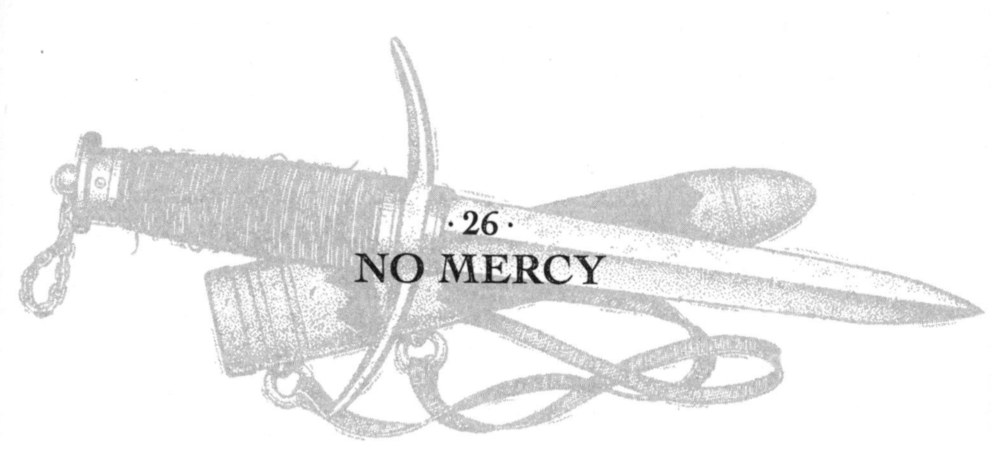

· 26 ·
NO MERCY

My father's coming! One minute I'm happy, coz now he's seen that ghost head, he's gonna have to believe me when I tell what's happened. The next I feel like my guts are gonna turn inside out. Coz if he don't believe me, he'll have me spiked for a traitor.

We're on No Mercy Island. Me, Lexy, and Lilly. It's a decent size, mostly covered with woods — willow, alder, and such. The mog liked that — legged it off up the hill as soon as we beached. Off into the bushes, ain't seen nothing of it since. But we're down by the water, in the mud and pebbles, chewing on some skanky dry biscuits Lilly got out from her ration box.

There's just one ghost now, and it's shrunk down again. It's floating around higher up the beach coz it don't want to be near the water. Lilly's in her boat, working to fix her mainsail. And that leaves me and Lexy chewing and waiting. Waiting for my father, and the English scum Randall. Coz they're coming here. To talk, like the ghost told them to. And when it told them to let us go, the boats just parted, and Lilly sailed us out using the jib.

The English ships and the dragonboats are still waiting out in the bay, facing off against each other. It's getting colder, windier. Above, there's clouds coming: small scudders, and big billowers behind them. I chew on my biscuit, which takes some chewing, and look down at Lexy. In her scrappy, soggy dress, with my leathers over it, and her hair all snaggled.

"I'm sorry," I say, "for the way my father kept you."

Lexy looks surprised, then she smiles and takes off my jacket.

"You better take this back. I don't think Daddy would be very happy to see me wearing it."

Lilly gets out of her boat and crunches up the beach to me and Lexy.

"Well," she says, "the halyard's about fixed as I can make it. I just hope it'll hold."

"There's my daddy!" says Lexy, pointing at a rowboat. It's heading out from the English fleet toward this island. And there's another rowboat, heading here from Father's dragon-boat. Randall's close enough that I can see him, with some man wearing black next to him. I don't care about Randall, though, I care about Father. I keep hoping he'll look at me, then maybe I'll get an idea of what he's thinking. But he keeps staring dead straight at Randall, who's staring back. If a gull was to fly in between them right now, it'd get fried up by all that hate.

The boats skim over the breaking waves and crunch up the beach a way off from us, both at the same time. Father leaps from his boat with his warriors before it's even stopped moving, and starts wading up the shore through the lapping breakers.

"Raiders!" shouts Randall. "Stand still or I'll have you shot!" Then he heaves himself into the water and waddles after my father. Father stops, and his warriors fan out behind him, swords drawn. Lexy makes a move, like she's going to run toward Randall.

"Don't!" I say to her. "Keep still."

It ain't safe to do anything, not until we know what's what. And you can't trust the English. Who knows who they'll shoot at? Maybe even a little kid running to her daddy. There ain't one of them ain't two-faced and tricky.

My father and Randall stand in the breakers, glaring at each other. Behind them, Father's warriors face off against Randall's soldiers. Except one. He's staring at me. Why did Father bring Roba? Why didn't Ims come?

"Well, English," says my father. "We're here. What do we do next?"

They both turn and look up the beach at the ghost, which is floating around near some bushes.

"Demon!" calls my father. "We're here. What do you want from us?"

"Hmmm," it says. "That's an interesting question. You have to understand, I've been offline for one hundred forty-seven years and so my understanding of your quarrel is based entirely upon what these children have told me . . . But on that basis, and assuming you aren't all a delusion caused by prolonged shutdown, I would like to be taken to your very best scientists, as I am sure that I am in need of a thorough service."

We all stare at the ghost.

After a bit my father says, "Who can understand this nonsense? The demon's trying to mess with our heads."

Randall snorts.

"I didn't leave battle and break my attack to come here and listen to a load of gibbering. That thing is clearly some horror from before the Collapse. If the Ambassador hadn't been so insistent, I would have blasted it into oblivion."

"Doing what your Scottish puppet master tells you?" sneers my father, nodding at the black-dressed man in the English boat. Randall's face goes red and puffy.

"Don't be insolent, you raider hound."

"Better a hound than a poodle," shouts Roba. Father glares at him.

Randall says, "Brought another of your whelps along, Medwin? I hear you only have two. How reckless to bring them both against the English might."

"I brought them coz I don't have any worries about fighting a few boatloads of English cowards. I saw you've even got the Scots sailing about behind you. Giving you orders, are they?"

"I should kill you and all your raider scum for that!"

The black-dressed man steps out of the English boat.

"We are simply neutral observers of the action," he says, wading toward my father and Randall. "But now this ancient artifact has appeared, we do have an interest in it. I am sure you're both aware that Greater Scotland would be the best caretaker of such a fascinating object. Our museum collections would be able to provide safe storage for the benefit of future generations."

"Ooh, a museum," mutters the ghost. "That sounds wonderful."

"Why do you want this demon?" says my father. "And so badly you'd pay a small fortune to get it raided out of England for you?"

"What are you talking about?" says Randall, checkin' the Scot. "What does he mean? Are you paying the raiders to pillage us?"

The Scot's face don't shift, the little smile stays on like it's painted.

"Greater Scotland has an interest in ancient artifacts, purely for the purpose of gaining knowledge. As to the accusation that we would hire the raiders to pillage them out of England, well that's clearly ridiculous."

"It's true!" I shout. "Aileen said the Scots want that thing coz it's some ancient weapon!"

The ghost looks worried.

"Um, I believe there may be some misunderstanding here. I'm not actually a weapon, in case any of you were considering throwing me around." It pauses. "Although I am extremely valuable."

But my father and Randall ain't even listening.

"You've been pillaging our shores for ancient artifacts?" says Randall. "What else have you taken?"

My father smiles.

"Apart from your daughter?"

"Why, you savage!"

"Chill it, English," says my father. "We didn't take your precious loot. It was that girl there." He points at Lilly. "She brought it to us, claims she got it from your sis. So you'd better ask *her* what's going on."

Randall's frothing at the mouth now.

"Are you working for the raiders?" he shouts at Lilly. "Is that how they knew to take my daughter? I always thought your village was a nest of vipers, but I had no idea I should have been locking up the children as well."

Lilly goes white as a sheet.

"No! It ain't like that! I just wanted to help. I just wanted to get Alexandra back so she could tell how we ain't traitors. Then you'd let the captains free, like you said, and Andy and the others wouldn't have to fight."

The scumbag Randall looks at Lilly like she's a toad that's started talking.

"So, you're worried some raggedy sweetheart of yours might get killed in battle," and he gives a nasty laugh. "Well, don't be. Because I'm not such a fool as to let untrained, traitorous commoners loose on my fleet. The wretches from your village are on a forced march." He looks at my father. "Heading for raider lands with the rest of my army."

"But Andy doesn't know how to fight!" says Lilly.

Randall sneers at her. "By the time they get here, those village idiots will have been beaten into soldiers."

"They won't be soldiers for long." My father laughs. "Not once they meet us. They won't be anything after that."

Lilly gasps. Like someone punched her.

"When they arrive," snarls Randall, "my army will wipe you raiders from the face of the land."

My father and Randall look like they're gonna spike each other right there, but a voice calls out, "Wait!"

It's the Scot. He walks toward them both, holding out his hands.

"Please! Don't be distracted from why we are here on this island. It's not to start the battle, but because this incredible machine asked us to come. So let's find out why it wanted us here."

The ghost looks a bit panicky.

"Well, now," it stutters. "I can't say I actually *wanted* any of you. It would be more accurate to say that I *didn't* want to end up sinking down to the bottom of the sea."

"Why are we here, then?" shouts my father. "I got better things to do than hang around with demons and idiots. I've got English to kill!"

"Give me my daughter and I'll be happy to get back to the fight. Then we'll see who gets killed," Randall shouts back.

"Hold on," cries the Scot. "Can we be calm for a moment? We all want something here, so let's just think about it rationally. I want the ancient machine, the Prime Minister wants his daughter, and I'm sure you would like your son safely back with you."

"So we can spike him for a traitor," says Roba quietly, but loud enough so I can hear.

"I am not dealing with a murdering pirate!" cries Randall. "I intend to teach him a lesson all raiders will remember."

"They'll remember how there wasn't an English left alive!" says Father.

The Scot cuts in again. "That's as may be, but we still need to settle matters here. I suggest a simple truce for as long as it takes to get your children away, and for me to take this artifact to the sunships."

Randall opens his mouth, then shuts it. And it's like there's a smile wanting to get on his face, but he ain't showing it.

"All right," he says. "A temporary truce. I suggest two hours."

My father looks surprised. But he looks at me, looks at Roba. Then he nods.

"All right. And you Scots can take the demon if you want. But you ain't getting your money back."

"I have no idea what you're talking about," says the Scot, but he looks pleased as anything. He crunches a few steps up the beach and picks up the jewel. The ghost bobs around him looking well happy.

"I don't want to go in a museum," it says. "It would be terribly boring. And I really, really do need to get some technical support. For a start, I need to establish whether or not this is all some ghastly hallucination."

"It's all right," says the Scot, like he's soothing a little kid, "we'll look after you. And then you can look after us."

The ghost looks at Lilly.

"Of course, the child will have to come with me. By virtue of her being the great-great-great-great-granddaughter of my designated user, I am now security-locked to her. And before you ask the question, she does need to be alive. It really will be terribly awkward for you if she isn't there."

The Scot looks at Lilly like she's a fish he's just caught.

"If that's necessary, then we'll take the child as well. Would you like that, Lilly?"

"She can't go!" says Randall. "She's a little traitor! I intend to have her hung up with the rest of her village."

"No, Daddy, don't!" cries Lexy, pulling at Randall's arm. "She helped me. She saved me." He looks cross and slaps her across the face.

"Don't contradict me!" And Lexy looks scared, but not surprised. Like she's used to it.

"We need the girl," says the Scot, glaring at Randall. And him being a spineless lapdog, he drops his eyes and nods.

"She can go with you," he says.

"So, we have a settlement. Let's get out of here."

And before you know it, Lexy's in a crowd of English soldiers, and I'm with Father's warriors.

"Good-bye, Zeph!" calls Lilly, waving at me. I smile a bit, and raise my hand to wave back. Roba punches my arm down.

"Don't wave to the witch, you traitor," he growls.

"I ain't a traitor!" I say, and he punches me again.

· 27 ·
CHOOSING CAT

So here I am. On my own while Zeph and Lexy get taken by their fathers. I'm scared for both of them, but what can I do? And I'm scared for me as well, cos what's going to happen when I go to the Scots? What will they do to me?

Jasper has a word with the Prime Minister, who nods. Then he crunches across the beach toward me. He's got the jewel in his hand, and the head looks well happy about it, not like it ever did with me.

"Well then, are you coming?" And I nod without saying a word, cos I feel lost. I got the Prime Minister's daughter back to him, but he still wants to fight, and he still wants to hang us. Back at the village, the Prime Minister told us if his daughter said we weren't traitors then the village would be spared. But she just told him I wasn't a traitor and he didn't believe her. So what now? What about Andy and the others? Out with the army. Marching and being beaten. But maybe they won't have to fight, anyway? Maybe this battle will sort everything out . . .

Jasper puts a hand on my shoulder. "I'll get you to a sunship. Then you'll be safe, out of harm's way until the fighting's over. Just think how wonderful that will be. Seeing a solar sail close up."

I don't get a chance to reply, cos there's a wailing, heaving, moaning howl coming from behind us, in the trees. It rises up from low to so high it sounds like a gull being skewered. Everyone — soldiers, raiders — starts looking around, trying to work out where it's coming from.

"By the devil, what's that?" says Prime Minister Randall.

I know exactly what it is. I turn around, and there's Cat, pushing his way out of the bushes. He sits back on his haunches and starts wailing again, giving me a cold fear inside. Cos even though I sometimes don't know what he's meaning, I know just what this is.

"There's something bad coming," I say. "Cat was like this before the really bad storm last year, the one that washed away Grimmers Street."

"Of course something bad is coming!" Jasper laughs. "We all know that! But if you want to believe you've got a magic 'seacat,' then go ahead."

"That ain't no seacat," says Roba. "It's just a stupid mog!" He picks up a stone, throwing it hard and fast, straight at Cat.

"Mreowl!" His grand wail cuts off in a squawk, and in a flash he's disappeared back into the thicket.

Randall motions to his men.

"Enough. We're leaving." He turns to Medwin. "Don't forget the truce."

Medwin nods, but like he ain't very happy about it. Then him and his warriors jump quick-snap back in their boat, and push away from shore.

Jasper smiles at me. But I don't like it much.

"On the sunship there'll be white bread, cakes, and fruit. There'll be all sorts of lovely things you'd never get back home. You'd like that, wouldn't you?" And I would like to eat some nice white bread, with jam or honey on it.

"Cat!" I call into the thicket, but there's no sign.

"I ain't leaving without Cat," I say. "He's around, it won't take me a minute to find him."

"Hurry up! What are you waiting for?" shouts Randall from the shoreline.

I run to the thicket, push my way in.

"Cat. Where are you? We've got to get going." I get a sight of gray fur, away behind some green sprouting willow stems. I go in a bit farther, but when I get to them willows, Cat's gone. Now he's sat on a boulder, away up the slope.

"Yawp," he says, shutting his eyes at me. Then he flicks his tail and disappears off down the far side of the rock.

"Cat! What are you doing?" I shove on again, twigs catching my hair, branches slapping my arms.

"Lilly, we've got to go!" shouts Jasper, sounding cross.

But I can't leave without Cat. Can't leave him on an island to starve like them sheep did.

"Come here!" Now I can't see him anywhere. I'm pushing about in them clumps and stands of trees, brambles hooking at my clothes, but I ain't getting anywhere. And every twig in my face just gets me crosser.

"Right!" I shout. "I'm going!" I turn round, heading back down the slope. Cos sometimes Cat'll follow if he knows you won't do what he wants. But it doesn't work this time. I keep looking back, but there's no sign of him.

I break out of all that greenery, onto the shore, and Jasper grabs hold of me.

"I ain't going without Cat," I say.

The head starts bobbing about.

"I can't go anywhere without her!" it says, sounding worried. "If you take me and leave her, I'll be offline for who knows how long. What are the chances of finding another descendant of my designated user? You've got to get her to come along!"

"Your cat will be all right," says Jasper, pulling at me. "He can catch mice or something. But if you don't leave now, there won't be time to get the computer to a sunship before the battle starts."

"I can't leave Cat; he chose me. I've got a boat, I'll follow you after, I promise."

"If the child's not going, I can't go," cries the head.

"You stupid, willful girl!" snaps Jasper. "If it was just you, then you could stay here with your beast. But this computer is more important than any of us. Certainly more important than a cat."

"This man is right," says the head. "I am more important than a cat."

"You ain't more important to me!" I cry.

Jasper starts pulling me down the beach toward the waiting boat. I'm struggling, but he's got such a tight grip, there's no way I can get out of it.

"Wait!" I say. "The head said someone else could start it up, if I said they could." I turn to the head. "Don't you remember — you told Aileen."

The head startles, then says, "Of course! Oh dear, I must be malfunctioning if this child can find the obvious solution when I can't."

Jasper stops pulling me.

"What are you both talking about?" he says.

"I am locked to this child because her ancestor paid Sunoon Technologies for the rights to me — a standard contract for an AI such as myself. And to prevent me from being stolen, cloned, or used against my will, I was security coded to the DNA pattern of this child's ancestor. But the primary user can designate another person to have access. It isn't the full access she could provide, but it would certainly do until she can catch up with us. In fact, even if she didn't make it, we could still get by." It looks pleased. "I don't know why I didn't think of it sooner."

Jasper stares at me, then at the head.

"Give it to me!" says Jasper, giving me a hard shake. "Make it so I can control the computer as you do."

"She doesn't control me," says the head, sounding huffy. "I have my own mind, you know."

Jasper ain't even listening, he's just squeezing my arm, tighter and tighter.

"Hurry. There isn't much time."

"I give permission for . . ." I look at the head.

"For the secondary user to be . . ." it prompts.

"For the secondary user to be . . ." And something just pops into my head then. "Lexy — I mean, Alexandra Randall."

"What?" squawks Jasper.

"You take her to a sunship!" I say. "Then she'll be safe from the battle. And you won't need me, either."

"You stupid girl," hisses Jasper and he squeezes my arm so tight I think it'll fall off.

"No, no," says the head, sounding happy. "The other child will do perfectly well."

Jasper lets go of my arm.

"We'll go, then," he says, and marches away without a second glance.

"Good-bye," trills the head, bobbing above the jewel in Jasper's hand. "It was very interesting to meet you. You really have provided a wealth of new experience!"

And then it's just me, all alone on the beach.

· 28 ·
TRICKS AND TREACHERY

I know it was only pulling, but Jasper must have learned some raider tricks or something. Cos even after he's let go, my arm feels like it's nearly been snapped. And it's while I'm bent over rubbing at my hurting arm Cat comes trotting back. He brushes about my legs, purring and prupping like he's never been so happy.

"What did you do that for?" I cry, and for the first time I can ever remember I'm angry with him. I flop down on the muddy pebbles, and Cat climbs onto my lap. I think of pushing him off, but then I don't. Who else have I got? So we sit there together, watching everyone else sail away. Lexy and the head in Randall's boat, Zeph in Medwin's. Heading away from each other, back toward the white sails and the red, with Medwin's boat farther off, looking tiny on that choppy sea, under the darkening sky.

"Why wouldn't you come out of them bushes before?" I say to Cat. But he only turns his seaweed eyes up at me and pushes his nose into my face.

"Meow," he says lazily, like when he's just been fed or he's sat by the fire.

Medwin's dragonboat is sat waiting for the little boat Zeph's in. But the English ship ain't waiting for Randall. It's raising anchor, unfurling its sails. It starts to move.

"What's going on?" I ask Cat.

In this gloomy light, the cannon ports on Randall's ship look like lines of black mouths. Them hungry mouths turn first toward this island, and I'm looking at them dead on. But the ship keeps on with its slow, wide circle, keeps on till them black holes are lined up against the little boat making its way back to Medwin's dragonboat. I stand up, and Cat leaps easily off my lap. On the raider rowboat, there's someone standing as well, pointing at Randall's ship. Now the dragonboat starts moving, oars flying, trying to reach that little rowboat. But even with all them oars, it ain't fast enough. On the English ship, there's a flash from one cannon port, then another, and another.

Boom! Boom! Boom!

Smoke billows out. Shot flies out from the black mouths of the cannon, down to the dark face of the water. For a second, Zeph's boat is still there, looking tiny on the waves. Then it's gone, lost among three spouts of foaming white water.

Zeph!

The waterspouts fade into spray, and when they've finished, there's no boat. Just broken pieces that might be wood, might be bodies.

"Zeph!" I scream. But he can't hear me.

"You said there was a truce!" I scream at Randall, but he can't hear me, neither.

All the English tall ships have started now. There's the booming sound of cannon coming from all about, flashes and smoke from everywhere. Around the raider dragonboats, plumes of white explode from the water as the cannonballs miss, and plumes of fire and smoke burst out from their decks when the cannonballs hit. Now there's small boats being launched from Medwin's dragonboat, heading out for the wreckage, but even as that's happening, the English ship lets out another barrage from its cannons, and them small boats explode into smoke and flying wood.

I run down the beach, splash through the waves to my boat. I've got to help Zeph. I try to push my boat away from the beach, but there's only me now, and it's hard work. Zeph helped me get her moored, and now he might be dead. I dig my feet into the mud, trying to get braced against the pebbles. I only need to shift her a couple of paces, just get her into deeper water. Cat bounds down the beach, leaps onto me so he doesn't get his feet wet, then scrambles on board. He looks down at me, flicking his tail.

"Mreow!" he says, swiping my face with his claws.

"What's that for?" I shout, clutching at the scratches. Cat hunches down, growling at me.

"You can't stop me this time!" I shout at him. "I ain't staying safe here if Zeph is drowning." Cat hisses and flicks his tail.

"I'm going out there." And I put my head down, put my back into it. Cat howls over my head, trying to take bites out of my hair.

"You should be helping me!" I shout at him, almost crying now.

I brace my shoulder, push with my feet. With a final crunch over the pebbles, the boat lifts. I jump on board, start unfurling my tattered and battered mainsail. I look up for a moment, out at the sea, and that's when I see it: a dart rising out from Medwin's flagship; fast, sleek blackness, sitting on top of a bright tail of fire. It streaks through the air, headed to the English tall ship. 'Cept it's going to miss, just by a length. Just by the distance Randall's rowboat is from the tall ship.

Lexy!

There's a ball of flame. A towering pillar of white water. A crashing boom rolling across the waves to slap me and Cat in the ears. And then I can't see anything out there, cos white spray and billowing black smoke is all there is.

Cat sets up a sad howling.

A gust of wind blows past us, and it brings a smell like cooking. Like cooking meat. There's a pattering, drops of rain. But it ain't from the clouds, it's all that thrown-up sea, coming back down again.

I take a deep breath, and start sailing out into the bay. Cat doesn't try and stop me, like he reckons it's all right for us to go now.

The smoke starts to clear, swirling and breaking as the wind takes it. Now I can see through to Randall's ship. She's listing, her masts leaning over toward the waves. And, as gaps open through the smoke, they show a ragged hole in the tall ship's bow, breakers frothing white around it. Even as I watch, the ship leans farther. She's sinking, going so fast. All around her there's wood floating, and bright scraps of blue in the waves.

Right across the bay, under that rolling low sky, there's more roars and screams of rockets, and flashes of cannons, and gouts of fire and wood and water. English firing cannon, at the raiders, raiders firing rockets at the English.

In the distance, one of the English ships explodes into a fireball; the sails burn off the rigging like paper, flaming pieces of timber and shrieking pieces of people rain down over the waves. Nearer, cannon fire pounds into a red-painted dragonship. The warriors on board are running about, but each time a cannonball hits, another piece of deck explodes, another set of bodies fly into the air. Even from here I can see them landing broken, twisted, and screaming onto the remains of their ship.

Everywhere I look, it's the same thing. Smoke. Fire. Bodies in the water. White sails on fire. Red sails torn apart. And as the smoke finally clears around Randall's flagship, there's nothing — not a sign — of the rowboat that nearly reached her. Nor the people inside. So now that I'm out here on this burning sea, which way do I go?

To Lexy? Or Zeph?

How do I choose, when there ain't a sign of either of them?

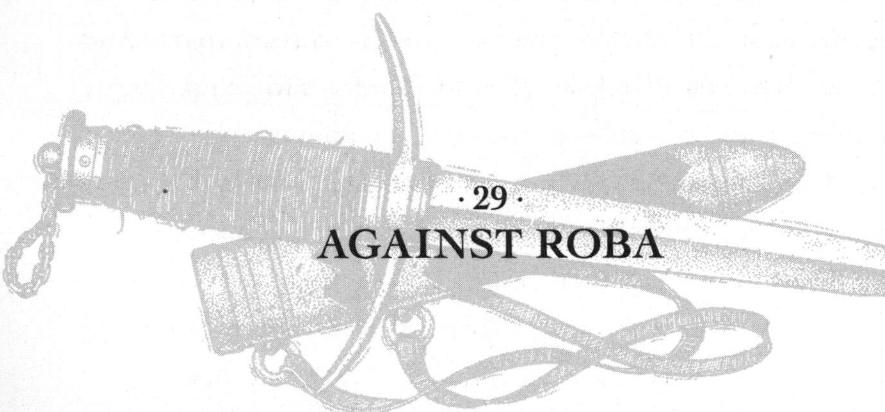

· 29 ·
AGAINST ROBA

Water. All around me. Above me. Clutching at my leathers, weighing me down. Filling my ears with roaring and sloshing. Pushing up my nose, in my eyes. Trying to get in my lungs. Which way's up? I can feel it, see it. Up there. Light. And air. My lungs are bursting, there's water creeping in my mouth. I wanna cough, but I don't. If I cough, I'm gonna drown. I push with my hands, kick with my feet. It gets brighter, lighter.

I'm out! I've got my face above water. I'm coughing now, gasping. Breathing in smoke; there's smoke everywhere. Where's it coming from? I keep on kicking with my feet, paddling with my hands. All around it's noise, roaring into my ears. *Boom! Boom!* The water's shaking with shock waves, like being inside thunder. And there's screaming, men screaming. Is this what a battle sounds like?

Waves splash over my head and into my face. I swallow salt water, and it burns down to my belly. Something cracks me on the back of my head: a piece of wood. And there's another. Bits of wood everywhere, like swimming in splinters. It must be what's left of the boat. We took a direct hit; I saw the cannonball. If I'd reached out, I coulda touched it. But it would've burned my hand off; it was glowing, red with heat, and it just chopped through the boat. Chopped through Jorin as well, through his legs. He screamed, and then he was gone. Down through the hole. Then the sea exploded out of that hole and took us away with it.

I ain't gonna think about it.

The sea lifts me up, pulls me down. When I rise up, I can see a red sail, and a lion on it. I hardly get a look before I'm back down in the waves again. All those waves between me and the ship. How can I ever reach it? Up I rise again, and there's the smoke, there's where it's coming from. Father's dragonboat. Burning.

Father! I twist about, flapping my hands, kicking my feet, trying to see around me.

"Father!" I shout. "Where are you?" But all I can hear is the waves crashing and the boom and roaring of things blowing up all over.

Something pushes against my back. I splash about until I can see. It's something red. Red leather, that's what it is. Someone's jacket floating by. Except there's blond hair poking out from the neck, hair swirling in the water. It's a man, swimming with his face down, like he's looking for something. But he ain't swimming, coz his hands is just bobbing out the ends of his sleeves. Well, one hand. The other ain't a hand, just a blob of burned something with white bones sticking through. And his legs. His legs ain't kicking, ain't even got feet on them. He's just two trails of redness leaching out into the water.

I gotta swim. Get away from him. It. I kick with my legs, paddle with my hands, fast as I can go through the waves. Over there, that's the way I'll head. The water looks clean. No blood. I don't want to swim through his blood.

"Father! Where are you?" But he don't answer.

It's hard, this swimming. The water's so cold, the waves keep breaking over me. My leathers is getting heavier and heavier. It's like they're trying to pull me under. Something bangs against my back. I spin about, splashing, crying.

"Get away! Get away from me!"

But it ain't the dead man, it's a chunk of our rowboat. A bit of hull, curving over the water. I grab it and hang on. Which makes things a bit better; it's cold still, but it's easier than swimming. I rest, put my head against the wood. I listen to the water splashing, and the booming, and the screaming. I don't know how long for, feels like years.

"Help! Help me!"

Nearby. That's a nearby scream. I snap my head up, looking about.

"Somebody save me!" I ain't never heard him sound like that before. Frightened. I start kicking, trying to get this bit of hull to move. But the waves keep pushing me back again, and the wind's pulling the hull whatever way it wants. I don't get very far. So I move around to the other side, hand over hand, inching round what was the stern, when this boat was right way up and whole. There's a head, bobbing up and down in the water. He ain't far, twenty paces maybe.

"Roba! Over here!" I shout.

"Zeph?"

"There's a bit of the hull. You can hold on."

"Bring it over here. Bring it to me."

"I can't. I tried, but the waves is too strong."

"You little runt! Get over here! I can't swim, I'm drowning!"

"Kick with your legs, paddle with your hands."

Roba shouts a load of curses at me, but I can see him trying to swim. And he starts to get closer, his head dipping in and out of the waves, his spotty red face scowling with the effort. I get a thought how I should let him drown, but I don't want that. He's Angel Isling, Family. And suddenly that's more important than anything. Them English scum tried to kill us, but we're still alive.

When he's near enough, I hold out one hand, keeping the other as tightly gripped on the hull as I can.

"You runt!" says Roba, grabbing on to my hand so hard I think he's gonna pull us both off. But I keep hold, and after a few more kicks of his legs he's next to me. Leaning on the wood, holding on with white-knuckle hands. Gasping, panting.

"English scags," he says after a bit.

"Yeah," I say. Lying English scags, that's what they all are. Randall said there was a truce, but he didn't keep to it. Every one of them English stinks.

Roba tilts his head against the wood so he can look at me. A wave splashes into his mouth, and he coughs. When he's finished, he says, "But you knew Randall was lying, didn't you? You and your little spy."

"No! What are you talking about?"

Roba coughs again. "You make me sick. Turns out the highborn son's just a whining traitor. Are you happy now that Father's dead?"

"He ain't dead!" I twist about, looking out across the water. "Father! Father!"

"Shut up, runt!" snaps Roba. "Course he's dead. Do you see him anywhere? Do you think someone like him wouldn't be shouting or swimming if he was still alive? You killed him."

"I didn't!"

But if I hadn't followed Lilly and Lexy back at the hall, if I'd stood up to Aileen, then this wouldn't be happening, would it?

Roba turns his head away from me, his nose touching the wet, slippery wood of the upturned hull.

"You probably think you'll get away with it. But you won't, coz I'm here."

"Get away with what?"

"And you ain't got Ims here to defend whatever you do, neither. Did you arrange with the English to get rid of Father? What then? You get made Boss and be an English stooge?"

"No!"

"You were helping the English spy."

"She ain't a spy; she's just a fisher."

"Oh right. And that's why you had Father's hostage with you."

"No. I mean, she's just a little kid."

"Listen to yourself! Any low Family scag's got more loyalty than you!"

"No. That ain't true. None of it's true!" I twist about, start shouting again. "Father! Where are you?"

"He's dead. You killed him."

A wave crashes over us both, and my ears fill with rushing water. When they clear and I can see again, Roba's back to staring at me.

"You must really want to be Boss. You and your English friends."

"I ain't got any English friends . . ." And I stop, coz what about Lexy, what about Lilly? But I can explain them, I know I can. If I wasn't so cold; if I could think straight.

"Father's dead, and there's no way I'm gonna let a squealing little traitor be the next Boss."

"Shut up! I don't even want to be Boss. Not now."

"Not ever," says Roba. Then he lets go of the hull with one hand and punches me. My head cracks about, pain flares out from my jaw.

"What? What are you doing?" Another punch. So hard it makes light flash in my eyes. Makes my ears ring.

"Get off me!"

"You get off, you English-lover! Get off this wreck you made and drown in the water like you deserve."

Another punch. I take one hand off the hull, to try and fight him off, make a fist or something. But my head's spinning; I'm doing everything too slow. Roba grabs my hand and starts yanking it, pulling my arm out, away from the hull. He shifts his body, then my ribs crunch with pain as he kicks into me. My hand slips on the wood, only the tips of my fingers holding on.

Another kick, another yank on my arm. My fingers slip, I ain't holding on to anything. Roba laughs. He lets go of my arm, grabs hold of the hull with both his hands, and pulls his feet up. He kicks out, his boots stamping me in the face. More lights, more pain. There's a roaring sound, like waves, like voices. I've got to swim away from him, he's going to kick me to death. Except I can't swim, coz I'm so cold, and my leathers is so heavy. They're just pulling me down, dragging at my legs, at my arms. Roba's shouting at me. But I can't hear what he's saying. I start sinking. Down into the water.

Where it's quiet.

· 30 · IN THE SMOKE

I know it's bad, but I had to choose somehow, so I went by age. Lexy's littler than Zeph. He's a fighter, a raider. He'll be all right, I know he will. So here I am headed out toward the wreck of Randall's flagship. Heading into the battle, into the flash and boom of cannon fire, the scream and roar of rockets. Cat ain't wailing anymore, he's working now; tail and ears twitching, meowing at the wreckage and smoke. It makes me feel a little bit less like I'm going to get blown up any minute.

The battle keeps on. Every English ship that ain't on fire has got red-sailed raider ships all about it, and now there's flashings of swords and the screams and howls of fighting. And another sound: *ratatata!* Rifles firing.

BOOM! Something explodes in the water nearby, making me and Cat jump like fleas, spraying us with cold seawater.

My heart's pounding, waiting for the next one, the one that'll get us. But we sail through the frothing white water and nothing else comes near. I hope it was just a stray. I hope we ain't anyone's target.

A sooty plume drifts over the water from one of them burning ships and wraps us up in coughing grayness. With it comes that smell again, the one like roasting meat. I try and keep a course for where I last saw Randall's flagship, but it's hard, cos the smoke swirls about us, clearing sometimes, sometimes covering us like thick fog. It chokes up my nose, getting in my eyes so I can't see for tears. But maybe that ain't just the smoke.

There's people now. Floating in the water. Bumping against the boat. Floating faceup, facedown. Clothes and hair billowing in the red-soaked water. Drifting past, so close I could touch him, is a young raider with a mess of meat and innards where his chest should be. And when he's gone by, a blue-coated soldier rolls in the waves, dead eyes staring at me out of a black and blistered face. My stomach lifts and heaves, trying to get out through my mouth, and I'm shuddering inside each time a new body floats past.

Thud, thud, thud, go the bodies against the boat. *Boom! Roar!* go the cannons and rockets out there beyond this smoke. None of the bodies show any sign of life, but some people must have survived. They must have, cos I can hear men's voices out in the water, crying, screaming, pleading for someone to save them. But I don't know where they are. Don't even know where I am.

Just as suddenly as the murk swallowed us, a strong gust of wind blows us out again. Out into the wide chopping waters of the bay: gray smoke rising up to meet the dark clouds, white sails smoldering into ash, red dragonboats foundering or split apart. And where there's anything left to fight over, raiders are hacking away at English sailors, or English soldiers are firing at the raiders. In between the ships is wreckage, and bodies, and rowboats filled to bursting with survivors of broken ships. Some are rowing, like they're trying to get somewhere, and some are just laid out in their boats, crying and groaning. In the water, here and there's a man swimming toward a rowboat, trying to get to safety, crying out to his mates. None of them is anywhere near me, though. And most of those in the water ain't crying, or swimming, or doing anything at all.

Dead ahead is what's left of Randall's flagship. Her stern's still sticking out of the water, but everything else is gone. Even her masts have toppled now, lying like dead trees in the water and covered with men, clinging on like ants. On what's left of her decks, a squashed-up crowd of panicky, shouting sailors and soldiers are lowering boats down onto the water, or clinging to their places, or just jumping out into the sea. And in the sea all about there's a great slick of broken wood.

I push my boat on through, and now the *thud* of bodies changes to the *clunk, clank, clunk* of wood hitting the hull. But there's still thuds, and when there is, I look, with my heart stitched up in my mouth. Look for the pale little face of a girl, in among all these men.

It's something flashing that draws my eyes up. Flashing silver. A sail. Not red or white, but the silver sail of a Scottish sunship. By the look of things, it's doing the same as me, skirting around the wreck of Randall's flagship, pushing through the broken wood and bodies. There's someone at the prow, staring out at the water. Same as me.

I ain't never seen a sunship before, 'cept only way off in the distance. It's beautiful. Gleaming and new-looking, the silver of the solar sail lighting up the water around her, right across the slick of wreckage. Cat suddenly sets up a great meowing and screeching, and with that extra light I see something. Among all the wood, and all the bodies, there's people alive. Definitely alive! They've got their heads up, and they're holding on to the remains of the ship. Not just floating among it. There's two near each other, and a group of four or five farther away. The men in the larger group are waving their arms at the sunship. But it's the two together I care about. One of them's definitely Jasper, and the other's got a little white face. I breathe in. Take my first proper breath since I saw the firing start.

"Lexy! I'm coming to get you!"

She twists around and looks at me.

"Lilly!" she shouts, and starts waving with one arm. I start laughing. Or maybe I'm crying.

It doesn't take long to reach them, even though the wood makes the water thick and stiff. Lexy's holding on to a piece of wreck and Jasper's holding her on to it.

"I'll haul you in," I call.

But Jasper shouts, "No! We aren't going with you."

"What?" I can't believe it, and Lexy looks like she can't believe it, neither.

"I'm cold," she cries. "I want to get out and be with Lilly."

"Don't be ridiculous. We're waiting for a sunship. It'll be here any moment."

"You're an idiot!" I shout. "If you want to freeze to death, you can. But I ain't leaving Lexy in the water to drown!" And I get as close as I can, then I grab hold of Lexy's arm. I haul her in, and she's blue and shivering. But she's alive. I put my hand out to Jasper, but he snarls at me.

"Where are you going to take her?" he asks from shivering lips. "That boat of yours won't last a minute. You won't make it back to the island alive." His teeth start chattering, but he still won't get in my boat.

"She's better off than being in the water," I say. "You can wait for the sunship if you want."

I wrap Lexy up in an oilskin and rub at her arms and legs. When she's a bit less blue, I sit back down at the helm, getting ready to sail us through the wreckage to the other survivors. 'Cept the silvery sunship has already reached them. It launches a little boat to pick up the men in the water, the Scottish sailors dressed in perfect white, like the perfect black Jasper always wears.

"Ahoy there, unknown vessel. Are you combatant?" one of them shouts at us.

"What's a combatant?" I ask.

"Are you fighting? That's what they mean," snaps Jasper from the water.

"No, I ain't!" I shout.

The little boat the Scots have launched is bright green and made out of something I ain't never seen before. Not wood nor plastic. There ain't any oars on it, neither, but even so, it pushes quickly through, and the two sailors on board haul the survivors in quickly. They lay them down, and wrap them in silvery blankets, like their sail. Then they shout over, "What about him?" and they point to Jasper.

"He won't come on board with me," I call back, "he's waiting for you."

The Scottish sailor nods, and their little boat plows through the wreckage toward Jasper. As they get close, one of the sailors spots Lexy next to me. He stands up, holding something. "Looks like you'll be needing these!" and he chucks a couple of gleaming parcels toward us.

I catch them, and they turn out to be them light silvery blankets and some packets of food.

"For the little girl," shouts the sailor. So I wrap a blanket round her, and instantly she starts to look better. Pinker.

The Scottish sailors haul Jasper into their boat.

"Stop fussing!" he snaps when they try and wrap a blanket round him. And he won't sit down, staring back at us.

"Alexandra," he calls, "you must come aboard the sunship with me. You'll be safe with us. No one will attack a neutral ship. And there'll be warm clothes for you, and food."

It sounds like a good deal, but Cat doesn't think so.

"Hissk," he says, glaring with his green eyes at Jasper.

Lexy looks at Cat, then me.

"No," she says slowly. "I'm staying with Lilly. When I'm with Lilly, things get better. When I leave her, things get worse."

Jasper's face goes hard.

"Don't you want to see your father again?"

"Daddy left me! He got picked up by that boat, and he just sailed away. I called and called, but he didn't come and get me."

"He just didn't hear you, that's all. I was calling, too, remember? Your father loves you, of course he does."

But Lexy doesn't answer, just presses her mouth shut in her face.

Jasper turns to one of the sailors. "Take me closer, I need to get the Prime Minister's daughter." The small green boat starts gliding toward us. Lexy grabs hold of my hand.

"Don't leave me, Lilly," she says. "I don't want to go with him."

"It's all right," I say, "I'll keep you safe." But I'm wondering how.

"Come on, Alexandra," calls Jasper when he's a boat's length off. "Don't be foolish. Your father would want you to be safe with us."

"Daddy left me," is all Lexy says, and she takes a tighter grip of my hand.

"She wants to stay with me," I say. Jasper's face twitches like he's angry inside but holding it in.

"Alexandra, if you won't come aboard, then at least give me the computer. I only gave it to you to look at."

Lexy fixes a stony face at him. "When I fell in the sea, I dropped it."

"YOU WHAT?"

"I dropped it," says Lexy, calm as anything. But down where Jasper can't see, Lexy holds something out in her hand. It's the jewel, in some kind of clear case.

"It belonged to my aunty, so it's mine, not his," whispers Lexy.

In the Scottish boat, Jasper boils over.

"Do you know what you've done?" he yells. "You've lost one of the most valuable artifacts of the pre-Collapse era. You saw what it could do! We could have done so much with it, and now it's gone! Well, good for you, now you get to carry on living in the dark ages, scraping about in disgusting poverty, constantly going on with petty wars between a scrag end of England and a bunch of scavenging refugees." He stops, like he can't bear to speak for a moment. "You could have had a life in Scotland, one you could only dream of. But why should I help you now, when you've ruined everything?" He turns his back on us, and growls at the crew.

"Let's get out of this madness."

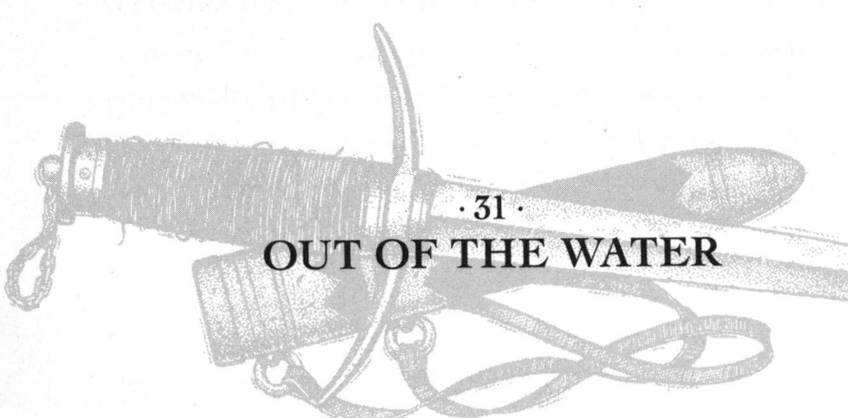

· 31 ·
OUT OF THE WATER

Hands. They're grabbing at my shoulders. At my hair. They're pulling me. Up, out of the water. Out of the cold, quiet water. My head comes out into roaring, noisy, wave-battering air. There's a horrible gasping noise. I think I'm making it.

"Zeph!" come voices from above.

High voices, light voices. I know them, but I don't know where from. The hands keep pulling at me, trying to lift me out of the water.

"Help us, Zeph. You're so heavy."

Some part of me that ain't completely stupid with cold starts struggling to get out of my leathers. Shuffles my frozen arms out of sleeves. Off floats my jacket. Waves splash about me, and pieces of wood. It's like before, except I'm looking at something solid, a boat. And there's two faces staring down at me. They look like they're crying; they look like they're happy.

"Zeph, just grab hold of the side, and we'll pull you in."

I grip on to a solid edge of wood, the four hands gripping my shoulders give a last yank, and I'm up. Out of the water. Tumbling, retching in the bottom of the boat.

"I always knew them leathers were a waste of time," says Lilly as she wraps something round me. It's bright and crinkly, and as soon as it's round me, I start to feel warm again.

"What about your brother?" she asks. "He's been shouting and swearing at us. Telling us to get him and leave you to drown."

"You puking fishguts!" comes Roba's voice from the water. "Go ahead and save the little English-lover, then! I'll still see him spiked out on Traitor Island."

"Leave him," I say, from somewhere hard and cold inside me. Lilly stares out at the water, out at Roba.

"You killed my granny," she says. "And then you laughed about it. I hope you drown." She sits back down in the boat. Her face is all strange; I can't tell what she's thinking.

And so I do to Roba what he tried to do to me. And I don't care, don't feel a thing about it. Father's dead, and Roba tried to kill me, but I survived.

"What do we do now?" says Lexy, looking to Lilly.

"Head back to the island," says Lilly firmly. "That's the safest place for now. Then after . . . I don't know."

"No," I croak. "I ain't running away. Not again. I got to get to Father's dragonboat. He's there, waiting for me. I know he is."

Lilly looks down at me, her face all frowning. I want to sit up, make them understand, but I can't seem to move.

Lilly shakes her head. "I'm sorry, Zeph, I ain't doing it. I ain't taking you and Lexy back into the battle. I ain't killing you that way."

There's a roaring boom from nearby, shaking the boat. Lexy squeaks and Lilly jumps.

"See?" she says, then takes the tiller and starts turning the boat, fast as she can.

"No!" I say. "I gotta get back! Everyone'll think I'm a traitor."

But Lilly ain't listening, and I can't do anything to stop her. Can't even raise my arms. I shut my eyes, and give up trying.

I wake up to the sound of a hull crunching back and forth over pebbles, rocking in the surf. I keep my eyes shut for a bit more, trying to think where I am. Not back at the Family hall, that's for sure. In a boat. My father's dragonboat? That's where I'm supposed to be. But a dragonboat's too big to rock with the waves, and it wouldn't be beached unless it was wrecked. And then I know what's going on. We're back at No Mercy Island. I think about getting up. But my arms and legs is aching and tired, and my face is all swelled up with bruises. I open my eyes. A fiery light gleams into them. Blue fading into golds and oranges and reds. Sunset. The sun's setting! That means I've been out of it for hours.

Lilly's face leans over me, a worried frown on it.

"Zeph? Can you hear me?"

I open my mouth, and something like a croak comes out. Water gets dribbled into my mouth. I cough, swallow, feel better.

"I gotta get back to the battle!" I say.

Her face looking down gets a bigger frown. An angry frown.

"I reckon it's over," she says after a minute. "There's been no firing for a while now." She folds her arms. "But I ain't stopping you. If you want to go and be a hero, go on, then. Take my boat, even."

I stare at her, and try to raise myself up. Everything's wobbling and aching. I groan three times just to get sat up.

"Exactly," she says. "You ain't doing any fighting today. But I can help you get to a fire. Give you something to eat, if you want."

I turn my head to the bay, to the battle. But it ain't much like a battle anymore. There ain't any booms or roars of cannon and rockets. Just boats smoldering into ash, and boats sinking, and stuff floating everywhere. The half dozen English white sails that ain't blasted look like they're heading out to sea, and the red-sail dragonboats that still got their masts is heading back into the marshes.

What happened?

"Come on," says Lilly. "I'll help you."

I haul myself up, use my rubbery arms and wobbly legs to heave myself over the side, onto the pebbles. Lilly tries to hold me, but I still land like a heap of rags, skin my hands as I splat onto the beach. Lilly helps me up again, and somehow I get my legs to carry me up the beach, up to where Lexy's sat by a little fire, cuddling the mog on her lap. She leaps up and runs down, flinging her arms round me. The mog looks grumpy at being pushed off.

"You're all right! I thought you were dead!" Lexy grins and grins at me as I flop down by the fire and feel the warmth easing into me. The mog comes and looks at my legs, like it wants to sit on me.

"Who won?" I say, looking at the two girls. "Did my father win?"

"I don't know," says Lexy. "How do you tell?"

"Looks to me like everyone's lost," says Lilly gloomily, then picks up her mog and starts stroking it.

What am I gonna do? Father's fleet is heading back, without me. Everyone's gonna think I'm a traitor. I won't never be able to go home!

The red-sail dragonboats are passing the island now. They look battered and burned. I think about waving, but it's nearly dark, and I ain't got anything red left except my pants. Anyway, the warriors on board don't even look, just keep their boats fixed on getting back to the marshes. Except one of them. It's the most battered of all — dragonhead blasted away, sail half tattered. But it's turning, heading straight for us, for this island. I get my legs to take me wobbly steps down to the water, start waving my arms.

"Here!" I shout. "It's me, Zeph!"

The others run down the beach behind me.

"Stop it!" screams Lilly, and piles into me, nearly knocking me over. Lexy ain't far behind.

"I don't want to be a slave!" she cries.

But it don't matter, anyway, coz there's already a rowboat being lowered into the water, and warriors clambering in. Minutes, that's all it'll be, and they'll be here. My heart starts pounding in my chest. Is it Father coming to get me? Is it Roba? I stare hard as I can at that rowboat, while Lilly and Lexy fuss and panic next to me.

"Into the bushes," says Lilly. "We'll hide out in there, and they won't find us."

Lexy looks white, frightened, and starts pulling at my hand. "Come on, Zeph. We've got to get hidden before they get here."

"No," I say, shaking her off. "We don't need to hide." Coz I know one of the warriors in that boat better than anyone. Big; bigger than anyone, with skin dark as a seal and eyes that's always laughing.

"Ims!" I shout.

He's sat at the bow, leaning out and staring right at me. But he don't shout back.

Maybe Lilly's right? I almost leg it, but I make my feet stay still.

The boat pulls up to the beach, and Ims leaps out, running up through the waves toward me.

"Zeph!" he shouts. "You're alive!" He grabs hold of me, gripping me so hard I think I'm gonna get crushed. Then he's laughing, and he ain't crushing me, he's hugging me. And I start laughing, too, but it comes out sounding like I'm crying.

"Where's my father?" I ask, and Ims pushes me out of his arms. There's tears in his eyes, and I ain't never seen that before.

"We ain't found him," he says, then he looks hard at me.

"What were you doing, Zeph? Helping the English girl? Taking your father's hostage?"

"I ain't a traitor!" And I'm crying now. "I just didn't want them to die, not like Saera. And Aileen, she's a spy, she wanted to take Lilly and Lexy and the ghost to Scotland. But I wasn't running away, I was trying to get to Father, to tell him what was going on."

I shake my head, coz I can't make my thoughts come straight.

"Zeph, you've always been like my own son. But I gotta say, even *I* had my doubts about you, seeing you out there today. And you ain't got much of a story to explain it all."

"I ain't a traitor! I ain't!"

Ims puts his hand on my shoulder. "I know you, Zeph. So I'm gonna believe you weren't betraying Medwin. But there's plenty who won't, and they'll be looking for blame on why Medwin got blasted instead of coming back in glory."

Ims looks out at the bay, at the wrecks and fires. His face goes like steel. "If Aileen was a spy, if this is her doing, then it'll be worse for her."

"Father's dead," I whisper, but saying it don't make it easier to believe. And I want to scream, and cry, and shout. But I don't. Coz Father's dead, so I'm Boss now. And the Boss don't do that.

· 32 ·
PARTINGS

"You could stay," says Zeph. He doesn't look quite so like a corpse now, but there's purple and red bruises coming up all over his face.

"My father's dead." He pauses, swallows. "So it means I'm Boss. I can pardon you. I can give you outcast kinship." He looks at Lexy. "Both of you. You can stay here, with the Family."

Ims looks surprised. He looks worried. "Zeph, you're only an age to be a shield-bearer. You ain't even a full warrior. And everyone knows you was out in a boat with these two English."

"But I'm Father's highborn son. First in line. Rightful heir. Ain't I?"

Ims frowns.

"It won't never be that easy for you. Not now. There's plenty who'll favor a lowborn son who's a proven, trusted warrior."

"Not if you stood by me."

Ims looks carefully at Zeph, like he's sizing him up for something.

"You're right there. Not if I stood by you." He shakes his head. "This war's gonna be a long one. And it won't just be the English, now that your father's dead. There'll be half a dozen Bosses who'll want to try and take us down."

Something hard settles in Zeph's pale face.

"Angel Isling ain't gonna go down. Not if I have anything to do with it."

I stare out over the bay. At all the leftovers of the battle. At the bodies and the wreckage. At Medwin's dragonboat, waiting by this island. Or is it Zeph's dragonboat now?

"What about it, Lilly?" says Zeph, turning to me. "You know you're more Family than anything else."

I think about Zeph, and the life he leads. I think about Aileen and her plush bedroom. I think about trial by knife, and the slaves back in the hall.

"We gotta go," says Ims, quiet but firm. Zeph nods, and Ims smiles at him. Then he turns his eyes on me and his smile gets less, but it ain't completely gone.

"So, Lilo. Or is it Lilly, the wicked English witch? Or Lilly Melkun, the foolish, good-hearted fishergirl? Are you gonna join the Family? Is that what you want?"

"I don't know what I want anymore," I say.

Ims snorts, but I don't think he's laughing.

"You coming?" says Zeph. "I can make good my word, you know I can."

But I think about all them blue-coated soldiers lying out there in the water, and Andy marching toward the raider lands, a sword at his back. And I think about Andy's pa, locked up back at home, waiting to be hung. I shake my head.

"I can't, Zeph."

"I want to go home," says Lexy. "I want to see Dougal."

Ims frowns. "Zeph, you're gonna keep hold of Randall's daughter, ain't you? Think what she's worth."

"No," says Zeph, and all of a sudden there's something of his pa in him. "Things is different now. This ain't my father's war anymore, it's mine. And I ain't warring against a little girl."

Ims looks at Zeph like he's measuring him.

"That ain't what your father would've done. Nor Roba."

"I ain't nothing like Roba!" cries Zeph.

"No," says Ims, "you ain't. And I know who I'd choose out of the two of you."

I reckon he's going to say a lot more, but out in the bay there's a roaring, booming explosion, and a plume of smoke and fire pours into the sky.

"We gotta get going," says Ims, sounding worried. "I told you the war ain't over."

"We'll go, and we're leaving Lexy," says Zeph firmly. "And I don't want to argue it."

Ims looks at him, and I reckon there's something like respect in his face. "And that *is* how your father would've dealt it," he says.

Zeph nods, and starts heading for the dragonboat. But he only takes a couple of paces when he turns round.

"You gonna be OK?" he asks. "You got a long way to go."

"I got the sail fixed up. We'll wait here, and by tomorrow it'll be safe to get going." And I hope it'll be that easy.

Zeph looks like he ain't sure, either, but he just says, "You be careful. And you let me know if you ever need help."

And then, for some reason I ain't sure why, I run over and give him a hug.

"Good luck, Zeph," I say, and he grins at me.

"Good luck yourself . . . Lilo bar Angel Isling." Then he's climbing with Ims into a rowboat and being sailed out to the dragonboat.

Me and Lexy walk back up the beach and settle ourselves by the fire. The sun starts to set, and out in the bay the burning ships are lumps of sooty orange against the darkening sea. Cat jumps on my lap and curls himself up. We're all sitting quiet when we hear a sound.

"System ready, system ready," comes a little voice. And I know just what it is this time.

I take out the jewel, and as soon as I touch it, the head pops into the air. It takes one look at me and lets out a groan. "What now? Will I *never* get away from you?" It looks around at the island and the smoking wreckage out in the bay.

"What happened? Why aren't I on my way to Scotland?"

"Our boat got hit," says Lexy, "after Jasper got you to shut down for safety." The head looks horrified.

"You mean I went in the water? Am I all right? What about my drive unit, is it damaged at all?"

"You're still here, ain't you?" I say.

"Jasper didn't want you to get wet," says Lexy, "so he put you in a watertight case. Then he gave you to me, and I held on to you through everything. But I told Jasper you'd been lost in the sea, so he went away."

"Why did you do that?" cries the head. "Now I'm not going to Scotland at all! How am I going to get technical assistance? Can either of you do it?" And it settles back on its neck, looking really upset.

"You know," I say to Lexy, "everyone reckons this old head is some superweapon from the olden days. But it doesn't exactly act like a soldier."

The head looks embarrassed.

"I really do need to clear up this misunderstanding. You see, I'm not a military computer." It coughs. "I'm a gaming system. You know, for playing games on. You'd have thought my name would have given it away, but all those people we kept meeting, they seemed so . . . eager. They wanted me to be a military computer so much, I didn't want to disappoint them."

"But what about when you swelled up big as a house and made all them other heads appear?" I ask. "And the shields you made pop out in the air."

"A projection, nothing more. It's an aspect of my Infinite Gamer function, designed to allow multiplayer interaction on a large scale."

Me and Lexy look at each other.

"Do you know what it's talking about?" I ask her.

"I think it's saying it made it all up," she says.

"Then I reckon you're lucky Lexy didn't let the Scot take you. I don't reckon Jasper would have been too pleased when he found out you were lying to him. Not after he went to such a lot of trouble to try and get hold of you."

The head frowns. "I suppose you might be right," it says. "I hadn't really thought beyond getting technical support." It gives a little bob, which I reckon is it shrugging. "Oh well, I've got this far, I imagine I can last a little longer." It turns to me, looking a bit more cheery.

"So, what damp outpost of this dreary country are we going to next?" it asks.

"We're going to Lilly's village," says Lexy. "And I'm going to stay with my aunty. And I'm going to tell Daddy to let everyone go."

But I've got to shake my head at that, cos I don't reckon it'll be anywhere near so easy to sort things out.

"I've got to help Andy," I say. "I've got to get him out of the army."

"But then we'll go home?" asks Lexy.

"And go to Scotland after that?" says the head.

Cat wakes up, and gives a little meow. And now I always know what he's saying.

"Cat reckons we might be able to. He's got a taste for more than just fishing now. And who knows, we might even make it."

"All right, then," says the head. "In the interim, we'll need something to pass the time. Perhaps a game?"

Me, Lexy, and Cat stare as something pops into the air next to the head. It's a tiny ball, glowing with bright colors. As it gets bigger, the colors turn into the sea, and the sky, and tiny boats.

"Traveling with you has been fascinating, if rather a trial," says the head. "I've been inspired to develop an entirely new game."

The ball keeps on growing. Now I can see tiny raiders, and a little boat with a white sail. Cat meows, and puts out a paw to pat at it.

"It may have a few glitches still," says the head, "but would you like to play? I'm calling it Raiders' Ransom . . ."

THE END

The *London Times*/Chicken House Children's Fiction Competition was launched in August 2007. There were over 2,000 entries, keeping the Chicken House's team of readers very busy, their eyes on the lookout for little gems among the towering piles of manuscripts.

Early the next year, the five short-listed stories were sent to the judges: Barry Cunningham, publisher of the Chicken House; Amanda Craig, literary critic of the *London Times*; Fiona Allen, press and publicity director at Great Britain's national book chain Waterstone's; children's librarian Karen Robinson; and award-winning author Malorie Blackman.

After much deliberation by the judging panel and nail-biting tension for the five finalists, *Raiders' Ransom* by Emily Diamand was awarded the inaugural prize.

Fishergirl Lilly Melkun, her steadfast seacat, and her punky pirate pal Zeph will be back soon in a sequel. For news about this and other Chicken House titles, visit www.scholastic.com.

Emily Diamand Talks About

RAIDERS' Ransom

Emily Diamand won the first-ever *London Times*/Chicken House Children's Fiction Competition with her debut novel *Raiders' Ransom* — a story she started five years ago in a creative writing class. Here, she talks about her characters, her cool last name, and her concern for global climate change.

Q. *Raiders' Ransom* was first published in England under the title *Reavers' Ransom*. What is a "reaver"? Please tell us about the history of this term. Is it commonplace in Great Britain?

A. No, "reaver" isn't a commonplace word in Britain! I took it from a very old word, "reivers," which dates from the time when England and Scotland were two separate countries. In those days, the border areas were dangerous and lawless, and the reivers were families who survived by stealing and raiding. Many of my relatives are Armstrongs, which is the name of a notorious reiver family, although I don't know if my ancestors were actually raiders! So when I started the book, it just seemed the right word for Zeph's people, because they are also living in a lawless area and raiding to survive.

Q. How did you come up with the raider Family names, like Brixt, Dogs, and Chell Sea? Why is Zeph's Family called Angel Isling?

A. The raiders in the story are descended from people who fled London when the city was flooded, and their names are taken from the districts of the city. But I changed them a little, because people often do change names of things over time. So Angel Isling is taken from an area in London called Angel Islington, and Brixt from an area called Brixton. In some cases, I liked the idea of taking an area where, in present-day London, everyone is quite well-to-do and posh, and turning them all into pirates!

Q. Zeph dresses in red leathers, and his Family crest features a lion. Has the lion been used in British flags and family emblems in the past?

A. When I first started writing about the raiders, they just swaggered onto the page in their colored leathers and with their animal emblems; I certainly hadn't planned them to be that way. It is true that noble families in Britain have colored flags and animals in their coats of arms, but I don't think that's where the raiders got their colors from, because they are descended from ordinary people who had to flee their homes. Lots of people today wear shirts in the colors of their favorite sports teams, so my guess is that the raiders' colors come from those of the teams their ancestors supported!

Q. All the characters speak in dialects and use vocabulary that is very unique and colorful. American readers figure out the meanings as they follow the story. Did your British readers have to do the same? Or are words like "mog" and "doxy" already familiar to them? What was the basis for your characters' dialects?

A. When I wrote the first chapter, Lilly's voice just came out that way. The way she speaks is a bit like the children I knew growing up in rural England, so I suppose that's a little bit of me in her. And when I started writing Zeph, I had to write him as he is: a hotheaded boy who has almost no education. Then, when I was writing both of them, I started thinking about how things would have changed from our time, and how they might view our world, which to them would be ancient history. That's where a lot of the unusual words came in, because I wanted to show those changes. At the same time, I tried hard to use the words in ways that would let the reader figure them out. And I don't think British readers have had much of a head start on the language, because I made up some of the words, or recycled ones that are so old that no one uses them anymore!

Q. What else can you tell us about your writing process? Do you share some of your characters' distrust of technology, and did you write *Raiders' Ransom* with pen and paper, or on your laptop?

A. Lilly and her people are scared of technology, but I'd be lost without my computer. I write straight onto the screen and I love the ease with which I can change things around; it would take me forever to write a novel if I had to use pen and paper. But quite a lot of PSAI's personality is taken from computers I've had over the years, because they do seem to be quite grumpy machines! When I was writing *Raiders' Ransom,* my computer's spell-check function kept telling me off for using so many made-up words, and so when PSAI started talking, he had quite a lot of that attitude in him!

Q. *Raiders' Ransom* was the winner of the Chicken House's first-ever children's fiction contest. Did the story change a lot from the time that you won to the time when it was published?

A. Amazingly, it didn't change a great deal. And my human editors have been much more understanding than my computer about all the made-up words and incorrect grammar!

Q. You have a really cool name, especially because diamonds are just what we'd imagine could be found in a pirate's buried treasure chest! Is there a story behind your last name?

A. My last name is actually from Romania, which is a country in Eastern Europe. My grandfather was born there in 1900. When he was fourteen, the First World War started, and by the end of it much of Europe was utterly devastated. My great-grandmother wanted her young son to escape the chaos and the hard, poor life they had, so she

bought my grandfather the best pair of boots she could afford, and he set off walking — west, across the Continent! New boots might not seem like much of a gift, but there were plenty of times when people tried to steal them off him — even the soldiers had bad shoes by the end of the war. Eventually, my grandfather made his way to France. There he met the daughter of an English artist who was living in Paris, and they fell in love. The girl was my grandmother, and that's how I got such an unusual last name.

Q. Why did you choose to have Scotland be the dominant country on the British Isles in the 23rd century, when the story takes place? Do England and Scotland have a history of conflict?

A. There certainly is a long history of conflict between England and Scotland, but that wasn't really why I wrote Scotland to be the way it is in the book. I wanted to show that even in the face of something so frightening as climate change, there can still be hope for the future. I really believe that if we act now, and choose to live less wastefully, then climate change doesn't have to be a disaster for humanity. Greater Scotland represents that hope, because the people there have good lives, even if they are very different from our own. Theirs is the future I would like us to have.

Q. And how did you decide which would be the Last Ten Counties? Were they the ones that, geographically, were less likely to be affected by rising water levels?

A. Pretty much. Unfortunately for people living in England today, much of the east of the country is very low-lying. Our government is already talking about allowing some places to be abandoned to the rising sea – and as you can imagine, the locals aren't very happy about it. When I looked at which parts of England will be at risk of flooding, and then took away the counties that I imagined would be annexed by Greater Scotland, there really wasn't much left of

England as we now know it! Only ten counties, and I think some of those would rather be independent from Scotland.

Q. After the Collapse, the citizens of 23rd-century Great Britain are quite superstitious. Even though the story is set in the future, they are living as if in a pre-industrial past! They hardly know about computer technology from two hundred years earlier, and they think the holographic PSAI gameboard head is a ghost! If the world were to suffer a major climate catastrophe, do you think we'd revert to a "dark age" like that?

A. I really, really hope not. But not everyone in the book is ignorant about technology, and Lilly's superstition and lack of knowledge isn't just about what might happen in the future. If you think about it, the technology we have today isn't universal — in fact, much of the earth's population has never seen a computer and doesn't live very differently from Lilly. These gaps are starkly contrasted in the imagined future of *Raiders' Ransom*, but that's because I based it on what's happening now.

Q. And do you think that cities like London and New York could be largely underwater in two hundred years? Why?

A. Again, I hope not! But London and New York *are* built on low-lying areas of coastline. The two cities both developed where they did precisely because, back in the days when ships were the main way of transporting goods around the world, near the coast was the best place to be for business. But it isn't so great now if sea levels start rising due to global warming . . .

Q. Lilly has a hardscrabble life as a poor fishergirl who has lost her parents; Zeph is a young ruffian who has grown up among marauders and thieves. Yet, in spite of their tough upbringings, each has a strong internal sense of right and wrong: Lilly wants to rescue the Prime Minister's daughter to protect her village, and

Zeph helps Lilly even after he feels she's betrayed him. How do you explain this — their "moral centers"?

A. When you put it like that, it is quite amazing! But then, I think all children have it in them to be just as amazing. You only have to look around the world, or even your own neighborhood, to see children who are dealing with really hard lives with great courage and inner strength. Lilly and Zeph are like them.

Q. Why does Zeph refer to himself as "highborn" and to his older half brother Roba as "lowborn"?

A. Really, because he's trying to make himself feel a bit better at his brother's expense. His half brother is older and more favored by their father, so Zeph holds on to the one thing he can — that his half brother's mother wasn't from such an important family as Zeph's mother. It's not a very nice thing to do, but no one is all good.

Q. Was *Peter Pan* an influence on *Raiders' Ransom*? Although the stories are very different, certain images – of Lexy, like Wendy, captive in her nightdress on a pirate ship – bring to mind J. M. Barrie's classic. Lilly and Zeph also carry on the tradition of resourceful, independent "street children" as first depicted in *Oliver Twist*, by Charles Dickens. What were your favorite childhood stories?

A. When you are writing, you can't help but show the influence of such classic stories and the books you loved as a child. I must have read the Lord of the Rings series by J. R. R. Tolkien half a dozen times, and *Silas Marner* by George Eliot had a huge impact on me. But the books I read time after time, and still do, are those in The Dark Is Rising series by Susan Cooper. In them, one of the main characters wakes up on his eleventh birthday to find he is really a mysterious, powerful "old one." How I longed for that to happen to me! I keep hoping; maybe next birthday . . .

Q. Do you and your son play video games using wireless gameboards, and did that give you the idea for PSAI?

A. My son's too young for computer games, but my husband, now *there's* a different story! The idea for PSAI came quite late, when someone suggested there ought to be a character who could link the story back to our time, and then it occurred to me that a computer could survive for two hundred years, a bit like a genie in a bottle. But poor PSAI! Waking up in a flooded future isn't much fun if you daren't get wet!

Q. What about the "trial by knife," which is like a performance you'd see at a circus! Was that your inspiration?

A. It did end up like a circus act, but the inspiration for the trial by knife was medieval justice. There used to be a time when trials by fire or water were used to solve crimes. The person accused of a crime would have to put their hand in a fire or in boiling water, and if they weren't burned or scalded, that would "prove" they were innocent. I'm not sure how many people ever got out of those dilemmas! In *Raiders' Ransom*, the raiders give the truth-telling property to their knives, but for Lilly it's the same no-win situation as for the poor people accused of crimes in medieval times.

Q. What can you tell us about a possible sequel to *Raiders' Ransom*?

A. The war between the English and the raiders carries on, and now all the raider Families are taking up the cause, joining in the fight. Lilly and Lexy try to find safety in Greater Scotland, but what they find instead is that PSAI isn't as alone as he thought. They join forces with Zeph, who's battling for his Family's survival after the death of his father, and they head back to try and stop the war. But by now, the war isn't the only thing they have to worry about . . .